THE
ANATOMY
OF
DESIRE

FROM THEODORE DREISER'S
An American Tragedy

First published in the United States in 2021 by William Morrow
HarperCollins Publishers, 195 Broadway, New York, NY 10007

This edition published in Great Britain in 2021 by Trapeze,
an imprint of The Orion Publishing Group Ltd
Carmelite House, 50 Victoria Embankment,
London EC4Y 0DZ

An Hachette UK company

1 3 5 7 9 10 8 6 4 2

Copyright © 2021 by Matthew R. Dorff and Suzanne L. Dunn

The moral right of Matthew R. Dorff and Suzanne L. Dunn to be identified as
the author of this work has been asserted in accordance
with the Copyright, Designs and Patents Act of 1988.

All rights reserved. No part of this publication may be
reproduced, stored in a retrieval system, or transmitted
in any form or by any means, electronic, mechanical,
photocopying, recording, or otherwise, without the
prior permission of both the copyright owner and the
above publisher of this book.

All the characters in this book are fictitious, and any resemblance to
actual persons, living or dead, is purely coincidental.

A CIP catalogue record for this book is
available from the British Library.

ISBN (Hardback) 9781398705166
ISBN (Trade Paperback) 9781398705173
ISBN (eBook) 9781398705197

Designed by Elina Cohen

Typeset by Born Group
Printed and bound in Great Britain by Clays Ltd, Elcograf S.p.A.

www.orionbooks.co.uk

THE

ANATOMY

OF

DESIRE

L. R. DORN

For our parents

It's not enough just to ask questions and listen to the answers. We have to read between the lines to find the truth. Every one of us wants to be heard, but the words we speak are only the first clues. The real meanings often lie beyond the words.

Duncan McMillan, Emmy Award–winning documentary filmmaker

A DUNCAN MCMILLAN DOCUSERIES
Print/Audio Version

EPISODE ONE

GIRL DROWNED

Hey everyone, Cleo here, and as the sun offers rays of light, I offer rays of well-being. Our bodies are designed to move. Our breath is designed to sustain us. Every single day I want you to do two things: move your body and breathe.

YouTube, CleoRayFitness Channel

CLEO RAY: I taped this quote above my sink: "What does it matter if an influencer gains all the followers in the world only to lose her soul?"

DUNCAN MCMILLAN: *This journey began with me looking for a crime. It took a while before I realized I was looking in the wrong direction. This narrative would not lead to a perpetrator. It would lead to a person.*

BAILIFF: "Jury's coming back in, they have a verdict!"

DUNCAN MCMILLAN: *The Inyo County Courthouse, 9:20 A.M., Thursday, October twenty-fourth. Independence, California, is on the eastern side of the Sierra Nevada mountain range, population 703. Inyo is a region that spans over ten thousand square miles, and includes Mount Whitney and Death Valley, the highest and lowest points on the continental United States. The small town of Independence looks and feels like a relic from a bygone era.*

Today, millions of people from around the world are tuned in to this hundred-year-old courthouse, designed in the neoclassical style and listed on the National Register of Historic Places. It's a building that stands as a proud symbol of American justice. Over the last several weeks a murder trial has been unfolding here, and the media attention it's gotten has been ferocious.

CLEO RAY: You want to know what I was feeling at that very moment? How much time have you got?

DUNCAN MCMILLAN: *Sheriff Fred Hite was born in a house just a few blocks from the Inyo County Sheriff's Office. It's a position to which he's now been elected for three terms in a row.*

FRED HITE, COUNTY SHERIFF: July ninth was a Thursday, and I was at my desk in our Bishop office on the north end of the county. My wife had filled an online shopping cart with winter clothes for our kids. It was summer, but Target was having a sale, so she wanted to get a jump on things. I had veto power and could delete any item—long as each kid got the same number of things. We have five kids, and the cart had twenty-five items.

Anyway, I saw a 911 call had come into dispatch from someone up on Rock Creek Road.

WALLY UPHAM, BOATHOUSE ATTENDANT: They rented our standard two-person recreational canoe for the three-hour minimum. Young ladies, pretty, one with brown hair, the other blond. I only saw the blonde at a distance, and she was turned away from me. Didn't think anything of it. They seemed fairly friendly with each other—I mean, I don't know. They paddled out on the lake and were gone from my sight in ten minutes.

FRED HITE, COUNTY SHERIFF: Guy up at Serene Lake said one of their canoes was found turned over and a pair of tourists had drowned. They'd recovered one body, but both life vests had been found in the water. The other gal was nowhere to be seen, so they were dragging the cove with nets. I called my chief deputy, Erin, and had her listen in as I dialed the boathouse.

The attendant was talking fast. He was upset. Only one of the women had signed a release. Could mean big liability issues. He read her name over the phone: "Beck Alden."

I said, "Sounds like a guy's name." He told me her driver's license said Rebecca.

WALLY UPHAM, BOATHOUSE ATTENDANT: The girl Beck—Rebecca—left her windbreaker on a peg in the little store next to the boathouse. It was in the mid-nineties that day, so I thought she might have left it there on purpose. Her shoulders were bare, and she bought a tube of sun block. I saw her friend rub it on her.

FRED HITE, COUNTY SHERIFF: I told him not to touch anything belonging to them and to keep looking for the other girl. It was two-thirty or thereabouts, and the lake's maybe an hour away.

DUNCAN MCMILLAN: *Erin Newcomb is the first woman to be appointed chief deputy at the Inyo County Sheriff's Office.*

ERIN NEWCOMB, CHIEF DEPUTY: Sheriff Hite asked me to come along. I grabbed the paperwork and evidence gear, and on my way out I ran into the admin for our D.A. Told her it looked like we had a double drowning up at Serene Lake.

Inyo County is very spread out, with less than 20,000 total residents. In the last decade, our county has averaged 1.8 murders a year. Lowest murder rate per square mile in the contiguous United States.

We weren't expecting to find anything but an accident, and I told her either the sheriff or I would check in with her boss from the lake.

FRED HITE, COUNTY SHERIFF: We got there around four and found Wally, the guy working the boathouse. Like I said, he was shaken up, both because people had died on the lake and he'd only gotten one to sign the liability waiver. The owner of the boathouse was away somewhere, and Wally hadn't been able to reach him yet.

ERIN NEWCOMB, CHIEF DEPUTY: They'd laid her on a tarp along the shore. Her eyes were only three-quarters closed and her lips were blue. Her face seemed twisted into this . . . twisted expression. You could see she was an attractive girl.

You could also see she'd been whacked in the face.

CLEO RAY: I cared about her so much. Look, I'm a good person. Maybe the people who know me best are my followers. You want the truth about Cleo Ray, read their comments.

FRED HITE, COUNTY SHERIFF: The victim had cuts and contusions across the bridge of her nose, on her forehead, and surrounding her right eye.

WALLY UPHAM, BOATHOUSE ATTENDANT: I'd seen the bruises. But I didn't want to say anything until the sheriff and deputy noticed it.

FRED HITE, COUNTY SHERIFF: They'd been using grappling hooks and nets for a couple of hours and hadn't snagged a second body. Which turned into a suspicion the other woman may not have drowned and been able to swim ashore.

ERIN NEWCOMB, CHIEF DEPUTY: So why didn't this other woman rush back to the boathouse to report what happened?

FRED HITE, COUNTY SHERIFF: The lake was calm, not a breath of wind. Those rental canoes are usually pretty stable. When Ms. Alden was found, she was not wearing a life vest.

WALLY UPHAM, BOATHOUSE ATTENDANT: I handed her two vests—they're standard with the rental. I showed her how to put it on and buckle it, in full compliance with the regulations.

ERIN NEWCOMB, CHIEF DEPUTY: The coroner got delayed, and it was a real scorcher out there. We'd secured the area, but we needed to get the body to a cooler spot, and the coroner agreed. I took video and photos of the deceased, the canoe, and the cove where she was found. Then we lifted her into the back of the truck and transported her to the store. We laid her down on the floor next to the freezer and opened the door to cool her off.

FRED HITE, COUNTY SHERIFF: Wally showed me where she'd left her windbreaker. I looked it over and noticed a cell phone in one of the pockets. I put on evidence gloves and took it out. The phone's auto-lock was off, and right away I saw the unsent text. Here's what it said:

> *Hi mom. We're up in the Sierras and I want to share a secret—we're getting engaged! Please don't tell anyone, especially not dad. I want to tell him myself. I'm ready to do it, finally. You can say you heard from me at the lake and everything's fine. Please don't worry about me. This was meant to be and I've never been happier. We'll be back late Sunday. Big hug and kiss. Love you—Beck.*

There were some heart emojis and such. But she hadn't hit send.

ERIN NEWCOMB, CHIEF DEPUTY: Two girls, one saying she was there to get engaged. From the beginning we suspected the victim meant she was getting engaged to this other girl, the blonde she rented the canoe with. That's fine with me, by the way. Personally I've got no problem with that.

FRED HITE, COUNTY SHERIFF: We have a strong Christian community up here, so it's not what we believe, but the law says they can and that's that. In six years, all the homicides I've investigated had male perpetrators. That these were two females and foul play was involved—it had an impact on me.

As I was reading Ms. Alden's text, two men and a boy approached the store wanting to buy more fishing supplies. Erin asked if they'd seen a woman around the lake.

ERIN NEWCOMB, CHIEF DEPUTY: They had seen a girl, by herself, headed back toward the boathouse. She acted *surprised* when she saw them. Or did they say *afraid*? Well, they were mixing English with Spanish. Anyway, they said she veered away from them and headed into the woods.

FRED HITE, COUNTY SHERIFF: They described her as *bonita*, pretty, and *rubia*, blond, which matched the description from the guy at the boathouse. I asked if he'd seen the car the women were driving.

WALLY UPHAM, BOATHOUSE ATTENDANT: No, there's a gravel parking area behind the building, and by the time I came back from getting the body out of the lake, the only cars there were mine, the sheriff's SUV, and the Mexicans' pickup truck.

FRED HITE, COUNTY SHERIFF: The Mexican men said her hair and clothes looked damp, *mojada*. This was between one and one-thirty, which fit the timing of when the canoe would have capsized.

ERIN NEWCOMB, CHIEF DEPUTY: This person had just been in a boat accident where her fiancée drowned and she doesn't ask for help? She turns away and takes off into the woods? I suggested we make that call to Mr. Mason.

DUNCAN MCMILLAN: *Owen Mason is the district attorney of Inyo County, an elected office. He has a reputation for being a fighter on behalf of crime victims. And he's a Republican.*

OWEN MASON, DISTRICT ATTORNEY: Is my aggressive pursuit of this case because an election's coming up and the polls showed me tied with my opponent? I did anticipate they'd ask that. And my answer would be consistent: "There are cases where we're compelled to seek the path of justice aggressively, and this is one of them."

FRED HITE, COUNTY SHERIFF: Two young women come to a lake that's off the beaten path, rent a canoe, paddle out to a remote cove. Their canoe is found overturned. One of them is dead in the water, the other missing. The missing one is identified by witnesses walking alone through the woods afterward. She says nothing, avoids them, apparently returns to the parking lot at the boathouse, and drives away without alerting anyone.

My first call was to my wife. Told her she should start dinner without me.

ERIN NEWCOMB, CHIEF DEPUTY: We were feeling sick in our hearts. Who leaves the person she's planning to marry drowned in a lake and takes off?

CLEO RAY: I made mistakes, big ones. And there's the difference between not guilty and innocent.

FRED HITE, COUNTY SHERIFF: One of the bystanders tweeted out a video of us lifting the body into our vehicle: #GirlDrownedBishopCalifornia.

Owen Mason was already watching it on his computer when he picked up my call.

DUNCAN MCMILLAN: *The world knows me as a documentary filmmaker, but I've always considered myself a journalist first. The common ground I share with journalists is that we all ask questions. What happened? Who was involved? Those lead to deeper questions. What really happened? The people involved, who are they really?*

When I start on a story in a place I've never been, the best people to answer my questions are usually the local journalists. Jake Crowe is a veteran reporter and editor for The Inyo Register, *a newspaper whose masthead declares "Serving the Eastern Sierra and Beyond Since 1870."*

JAKE CROWE, *INYO REGISTER*: The makeup of Inyo County is 64 percent white, 20 percent Hispanic, 11 percent Native American, with Asians and African Americans under 2 percent each. Historically, this is a very Republican county, and still a conservative stronghold, though there have been signs of a shift in certain districts. Median age is forty-six, eight years older that the national average. That's us.

Yes, I am very familiar with Owen Mason. And I knew he had not prosecuted a noteworthy criminal case in years. Two young women from the big city come up here. One drowns, one goes missing. After finding the body and seeing the head wounds, it's a safe bet our sheriff's first call was to our district attorney. That call would have gotten Owen Mason's attention.

OWEN MASON, DISTRICT ATTORNEY: The sheriff reached out to me before notifying the victim's family, and given the circumstances, that was the right choice. These matters need to be handled with care. The story was already out on social media and the sheriff was still investigating the crime scene, so I said I'd make the call to Rebecca's parents.

TITUS ALDEN: I was out in my workshop sanding a piece of pine. I was going to surprise Beck with a breakfast nook table for her twenty-second birthday. I'd already finished the benches. The phone was off, but I noticed the screen light up. I wouldn't have answered, but caller ID said *Inyo County District Attorney*. At first I didn't connect Inyo County with where Beck had gone, but I thought I should answer it.

OWEN MASON, DISTRICT ATTORNEY: Those calls are not easy. I am thankful I haven't had to make many of them.

TITUS ALDEN: He said, "Is this Mr. Alden?" I said, "Yes, it is." He said, "Mr. Alden, my name is Owen Mason, I'm the district attorney of Inyo County in the Eastern Sierra. Sir, I need to ask if you are the father of a young woman named Rebecca Alden."

I figured it was not going to be good news.

OWEN MASON, DISTRICT ATTORNEY: I knew it'd be a terrible shock when he heard, so I said, "I'll explain everything in a moment, but first a couple of questions. You have an 818 area code. Where are you located?"

He said, "Reseda, in the San Fernando Valley."
I asked, "Does Rebecca live with you?"
He said, "No, she's got a little apartment in Encino."
I asked, "Do you know where she is today?"
He said, "Up in the mountains."

TITUS ALDEN: He asked if I knew who she went up there with. I said I thought it was a girlfriend, wasn't sure which one. Then I said,

"Mr. Mason, I'm already feeling pretty nervous here, could you tell me what this is about?"

OWEN MASON, DISTRICT ATTORNEY: "I'm sorry, Mr. Alden. Your daughter was found in the waters of Serene Lake. She appears to have drowned. She's gone. I am very, very sorry."

TITUS ALDEN: I couldn't, you know, I just—when a parent hears those words, when a dad hears that about his little girl—no. *No.*

OWEN MASON, DISTRICT ATTORNEY: I got choked up myself. I have kids, and to hear something like I was telling Mr. Alden would be the worst thing I could imagine. Something told me even then it would become my mission to help this man and his family find justice.

JAKE CROWE, *INYO REGISTER*: It's July. The county election's in November. To get something like this pushed through the court that fast requires a lot of tenacity. Mason could see this would be an attention-getter, but I don't think he had any idea how massive the avalanche would be.

I was meeting with my editor when the call came in. Honestly, a single person drowning is tragic, but it's not big news. When it became clear who was involved and that there was a possible love triangle with these social media hotshots, we realized it could be big.

TITUS ALDEN: If that wasn't bad enough, I had to figure out how I was going to tell my wife. Grace has heart problems. I was seriously concerned she'd have a heart attack. I was thinking *I* might be having a heart attack—I could feel this heavy pressure on my chest.

It was my heart, all right. Breaking apart.

Then came a whole new world of hurt.

OWEN MASON, DISTRICT ATTORNEY: I said, "There's more to this, Mr. Alden. It's terrible and I sympathize with you deeply. But there are some other things you need to know. Take a deep breath, okay?"

TITUS ALDEN: Then came the words "We think there may have been a *crime*." My daughter was *dead*, and it may have been a crime.

OWEN MASON, DISTRICT ATTORNEY: I told him we'd found her cell phone and an unsent text to Rebecca's mother.

DUNCAN MCMILLAN, INTERVIEWER: You knew the text revealed information that Rebecca hadn't told her father.

OWEN MASON, DISTRICT ATTORNEY: I did.

DUNCAN MCMILLAN, INTERVIEWER: You told him anyway.

OWEN MASON, DISTRICT ATTORNEY: He would've found out soon enough. His daughter had died, that was the big blow. That it might have been foul play took it to another order of magnitude. I read him the text and told him we needed to know who Rebecca had gone to the lake with. And if he didn't know, his wife might.

TITUS ALDEN: In less than five minutes I found out my daughter was dead, may have been murdered, and was gay. And she was planning to get married to someone I'd never met.
    Yeah. Uh-huh.

OWEN MASON, DISTRICT ATTORNEY: It was clear from the text his wife knew. Mr. Alden said he'd talk to her and call me back. Meanwhile I called our chief medical examiner and let him know Rebecca's autopsy would take top priority. The results should be communicated to me only.

TITUS ALDEN: I sat my wife down, held her hand, and said, "Beck is gone." She screamed and fell on the floor. I knelt down and hugged her. We were both sobbing. After she calmed down somewhat, I said, "Do you know who she went to the lake with?"

CLEO RAY: It was a perfect day. She looked beautiful. And she was happy. Maybe the happiest I'd ever seen her.

OWEN MASON, DISTRICT ATTORNEY: Mr. Alden called me back and said his wife was too upset to talk on the phone. She told him she'd never met Rebecca's girlfriend, but Rebecca had said the girl was the niece of a man named Samson Griffith. He was someone Rebecca had worked for doing hair and makeup on video shoots. I told Mr. Alden not to talk to anyone else for the time being and asked him to come up to Bishop to ID the body, and so we could discuss things further.

I didn't know the name Samson Griffith, so I looked him up online while Mr. Alden and I were on the phone. I saw immediately he was kind of a big deal in that world. His company represented actors, singers, and internet celebrities—aka influencers.

TITUS ALDEN: My wife said Beck wanted to be the one who told me about, you know, her preferences—or orientation, I guess. And you saw in the text she would have as soon as she got back. I'd made crude comments from time to time, mostly about male homosexuals, but I was joking, the way people joke, or used to joke, about that. I'm not homophobic. I wouldn't have judged her. I may have felt sorry for her, because I believe it's a harder life than being normal. Sorry, I don't mean normal, I mean in the sense there are a lot of people in the world who will judge you for it.

JAKE CROWE, *INYO REGISTER*: Before law school, Owen Mason had been a mixed martial arts fighter. A grappler. Ten pro fights—five wins, five losses. You can see he'd broken his nose and never had it fixed right. I think he figured it made him look more fearsome in the courtroom. Deep down he's an emotional guy, a spiritual guy. That comes through. In fact it's a big reason he's been successful.

OWEN MASON, DISTRICT ATTORNEY: It wasn't until law school that I found I had a talent for public speaking. Otherwise I was an average student. But when it came to making an opening or closing argument, I felt in the zone. I got good at fighting for a point of view. And that made an impression on people in a position to hire me.

JAKE CROWE, *INYO REGISTER*: I wouldn't say his actions were entirely politically motivated. The guy's inclined to fight for people who can't fight for themselves. But there's no denying he also saw a huge opportunity, from the moment he learned L.A. people in the media business were involved.

OWEN MASON, DISTRICT ATTORNEY: I got Samson Griffith's office number from his company website and dialed it. I still didn't know the name of the woman who'd been in the canoe with Rebecca. But I had a hunch Mr. Griffith might.

His assistant said he was in a meeting and wouldn't be able to return my call for a couple of hours. I told her it was urgent. She asked what it was about. You don't want to give out much information in those circumstances, so I said, "Please have him call me."

SAMSON GRIFFITH: I frequently get calls from people with titles like *district attorney*. In most cases it's about them wanting to get their kid or relative a meeting with me. When this Mr. Mason didn't say what it was about, I assumed it was a personal matter.

I was unaware of the drowning incident at that point. That afternoon my head was completely wrapped up in a major negotiation for one of my clients.

TITUS ALDEN: I remember saying, "We have to drive up there to identify the body," and the second those words came out of my mouth, I broke down again. Neither my wife nor I was in any shape to make that drive. Much as we wanted to go to Beck, we had to settle our nerves.

SANDY FINCH: (YouTube) "These Argentine polo boots are works of art—while providing the player with maximum protection and functionality. They rise to just below the knee, zip up the front, and have a single buckle at the top. These babies from Pro Polo Co will set you back a mere eight hundred bucks and are built to last. They are crazy comfortable. I've worn mine out dancing."

DUNCAN MCMILLAN: *Sandy Finch is a sports brand ambassador and social media influencer. He's unique because he is not a specialist in any one sport. His trademark is embedding himself in the domains of different competitive sports and games around the world and acting as a guide and conduit for his five million plus Instagram followers.*

SANDY FINCH: A group of us drove up to Mammoth together. My friend's parents have a six-bedroom chalet with an incredible view of the mountains. Cleo said she had stuff to do in L.A. and would drive herself up there on Thursday evening. Friday at dawn we were off on a three-day hike. And we'd agreed to go off the grid. We left our devices at the house, forty-eight hours totally unplugged.

For this group, that was an epic sacrifice.

DUNCAN MCMILLAN: *Assistant D.A. Brian Burleigh is Owen Mason's prosecutorial right hand. At thirty-two, he also acts as an unofficial envoy to millennial voters in the county.*

BRIAN BURLEIGH, ASSISTANT D.A.: My wife and I were at LAX waiting for a flight to Cabo San Lucas when my phone buzzed. It was Owen. He said, "Sorry to do this to you, but I need you to postpone your vacation and get back up here. A girl drowned in Serene Lake, and it's looking like foul play. I'll make this up to you on the back end."

   I knew Owen wouldn't be asking me to postpone my vacation unless it was a big deal, so I didn't even question it. I told my wife we had to go back, and back we went. The law enforcement community in Inyo is tight-knit and dedicated, and my wife knows that. She was still disappointed, so I told her she could buy whatever she wanted from the duty-free store.

OWEN MASON, DISTRICT ATTORNEY: I met with our county public information officer, and we composed a press release: "On July ninth, in the early afternoon, the attendant of a boathouse at Serene Lake on Rock Creek Road notified the sheriff's office that a capsized canoe had been spotted in one of the coves. The attendant found a deceased woman in her early twenties submerged in the water. Sheriff Fred Hite and Chief Deputy Erin Newcomb responded to the scene. After a preliminary investigation, the victim was turned over to the Inyo County coroner. An autopsy is scheduled to determine cause of death. The victim's identity is being withheld pending notification of next of kin."

   I didn't want Rebecca's name released until we had a positive ID from the family. And because this other woman might still be in the area, I didn't want to say anything to scare her away.

TITUS ALDEN: We finally got to Bishop around ten at night and were met by Mr. Mason and his assistant and also the sheriff and a deputy. They took us over to the coroner's office. Grace and I stood there in the cold room looking down at our girl laid out on a steel table. Her face was bruised; you could see she'd been hit. I was feeling all these feelings, mostly grief and rage.

BRIAN BURLEIGH, ASSISTANT D.A.: It was pretty awful. I know I teared up. No parents should have to see their child like that.

OWEN MASON, DISTRICT ATTORNEY: Mr. Alden turned to us with tears streaming down his face and said, "Do you think she suffered?"

I said I didn't know, but if she did, it was only for a short time.

He said, "I want you to find the person who did this to her. Find her. And make her pay."

I said, "I promise you both, faithfully and dutifully as the district attorney of this county, nothing will be spared to locate, arrest, prosecute, and convict the person responsible for this."

ERIN NEWCOMB, CHIEF DEPUTY: Our D.A. is a powerful speaker. We were inspired by what he said to Rebecca's parents.

BRIAN BURLEIGH, ASSISTANT D.A.: Owen would've been a great football coach or pastor. We came away from the coroner's office motivated to do right by these parents. And the victim.

FRED HITE, COUNTY SHERIFF: We went back over to the D.A.'s office, and the six of us sat down to talk. Rebecca's mom and dad were emotionally exhausted, but we couldn't wait till morning. We needed to know all we could.

ERIN NEWCOMB, CHIEF DEPUTY: We'd heard Rebecca's girlfriend was a niece of Samson Griffith, who owns a talent management company down in L.A. I went to the website and clicked on their client roster. I knew I was looking for a blonde in her early to mid-twenties. There were a few who fit the description, but when I googled Cleo Ray, a snippet came up saying that she was managed by her uncle. I looked her up on Instagram and YouTube. She's this thing called a *fit-fluencer*. She posts videos of herself working out and talking about exercise and healthy eating. Companies pay her to advertise their products.

OWEN MASON, DISTRICT ATTORNEY: We showed a video of Cleo Ray to Mr. and Mrs. Alden. He didn't recognize her, but the mother thought she might have seen her in a photo Rebecca had taped to a mirror in her apartment.

CLEO RAY: From the lake I drove back down the dirt road and onto the highway, then pulled off at the nearest rest area. I couldn't stop shaking. I had to get myself together before I hooked up with Sandy and our friends in Mammoth.

Sitting in my car, I saw this family drive up in their SUV for a bathroom break. Mom, dad, three little kids. I thought, *Wow, they look so normal, innocently living their lives.* And I felt so separated from that normality.

I got out of the car, went into the restroom, and threw up in the toilet. Someone knocked on the stall and asked if I was okay. It was the mom of those kids. I didn't want her to see me, so I said, yes, thank you, but stayed inside the stall until I was pretty sure they'd moved on.

I went out and sat at one of the picnic tables and did my relaxation breathing. There was a tree nearby, and I heard the sound of birds chirping, and they were really loud. I closed my eyes. Inhale on four, exhale on six. Four in, six out.

OWEN MASON, DISTRICT ATTORNEY: Samson Griffith hadn't gotten back to me. Calls to his office were going to voice mail. I left a message and changed the word *urgent* to *emergency*.

SANDY FINCH: Cleo got up to the house around dinnertime. We were on the back deck grilling up rainbow trout we'd caught earlier in the day. When I saw her, I thought she looked great. I mean, *great*. I don't know if I should tell you this, but maybe it'll—when I showed her where our bedroom was, she shut the door, grabbed me, pulled me down, and got on top of me.

She kept saying, "I missed you, I missed you, I never want us to be apart." She was intense like that. Sex with her was intense—every single time.

CLEO RAY: Part of me was like, okay, I didn't leave anything at the lake, the guy at the boathouse saw me only from a distance. Same thing with the two men carrying fishing poles. I didn't sign anything. Beck didn't tell anyone where she was going or who she was with. How could anyone prove I was even there?

SANDY FINCH: Not going to lie, I was into Cleo. And it wasn't just her rocking body. She was fun. And smart. And her uncle is like my godfather.

She was also a great fitness coach, and getting better all the time.

CLEO RAY: Sandy was everything I wanted. He was hot and nice and had millions of followers. Okay, I know how that sounds. But everywhere we'd go, girls would see us together and look at me with massive envy. I got to be honest, I kind of liked feeling that.

OWEN MASON, DISTRICT ATTORNEY: I got back to the office around midnight, after getting Mr. and Mrs. Alden settled at the Best Western. The phone was ringing when I walked in and I picked it up. It was Samson Griffith calling from L.A.

SAMSON GRIFFITH: He told me a girl had apparently—he was careful with his words—*apparently* drowned in one of the lakes up there. Said her name was Rebecca Alden, and did I know her. I knew she wasn't an employee, and I didn't recognize the name. I work with hundreds of people. He said she did hair and makeup. Then he asked if we kept contractor files, and could I look her up. I said I'd be happy to do that when I got into the office in the morning.

OWEN MASON, DISTRICT ATTORNEY: Then I asked about his niece. Did he know where Cleo was yesterday or today? He said he didn't. I asked if he knew anything about a relationship between Cleo and Rebecca Alden.

SAMSON GRIFFITH: In my head I'm thinking, *District attorney. Emergency. Girl drowned. Relationship with Cleo.* He asked if I had a cell phone number for her. I said I'd look for it and call him back. I clicked off and took a beat.

CLEO RAY: I had the phone on mute, but I saw my uncle's caller ID. I almost picked it up. Then I thought, *Why would he be calling me after midnight?* I let it go to voice mail.

OWEN MASON, DISTRICT ATTORNEY: I wanted to meet with Mr. Griffith in person first thing the next morning. He requested we do it at his home instead of the office. I asked Mr. and Mrs. Alden if they'd be okay helping me get access to Rebecca's apartment. We might find something that would aid the investigation. Mr. Alden said he'd meet me at the building after I met with Griffith.

SAMSON GRIFFITH: When I hadn't heard back from Cleo by the morning, I called my daughter, Gillian, Cleo's cousin. She and Cleo were having one of their periodic falling-outs, so she hadn't spoken to her. She did say Sandy Finch and David Kim and some friends had gone camping in the mountains. I said to myself, *Don't let Sandy be mixed up in this. That guy has a huge future in front of him.*

OWEN MASON, DISTRICT ATTORNEY: I pulled up to the Brentwood address at nine sharp. Mr. Griffith has a two-story house at the top of a hill with a view of the Pacific Ocean. Man's worth millions of dollars, why not?

SAMSON GRIFFITH: Honestly, the encounter was a bit awkward for me. I'm a donor to the Democratic Party, strongly progressive, unreligious. When I googled Mason, I saw he was a conservative Republican from a small town in evangelical country. But I was happy to help him. A girl is dead, he's investigating, I get it.

OWEN MASON, DISTRICT ATTORNEY: He told me he had a call in to Cleo but hadn't heard back from her. I asked him to tell me about his niece.

SAMSON GRIFFITH: She's the daughter of my older and only brother. My brother and I, we've never been close or spoken much, you know? We took different paths in life, to put it mildly. I don't judge him. I *try* not to.

OWEN MASON, DISTRICT ATTORNEY: He described Cleo's parents as *urban Bible preachers*. I detected a bit of a sneer when he said it. Did it bother me? No.

SAMSON GRIFFITH: Cleo did not have it easy growing up. I wasn't in her life until she was a teenager. Her parents kept my side of the family out of her view. Clearly they don't approve of what we do. If it's not God's work, it's the work of the capital D Devil. Right after Cleo turned sixteen, she showed up on our doorstep.

She'd taken a bus from somewhere in the middle of the country and made it known she was not on the same path as her parents. She wanted to enroll in school and asked me for a job so she could support herself. I thought that was incredibly brave of her.

CLEO RAY: My earliest memories are being out at night on a street corner and my parents making me sing gospel songs with them. Oh yeah, I've got a library of gospel songs burned in my brain.

> *I heard the voice of Jesus say,*
> *"Come unto Me and rest;*
> *Lay down, thou weary one, lay down*
> *Thy head upon My breast."*
> *I came to Jesus as I was,*
> *Weary, and worn, and sad;*
> *I found in Him a resting place,*
> *And He made me glad.*

I associate those nights with being hungry and worried there'd be nothing but scraps for dinner.

SAMSON GRIFFITH: We got her enrolled at Palisades High, and in the afternoons, she interned at Griffith All Media. First couple of years we ran her ragged. But she proved she could take it. In what free time she had, she was teaching herself exercise and anatomy, learning about nutrition, turning her body into her best asset. She was also taking speech lessons and acting classes and studied the social media business to see what was working and what wasn't.

BRIAN BURLEIGH, ASSISTANT D.A.: The one thing we couldn't charge her with was being a slacker.

SAMSON GRIFFITH: From her parents she did get a *killer* work ethic. Oops, unfortunate word choice. You'll cut that, right? Anyway, yeah, Cleo was focused and disciplined and put in the time to watch and understand why one influencer's numbers would keep going up while another's would peak and stop growing.

OWEN MASON, DISTRICT ATTORNEY: I asked Mr. Griffith if he knew whether Cleo was gay or bisexual.

SAMSON GRIFFITH: Whoa, hold on. I knew she was dating a man who was straight, or at least projected that. He had that rugged yet sensitive thing that's attractive to both men and women. But these young people tend to be more fluid and less binary in their views of sex.

Mason looked puzzled. I took it upon myself to explain *pansexuality* to this law-and-order, churchgoing, middle-aged white guy from the hinterlands.

OWEN MASON, DISTRICT ATTORNEY: I could tell that Mr. Griffith was trying not to sound condescending. But when you have to try that hard, it comes across as condescending anyway.

SAMSON GRIFFITH: I'd called our office manager before Mason arrived and gave her Rebecca's name. She looked in the employment files and texted me that Rebecca Alden had worked hair and makeup for us on about a dozen shoots over the last three years. She wasn't our A-list. Frankly, not even our B-list. But yes, she had been hired as a contractor by Griffith All Media during the period that Cleo was working for us. There was a chance she and Cleo had crossed paths on one of our shoots.

OWEN MASON, DISTRICT ATTORNEY: At that point I asked if he had any idea why Cleo might want to harm Rebecca.

SAMSON GRIFFITH: There's a line from Shakespeare about a character of ambition having "a lean and hungry look." That came to mind when I was around Cleo. She wanted it, *really* wanted it. I'm not saying that translates into someone who would willfully take another human life. I told Mason I couldn't imagine Cleo harming anyone.

CLEO RAY: I didn't sleep at all that Thursday night. I lay against Sandy, trying not to let him sense what I was feeling. When the alarm went off at five A.M., I pretended to wake up. Imagine my relief when I found out everyone was leaving their phones at the house.

SANDY FINCH: We got dressed, grabbed our packs, took a group photo in front of the house. Then we left our phones inside and hiked out on the trail into the backcountry.

SAMSON GRIFFITH: I asked Mr. Mason if he had a warrant or any judicial guidance on investigating Cleo. He told me as long as Cleo had an alibi or could convince them she wasn't at the lake with Rebecca, she wouldn't be in any trouble.

Honestly, I didn't think there was any way Cleo could be involved.

OWEN MASON, DISTRICT ATTORNEY: "By the way," I told Griffith, "there was an unsent text on Rebecca's phone to her mother, and it said she was up there to get engaged to her girlfriend."

SAMSON GRIFFITH: Couldn't have been Cleo. She was going to marry a C-list hair and makeup person? She might not get Sandy Finch to commit, but Cleo's aim was a lot higher than Rebecca Alden. Not to demean the dead in any way, it's just the reality of this world.

OWEN MASON, DISTRICT ATTORNEY: *This world* meaning the one he lives in? I brought up what Brian told me as I was leaving Bishop that morning. He saw on social media that when she started dating Sandy Finch, Cleo added a couple hundred thousand new subscribers to her YouTube channel and even more on Instagram. She went from under fifty thousand to over a quarter million.

Griffith said, "I'm not surprised."

I said, "I guess not. But it does mean her relationship with Mr. Finch was something she'd want to protect." I thanked him and asked him to let me know when he heard from his niece.

GILLIAN GRIFFITH: My dad called me after the D.A. left. He said, "I hope to God your cousin has an alibi." He told me the story and I was like, "Yeah, Cleo liked pretty girls, she liked pretty people," but I mean, committing murder, that's bonkers.

You do know I'm the one who introduced her to Sandy? She begged me. So at my birthday dinner I seated them next to each other. She did her little number on him, and boom, he's smitten. With his money and his looks, he's the dream guy for a billion girls, but for Cleo it meant even more. Being with him equated to more followers, bigger endorsement deals, red carpets, celebrity selfies. He was her ticket to a much higher level of influencing.

Why would she risk screwing that up?

OWEN MASON, DISTRICT ATTORNEY: I drove from Brentwood through the Sepulveda Pass to Encino. I met Mr. Alden in front of Rebecca's apartment building. It was just north of Ventura Boulevard and the 101 freeway, which means something if you're from there. The fashionable people live south of the boulevard or some such nonsense.

We called the manager on the intercom. She let us in the front door, and we told her the news. She gave us permission to enter Rebecca's apartment.

The manager was upset and told us Rebecca had been a good tenant. I had a photo of Cleo Ray on my phone and asked if she'd seen her coming or going from Rebecca's apartment. She said, "I recognize her. I do recognize that one." Out of earshot from Rebecca's dad, she whispered to me, "That one spent the night quite a few times."

TITUS ALDEN: Getting the news, telling Beck's mom, driving up to identify the body—the only way I had anything left came from my desire to find the person who'd done this to her. I hadn't slept in twenty-four hours. If Mr. Mason hadn't been with me, I could not have gone into that apartment by myself.

OWEN MASON, DISTRICT ATTORNEY: Before entering, I asked Mr. Alden to put on shoe covers and latex gloves as a precaution, and I did the same.

TITUS ALDEN: The second I stepped inside I could smell Beck, and I got slammed again. That's how grief comes. It's not a consistent thing. You feel okay for a few minutes, even an hour or two, and then here it comes again to crush you.

The cat came out of the bedroom to greet us and was looking for Beck. I kneeled down and petted her and told her she was getting a new home. "Don't worry, Grace and I will take good care of you." That's what Beck would have wanted.

OWEN MASON, DISTRICT ATTORNEY: Once we were reasonably sure that Cleo Ray had been the other woman in the canoe, the next thing was to establish probable cause. That's where *motive* helps. I spotted the picture on the mirror of the blond woman and took a photo of it.

TITUS ALDEN: First drawer I opened I saw something I didn't want to see. Something I can never unsee. So that was it for Dad. I stepped back outside in the breezeway and waited.

OWEN MASON, DISTRICT ATTORNEY: In the bedroom we came upon a drawer of sex toys. I won't describe them more specifically because those details already came out at the trial. They spoke to the nature of the relationship between Rebecca and the defendant, the level of physical intimacy they shared.

TITUS ALDEN: Mr. Mason brought out a box of keepsakes and asked if I'd mind going through it. I stood there and looked inside. There was a swizzle stick from a Mexican restaurant. Ticket stubs from a concert. A map from Hearst Castle, other mementos from her relationship with that woman.

I could see she meant a lot to Beck. And it made me wonder, *What the hell happened that it would end that way?*

OWEN MASON, DISTRICT ATTORNEY: In another drawer I found a stack of cards that Cleo had given Rebecca. One was a black-and-white picture of two preteen girls hugging each other. The cards showed there was a period where Cleo had had high engagement in the relationship. Lots of hearts, XOs, happy faces. Some were dated. The most recent one stood out because Cleo had drawn a large sad face inside it. This is what she wrote:

> *Believe me when I say I never thought this would happen to us. The idea of you not being in my life makes me so sad. Why would you want to hurt me, given the beautiful experiences we've shared? Please let's not destroy those memories. Our time together has been wonderful and unforgettable. Let's respect and honor that and move on. I always want you to be my friend, my special, sweetest friend.*

"Why would you want to hurt me?" To me, there's one way to read that. They were going through a breakup and Rebecca wasn't taking it well. But Rebecca's unsent text to her mom said "We're getting engaged." How did it go from "Let's move on" to "Let's get engaged" to Rebecca dead in a lake?

TITUS ALDEN: The more I thought about it, the angrier I got. Beck got romanced by this person who dumped her when something better came along. Male or female, didn't matter. What a terrible thing to do to someone who'd given herself to you.

That woman broke our daughter's heart. Then she lured her into a trap and killed her.

OWEN MASON, DISTRICT ATTORNEY: The pieces were fitting together. What I didn't see yet was how Rebecca had threatened to hurt Cleo. Through angry words and emotional scenes? Did she threaten to go public about their lesbian relationship? Or did Rebecca know something else that would be damaging to Cleo?

CLEO RAY: The sun was coming up over the mountains as we climbed up to the first ridge. Gorgeous summer day. Blue sky and big mountains and green trees. Being totally immersed in nature helped distract me. And Sandy was being so sweet.

Still, every moment there was about 2 percent of my brain screaming, *Are you insane?*

SANDY FINCH: I can see some clues looking back, but at the time I didn't notice anything wrong. I guess that either makes her a phenomenal actress or me oblivious.

CLEO RAY: I ran away from the lake because I panicked. I panicked. But then I pulled it together. And it was real. Being with Sandy, that part was not a lie.

SANDY FINCH: I couldn't have done that. I couldn't have pulled that off.

CLEO RAY: Besides Sandy and David, there were Stuart and Violet and Wynette and Harley and Taylor and Jill. All with at least a hundred thousand followers. Fashion, food, beauty, and travel.

DAVID KIM: An elite group—but we're not elitist. We just like hanging out together.

DUNCAN MCMILLAN: *David Kim is a men's fashion influencer and a close friend of Sandy Finch.*

DAVID KIM: I knew Sandy before he posted his first video. We've been on this ride together for the last five years. People in this business tend to seek each other out and support each other. We're a community.

No, Cleo really wasn't a part of it—until she started dating Sandy.

CLEO RAY: Growing up, I never felt I belonged anywhere. We moved around a lot, never stayed in one place for long. I never had a real posse. I was always passing through.

DAVID KIM: Look, I told Sandy I had concerns about Cleo. But you know how it is when you're infatuated. He was seeing the world through sex goggles. Cleo's hot, I won't argue that.

SANDY FINCH: I kept reaching for my phone. It felt like I was missing a limb. I have wondered how different the experience might have been if we'd taken them with us.

DAVID KIM: I'd hiked that trail and camped there with my family for years. I know the area well. God's country. My friends were blown away. Everyone was like, "We're coming up here more often." Being an influencer can easily become a full-time obsession. The occasional deep dive into nature is a necessity. And going off-line every once in a while.

CLEO RAY: In that place, with those people, with Sandy holding my hand, putting his arm around me, calling me *sweetie,* I could almost convince myself the thing at the lake hadn't happened. Almost.

DAVID KIM: We didn't bring any weed or alcohol. We take our cultural positioning seriously. We're not one thing to our followers and another thing in real life. I know, ironic considering what we found out about Cleo.

CLEO RAY: We came to a lake. The sight of it made me queasy. Everyone was horsing around. Stuart pushed Wynette into the water, and she pretended she couldn't swim. "Help! Save me! I'm drowning!" I'm sure my face got red, but it was hot in the sun and no one noticed.

SANDY FINCH: Such a great day. The vibe with Cleo was amazing. David found a spot to set up camp, and Cleo and I pitched our tent. She had camping experience. Her folks taught her how to pitch a tent when she was a kid. I liked watching her take charge.

CLEO RAY: David got the campfire going and we all sat in a circle. Everyone was on a high. People were like, "This is awesome," "I feel so alive out here."

It would've been weird if I'd sat there and not said anything.

DAVID KIM: What Cleo said at the campfire was "You guys are the best people I've ever known, and I've never felt so supported and accepted." She thanked us for being her friends.

I thought, *The reason you're here is because you're Sandy's girlfriend.* Okay, maybe that's harsh, but I know the others were thinking the same thing. And this was *before* we found out about Serene Lake.

SANDY FINCH: We cooked up a good healthy dinner, penne pasta and veggies, then indulged in roasting marshmallows and making s'mores.

CLEO RAY: I fed Sandy his and he fed me mine. It was all warm and gooey and we were licking each other's fingers and giggling like crazy.

SANDY FINCH: Me and Cleo and David were the last ones around the campfire. David was being his usual hilarious self, cracking us up. I looked over and saw tears in Cleo's eyes. I thought that was from laughing so hard.

OWEN MASON, DISTRICT ATTORNEY: I was well aware from the moment we had an ID on the suspect that it meant proceed with care. It wasn't the suspect I was concerned about; I didn't think she'd give us any trouble. But her uncle and her friends and her followers, that world of social media stars—every action we took would come under a microscope. The worst thing we could do was come off as too aggressive or biased. We had to take one step at a time and follow the letter of the law.

The next step was to get an arrest warrant.

CLEO RAY: When we got up to go to our tent, it started hitting me. As long as there were people around and we were talking and hiking I was okay, but being in the dark and the quiet was not what I needed. I mean, I knew they must've found her and were investigating, trying to find out who else was in the canoe. I knew there'd be clues that we'd been together. I knew she still had texts from me, even though we'd agreed to delete them all. My name would come up sooner or later. They'd find me and want to talk to me. But I thought I had time.

I hadn't slept the night before. And I wouldn't sleep that night, either. The idea of having to lay still made me want to stay up with Sandy as long as possible.

SANDY FINCH: Wow, yeah, the night in the tent. The last night before...

It was the most physically intense Cleo had been. She made love to me like she knew it would be the last time. After everyone was asleep, we went at it for two full hours. Just when I thought we were going to stop and sleep, she would start up again.

That night blew my doors off. I felt so close to her, we went to a whole new level. And even though I hadn't planned to do it then, I dug the box out of my backpack.

CLEO RAY: He turned on a flashlight and gave me this little blue box. I opened it. There was a ring inside. A gold fucking ring.

SANDY FINCH: It was a promise ring. I wanted her to know how serious I was about her, about us. We hadn't known each other long enough to get engaged, so I asked her not to wear it on her ring finger. Not yet.

CLEO RAY: I had *everything I wanted*. A beautiful, successful guy who liked me, who was falling in love with me. And I had my own thing, which was amazing. I had this full life and all these people on social media I was having a positive impact on.

But the voice inside me is saying, *It's going to blow up*. I realized that night, that moment, might be the peak of my entire life. Ahead was a dead end. All downhill from there.

I was bawling my eyes out when he slipped the ring onto my right-hand ring finger. Sandy teared up, too. I thought I was going to tell him the truth right then, blurt it out and say how sorry I was and beg him to still love me. The confession was on my lips—but I lost my nerve, shut down my brain, and fucked him again.

ERIN NEWCOMB, CHIEF DEPUTY: We got Sandy Finch's mobile number. I wanted to be the one to make that call. As I was dialing, my face got hot, like I was back in ninth grade calling the cute guy in class for the Spanish homework.

It went straight to his voice mail, which was full. I didn't even get to leave a message.

Dang.

OWEN MASON, DISTRICT ATTORNEY: I got to the courthouse in Independence at ten minutes to five. Brian, Sheriff Hite, and I presented what we had to Judge Oberwaltzer, who didn't blink in issuing the warrant. Next step was finding Ms. Ray, taking her into custody, and having her explain, with all due process of the law, what happened at Serene Lake between her and Rebecca Alden.

FRED HITE, COUNTY SHERIFF: We were on our way out of the courthouse when a call came in from my chief deputy. She got confirmation that Cleo Ray was with Sandy Finch up in Mammoth at a private home. She had the address. For reference, the town of Mammoth Lakes is about ninety miles north of Independence.

OWEN MASON, DISTRICT ATTORNEY: Right there we made the decision to send the sheriff, five deputies, and three vehicles up to the Mammoth house. I thought with any luck we'd have our suspect in custody before the end of the dinner hour.

As you know, it didn't turn out that way.

EPISODE TWO

GIRL ARRESTED

———————————————————

Treasure your pleasure! Now check out these new high-waisted leggings from one of my favorite athletic wear labels Body-Be-Fit. They come with a cool side pocket for phone storage, and the Be-Fit compression knit will sculpt you in all the right places. My color picks for spring are electric citron and strawberry rouge. What colors will you be wearing?

                                        Instagram post, CleoRayFitness

DUNCAN MCMILLAN, INTERVIEWER: What was going through your mind that night in the tent with Sandy?

CLEO RAY: I could look up and see the sky and stars. Those stars were the brightest ever. I could hear a breeze rustling through the pines above us. The sound of an owl hooting. I had the feeling of being surrounded by pure nature, pure peace. Sandy had fallen asleep with his arm around me. My physical body could not have felt safer next to his.

But you asked about my mind, didn't you?

FRED HITE, COUNTY SHERIFF: We arrived at the Kim home in Juniper Ridge and found three cars parked in the driveway. One belonged to the suspect. We split up to cover the back and side entrances. I knocked at the front door and identified myself. No answer. I knocked again. "County sheriff, open up!" No answer.

We had an arrest warrant and reason to believe our suspect was inside, but I hesitated to break in. The house was owned by a wealthy L.A.

couple who were probably well connected with the media and represented by a big law firm.

A voice from next door called out: "No one's home! They all left to go camping!"

CLEO RAY: The sounds from outside the tent changed from peaceful to threatening. Or the sounds didn't change, the way I was hearing them changed. It sounded like footsteps approaching, people sneaking through the trees into our campsite.

I was afraid to fall asleep because I thought I'd scream out from a nightmare and everyone would hear me. I did doze off. I was instantly back at the moment the canoe turned over, plunging under the water, panicking that I couldn't breathe, fighting my way to the surface.

As my head came out of the water, I woke up in the tent drenched with sweat. Sandy was sleeping peacefully. It was pitch-dark. I listened for sounds, and the campsite was quiet again.

FRED HITE, COUNTY SHERIFF: I called the D.A. to tell him no one was at the house and that a neighbor saw them leaving early in the morning on foot with hiking backpacks. She didn't know what trail they were hiking out on but could tell they were camping overnight because of the amount of gear they were carrying.

OWEN MASON, DISTRICT ATTORNEY: I called the Kim home, also in Brentwood, not far from Samson Griffith, and explained the circumstances to Mr. Kim. I told him we had the authority to enter his Mammoth home and search for information about where the group was headed, but I decided to call him first. He told me David had mentioned he might take his friends hiking, and his father was sure if they were camping overnight, they'd be headed north toward June Lake. That was the trail their family always took on camping trips.

Mr. Kim said he'd been trying to reach David and his calls were going straight to voice mail. He suggested the group might have intentionally turned off their phones to unplug from the internet.

CLEO RAY: I was bouncing back and forth from paranoia to gratitude for every moment I got to press myself against Sandy.

ERIN NEWCOMB, CHIEF DEPUTY: We decided to bunk down at the Mammoth sheriff's station and head out on the June Lake trail at sunup. Six more deputies from Mono were joining us and a search and rescue H-40 helicopter was being deployed to give air support. The operation was now fourteen peace officers strong, with a mission to apprehend a single female fitness instructor, probably unarmed and all of a hundred and twenty pounds.

We also got approval to use the department's ATVs to track down the hikers. Yeah!

OWEN MASON, DISTRICT ATTORNEY: I drove up to the sheriff's station, where we spent most of the time planning the search. Again, we weren't concerned about the suspect herself, but she was with eight other people, one of them her boyfriend. How were they going to react? Were any of them armed? Because of their reach in social media, we didn't want to give them any reason to accuse our people of misconduct. That led to the decision to have the ground team wear body cams.

JAKE CROWE, INYO REGISTER: I was tipped off a manhunt would be launching out of Mammoth at daybreak for a suspect in the Serene Lake killing—the Information Office had changed the description from drowning to *killing*. I drove up to the sheriff's station after midnight and parked across the street. The lights were on inside, and I could see figures moving behind the blinds.

CLEO RAY: I kept touching the ring Sandy gave me and holding it against my heart. Then I got this panicked feeling they didn't let prisoners wear rings in jail, and I started obsessing over not having my phone to google that.

FRED HITE, COUNTY SHERIFF: Second week of July, lots of people are up here vacationing. With other groups of young people on the trails and in campgrounds, the operation had a fair amount of risk.

DAVID KIM: We were finishing breakfast when Cleo came out of the tent barely hiding her smile. Nobody missed the new ring on her finger. I was surprised. I looked at Sandy like, "Dude, really?"

SANDY FINCH: I was all in. I mean, that's the truth.

CLEO RAY: David was jealous because of all the attention Sandy was giving me. Not in a gay way. In a bro way.

DAVID KIM: The girls were saying how awesome it was. They were being polite. Knowing what we know now, I don't think they would have been so polite.

SANDY FINCH: We got up late, and while I was finishing my coffee, Cleo broke down our tent and packed up our gear. How's that for a camping partner? I remember thinking, *Could this girl be any more perfect?*

DAVID KIM: We headed out for another lake in the backcountry. We'd brought swimsuits. Cleo hadn't brought hers. It was like she'd packed for a different trip.

OWEN MASON, DISTRICT ATTORNEY: We met the helicopter and pilots at the landing field across the road. We looked at the map and made a plan to coordinate the search between air and ground.

FRED HITE, COUNTY SHERIFF: Usually the highway patrol folks are brought in for search and rescues. The mission was shifted to a SWAT enforcement detail, and the protocols changed accordingly.

JAKE CROWE, *INYO REGISTER*: I waited for the right moment and approached the D.A. and the sheriff. Now, understand, there's not a lot of love lost between the D.A.'s office and the local news media.

OWEN MASON, DISTRICT ATTORNEY: I bend over backward to keep my door open to the media. But it's the old story: give an inch, they want a mile.

JAKE CROWE, *INYO REGISTER*: I promised I wouldn't report anything until the search operation was completed. I wanted an inside view so my reporting would be the most informed it could be.

FRED HITE, COUNTY SHERIFF: Easy for reporters to make promises, but keeping them? The compromise was to let Mr. Crowe into the command center, but he had to surrender his mobile devices. That was fair.

OWEN MASON, DISTRICT ATTORNEY: Our relationship with the news media on this case started out peaceably. Unfortunately, that didn't last long.

ERIN NEWCOMB, CHIEF DEPUTY: The downside of using ATVs and air support is the noise. The person we were searching for would hear us before she'd see us. That would give her a chance to run. And we knew she'd run once already.

It was no joyride in the backcountry. We had to constantly work around other hikers on the trails and that slowed us down. Plus, we had a reporter observing the operation in real time from the command center. The pressure was on.

CLEO RAY: We were so wrapped up in each other, we kind of fell behind the group. The conversation was the deepest we'd ever had. It was about the things we most wanted out of life, how we saw our futures, our values.

Values. Sandy's were trust, honesty, and integrity. I won't tell you what mine were.

SANDY FINCH: We talked about having a big family, four kids because we didn't want one feeling like a middle child. We saw ourselves having two places, one in town, one in the country. We even said when we got back to Mammoth, we'd check places for sale. That's how in the moment we were.

CLEO RAY: We'd stop and make out, hike for a bit, then stop and make out again. At one point we thought we'd lost the others. We ran the trail until we caught up with them. Sandy's very fit. We'd do trail runs together in the Palisades a couple times a week.

After a night of making love and getting engaged to be engaged, we were feeling so connected. It was that perfect communion between two people.

He would tell you the same thing.

SANDY FINCH: No denying it. It felt really good.

CLEO RAY: I was on the brink of saying, "What if you found out something about me that sounded horrible? Would you give me a chance to explain and promise to believe me? Because you have to know I would never lie to you."

Never lie to you. Contradiction? But it was true. I ended up not saying anything because I thought it would only make it more confusing for him.

I'm so sorry, babe.

OWEN MASON, DISTRICT ATTORNEY: Early on the morning of our search operation, a story pops up in *Sierra High,* the local news publication for Mammoth and Mono County.

Headline: DROWNING VICTIM'S FEMALE COMPANION HUNTED BY INYO SHERIFF.

JAKE CROWE, *INYO REGISTER*: That did not come from me. *Sierra High* is our competition, so why would I give them that? Besides, the sheriff had my cell phone. The only way I could have gotten a message out was by smoke signal. To this day, I don't know how they came up with that.

DUNCAN MCMILLAN: *The first news story to go viral.* "Bishop, California, July eleventh. The body of 21-year-old Rebecca Alden, a resident of Encino in Los Angeles County, was found in Serene Lake on the afternoon of Thursday, July ninth. She had been seen in the presence of another woman, who has been identified as Cleo Ray, 25, also of Los Angeles County. Ms. Ray is believed to have been in the rental canoe with Ms. Alden when it left the dock, but she was missing from the scene when the canoe was found overturned in an isolated cove. A warrant has been issued by the Superior Court in Independence, and a law enforcement operation is currently under way to find Ms. Ray and arrest her on suspicion of murder. The suspect is reportedly hiking the backcountry near Mammoth Lakes with a group of friends. As more information becomes available, you'll find it here on the Eastern Sierra's number one independent source for news, from Lone Pine to Coleville along the 395 corridor."

ERIN NEWCOMB, CHIEF DEPUTY: Around noon we found their campsite. They'd left ashes in the pit, markings for four tents, and a matchbox from a sushi restaurant in West L.A. We could see the general direction they were headed, but there was a fork in the trail coming up. One way led to Bald Mountain Springs, the other to Grant Lake. We decided to split up, six and six. The helicopter would go back and forth between groups. I was in the group bound for Grant Lake.

Were we in competition for who found her first? Nah, we're professionals.

OWEN MASON, DISTRICT ATTORNEY: When the report about the arrest warrant and the search broke in the media, I decided to head back to our Bishop office. We knew the SWAT detail was closing in, and there wasn't much for me to do at the command center. Before leaving, I did confront Mr. Crowe of *The Inyo Register* about the news leak. He swore he had nothing to do with it. Since it wasn't his paper that broke the story, I accepted his denial.

But I considered it a bad sign.

CLEO RAY: I was getting a strong feeling something bad was going to happen when we got to the second lake. Sandy changed into his swimsuit. I hadn't brought mine, so he said I could swim in my underwear. Fine by me. But as he dove into the lake, I heard the sound of a helicopter. I saw it fly over and saw the police logo and *I freaked*. Extreme fight-or-flight kicked in. I looked to the lake and saw everyone swimming. I turned around to the woods.

What flashed through my mind was *I am going to get caught, but I'd rather get caught alone than in front of Sandy*. Not for his protection, for mine. From the heartbreak of having to look into his eyes.

ERIN NEWCOMB, CHIEF DEPUTY: I took a path east of the lake to cut off that angle of escape.

DAVID KIM: Suddenly this police helicopter is over us and a loudspeaker's calling out, "Stay where you are! Do not leave the area!" We're like, "What the fuck is this about?"

CLEO RAY: My instincts were telling me, *Hide! Dive under the brush and wait until they leave!* I kept moving deeper into the woods.

FRED HITE, COUNTY SHERIFF: The pilot radioed they'd sighted the group swimming in the lake, so we cut over to the shoreline. We saw the helicopter hovering and the hikers down below in the water.

SANDY FINCH: We heard the roar of the ATVs and five uniformed officers came racing up. They weren't kidding, this was serious. They're screaming, "Where's Cleo Ray?" I didn't process the implication. I spun around because I thought she was right behind me.

DAVID KIM: She wasn't in the water or on the shore. I shouted, "Hey, Cleo!"

FRED HITE, COUNTY SHERIFF: We knew what she looked like, and she wasn't with the group. I counted eight, one missing. I told them to get out of the water and line up on the shore.

DAVID KIM: I was like, "What for? What did we do wrong?" The sheriff said, "I'll explain, but right now I need you to get out of the water and where we can see you."

CLEO RAY: I could hear the ATVs and people shouting. My head was exploding, but I kept moving. I thought about what this would do to Sandy. Should I run back and throw myself at his feet? Should I resist the cops, get shot, become a martyr to police violence? Crazy things were going through my mind.

ERIN NEWCOMB, CHIEF DEPUTY: I was heading west toward the lake and suddenly I see her fast-walking in the opposite direction. I stopped my vehicle, pulled my weapon, and ran toward her.

CLEO RAY: I heard a woman shouting, "Stop! Get down on the ground! Spread your arms and legs!" I didn't need any help getting on the ground because my knees buckled.

ERIN NEWCOMB, CHIEF DEPUTY: I went over and stood above her. "What's your name?"

CLEO RAY: "Cleo Ray!" Then I remember saying, "Don't shoot me. Please don't shoot me."

ERIN NEWCOMB, CHIEF DEPUTY: I asked, "Are you with the Kim hiking party?"
   She said, "Yes."
   I said, "Are any of them nearby?"
   She said, "They're all at the lake. I'm alone."

CLEO RAY: Every ounce of energy drained from my body. I was paralyzed, couldn't move.

ERIN NEWCOMB, CHIEF DEPUTY: I identified myself and cuffed her hands behind her back.

CLEO RAY: Feeling the pinch of those handcuffs shot me full of adrenaline. "Why are you doing this? I haven't done anything wrong!"

ERIN NEWCOMB, CHIEF DEPUTY: I told her to stop talking and not to move. I patted her down and searched her backpack. Finding no weapons, I said, "We have a warrant for your arrest. Do you agree to come with me peacefully?"

CLEO RAY: "A warrant for what? I don't understand!"

ERIN NEWCOMB, CHIEF DEPUTY: I said, "I'll leave that for the sheriff to tell you. In the meantime, do you agree to come with me peacefully?"

CLEO RAY: I said, "I'll go with you, but do I have to have these handcuffs on?"

ERIN NEWCOMB, CHIEF DEPUTY: "Yes, ma'am," I said, "that's procedure."

CLEO RAY: She helped me to my feet, but my legs felt totally numb. I said, "Are you going to take me back on your motorbike?" She said, "No, we're going to join your friends at the lake. The sheriff will decide what happens then."

ERIN NEWCOMB, CHIEF DEPUTY: That's when she lost it. She'd been fairly calm to that point, but then she got hysterical.

CLEO RAY: I said, "Please don't take me back there! Those are my friends. I don't want them to see me like this!"

ERIN NEWCOMB, CHIEF DEPUTY: I'll admit, I felt sorry for her. She was about to be exposed as a murder suspect in front of her boyfriend. I said, "I can't make any promises because the sheriff is in charge here. We have to go back to where he is, and I'll let him make the call."

CLEO RAY: I put my head down and we walked through the trees back toward the lake. My legs were wobbly and I was sick to my stomach. I thought, *These are the last moments before Sandy finds out and I lose him forever.*

I told the deputy I felt dizzy and needed to slow down. She took out a tissue and held it so I could blow my nose.

FRED HITE, COUNTY SHERIFF: Once the hikers were lined up and quiet, I took Sandy Finch aside to question him. "How do you know Cleo Ray?"

SANDY FINCH: I was extremely skeptical. What could Cleo have done to justify sending a helicopter and a SWAT team after her? I said, "I want an attorney present before I answer any questions."

FRED HITE, COUNTY SHERIFF: I told him, "Sir, you are not accused of anything. I'm asking because we need to locate her as soon as possible."

SANDY FINCH: I said to the sheriff, "I thought she was right behind me, so I honestly don't know." Then I asked what she'd done to have all these officers chasing her down.

FRED HITE, COUNTY SHERIFF: I saw no reason not to tell him. "We have an arrest warrant naming her in the homicide of Rebecca Alden."

SANDY FINCH: Until the sheriff said it, I'd never heard the name.

FRED HITE, COUNTY SHERIFF: Before the questioning went any further, a radio call came in from my chief deputy. Said she had a sight line on me, so I looked to the trees and saw her motioning to me. I asked Mr. Finch to get back in line and went over to her. She led me down a hill and I got my first look at Cleo Ray. Pale as a ghost, shaky, red-eyed—not how she appeared on Instagram.

I still had to ask, "Are you Cleo Ray?"

"Yes, sir," she said.

ERIN NEWCOMB, CHIEF DEPUTY: I told the sheriff she'd asked about the charge. He looked in her eyes and said, "You're under arrest for the murder of Rebecca Alden." The suspect showed almost no reaction to that. I said she'd asked not to be brought in front of her friends wearing handcuffs. The sheriff asked if she'd been cooperative during the arrest. I told him yes, other than she seemed to be heading away from the scene when I encountered her.

FRED HITE, COUNTY SHERIFF: The suspect looked at me with pleading eyes. I thought about Rebecca's parents identifying her body at the coroner's, how completely heartbroken they were. And something inside me said, *This person does not deserve special consideration.*

CLEO RAY: The sheriff and the deputy went off to talk. My body felt icy cold, I was shivering uncontrollably. My hands were cuffed behind me. I couldn't even wipe my nose. I was standing less than fifty yards from Sandy, arrested for murder.

Shit.

FRED HITE, COUNTY SHERIFF: We had the helicopter land on the shore and put Ms. Ray inside to be flown down to our station in Bishop. And yes, that required her to walk past the people in her hiking party.

ERIN NEWCOMB, CHIEF DEPUTY: I didn't think she deserved any kind of break, either, but I still felt bad for her. Can you imagine a worse walk of shame?

SANDY FINCH: Yeah, that was surreal.

DAVID KIM: To her credit, she did look over at us. Her expression was part shame, part defiance, part "I'm so, so sorry."

CLEO RAY: I looked in Sandy's eyes. He held up a solidarity fist. It felt like he was holding my heart in his hand and squeezing it.

FRED HITE, COUNTY SHERIFF: We secured her into a rear seat, and the helicopter took off to transport her to the next point of custody.

CLEO RAY: First time I flew in a helicopter. As we were lifting off, I could see Sandy and David and the others watching me. I envisioned myself as someone so rich and important I got to fly while everyone else had to travel on the ground. Down below I could see the trail we'd been on. People were looking up and wondering what kind of megastar I was to rate my own helicopter ride.

Delusional? Yep. All that was holding me back from a total meltdown? That too.

DUNCAN MCMILLAN: *"Popular Social Media Influencer Arrested for Murder." I remember glimpsing the headlines in my news feed and skipping over them.*

JAKE CROWE, *INYO REGISTER*: The major outlets reported she'd been in the mountains with a group of her *co*-influencers. This lingo from social media kept taking on multiple meanings.

ERIN NEWCOMB, CHIEF DEPUTY: The other eight hikers were walked out to a service road, where a sheriff's van had been dispatched. We put them in the van and drove back to the house in Mammoth. We needed to find the suspect's phone, which she'd left at the house, and to impound her car. I rode in the passenger seat. It was a quiet trip. I sensed these guys were itching to get back to their phones. Cleo Ray's arrest was already viral and then some.

SANDY FINCH: I was gobsmacked. Couldn't believe it. The cops had gotten this really wrong. It would get cleared up in a day or two, and Cleo would be let go.

Right?

DAVID KIM: She was the niece of a big-league talent manager who's good friends with my parents, the cousin of a good friend of mine, the girlfriend of another good friend. Did I know Cleo Ray well? Did any of us? I kept thinking about my interactions with her and asking myself, *Who* are *you?*

ERIN NEWCOMB, CHIEF DEPUTY: Not Sandy Finch, but the other hikers started distancing themselves from Cleo Ray. None of them claimed to know much about her other than what was online.

SAMSON GRIFFITH: I got a call from my daughter, Gillian. She was in shock. This was a major crisis for our family and our business. After seeing the media coverage, I knew what I had to do next: call my brother, Asa.

DUNCAN MCMILLAN: *Cleo's parents, Asa and Elva Griffith, felt the calling as a young married couple to preach the holy gospel. Based out of Kansas City, Missouri, they are traveling missionaries whose church espouses living a life of Christian poverty—or the opposite of the American prosperity gospel.*

SAMSON GRIFFITH: I said, "Asa, I have bad news. Mary Claire's been arrested and taken to jail. There are no charges yet, but my understanding is, she's the main suspect in a murder." Long silence. Then comes: "Christ have mercy on her soul."

He must've covered the phone and told Cleo's mother, Elva, because she jumped on the line.

ELVA GRIFFITH: I said, "No. There's been a mistake. Our Mary Claire isn't capable of killing anyone."

SAMSON GRIFFITH: I said, "I agree, and I am on this—for the family." Then I said, "I have to tell you something before you hear it from another source. She had a relationship with this girl, the victim. A homosexual relationship." To my sister-in-law, I didn't feel right using the word *lesbian*.

ELVA GRIFFITH: Her father and I were stunned. God created us male and female, each for the other. The union God created and ordains is for husband and wife to come together in physical union, one flesh. It's not just what we believe, it's divine truth.

SAMSON GRIFFITH: After I dropped that little bomb, Elva must have dropped the phone because we got disconnected. So there it was. My first reach-out was to Cleo's parents. My next reach-out was to my law firm.

OWEN MASON, DISTRICT ATTORNEY: The helicopter delivered the suspect to the Bishop airport, and she was driven by sheriff's deputies to the station. This was midafternoon on Saturday the eleventh, forty-eight hours after the death of Rebecca Alden. We'd done a good job finding leads, tracking them, establishing probable cause, and making an arrest. On our end, the process had worked. We don't get many cases like this. It was an outcome we could be proud of.

In sports terms, that was the pregame.

CLEO RAY: In my head I kept repeating: *What doesn't kill you makes you stronger. What doesn't kill you makes you stronger.*

OWEN MASON, DISTRICT ATTORNEY: First we did a lineup and brought the two Lopez brothers, the ones who'd been fishing at Serene Lake, into the witness room. Separately, both identified Cleo as the person they saw walking alone around the time the canoe would have tipped over.

Did we hurry that first interview? No, we treated her like any other suspect. She even got a meal beforehand. The sheriff and I met with her in the interview room. And we did what we do in these cases, we asked her questions.

FRED HITE, COUNTY SHERIFF: Felony crime interviews are always recorded, starting when the suspect first enters the room.

CLEO RAY: I couldn't sit still. I had to get up and move. I started doing my trail-run warmups, lunges, and side stretches. After a few minutes the door opened and the sheriff came in with another man wearing a coat and tie. I thought that was weird because it was the middle of summer and hot outside.

> **SHERIFF:** Hello, Ms. Ray. This is Owen Mason, the district attorney of Inyo County.
> **DISTRICT ATTORNEY:** Hello, Ms. Ray.
> **SUSPECT:** Hello.
> **SHERIFF:** Before we begin, do you have what you need to drink?
> **SUSPECT:** I'll be needing more water soon.
> **SHERIFF:** We can get you as much water as you'd like. Do you need the restroom?
> **SUSPECT:** Not right now.
> **DISTRICT ATTORNEY:** Ms. Ray, have you been advised of your Miranda rights?
> **SUSPECT:** Yes.
> **DISTRICT ATTORNEY:** And are you familiar with Serene Lake?
> **SUSPECT:** I've heard of it.
> **DISTRICT ATTORNEY:** Have you been to Serene Lake?

SUSPECT: I can't remember right now. A lot's happened in the last hour, and I'm trying to get my bearings, okay?
DISTRICT ATTORNEY: Okay. Do you know the crime you're suspected of?
SUSPECT: Tell me again.
DISTRICT ATTORNEY: You can save us a lot of time, Ms. Ray, by answering this next question truthfully. Did you kill Rebecca Alden?
SUSPECT: No, sir, I did not.
DISTRICT ATTORNEY: Do you deny driving with Rebecca Alden to Serene Lake and renting a canoe together?
SUSPECT: I do not deny that.
DISTRICT ATTORNEY: So you did get into a canoe with Rebecca and paddle out on the lake?
SUSPECT: I don't deny that.
DISTRICT ATTORNEY: Why can't you answer a simple yes?
SUSPECT: Because nothing about this is simple.
DISTRICT ATTORNEY: Describe your relationship with Rebecca Alden.
SUSPECT: She was a girlfriend.
DISTRICT ATTORNEY: Was the relationship romantic?
SUSPECT: What do you mean, *romantic*?
DISTRICT ATTORNEY: Did you have intimate relations?
SUSPECT: What do you mean, *intimate relations*?
DISTRICT ATTORNEY: Did you have sex with Rebecca Alden?
SUSPECT: I'm sorry, that's private.
DISTRICT ATTORNEY: Did you and Rebecca ever discuss marriage?
SUSPECT: To each other? Not seriously, no.
DISTRICT ATTORNEY: Do you know why Rebecca would have told her mother the two of you were getting engaged on Thursday?
SUSPECT: I don't know why. We weren't getting engaged.
DISTRICT ATTORNEY: Rebecca had bruises on her face. Do you know how they got there?
SUSPECT: I never saw any bruises on Beck's face.
DISTRICT ATTORNEY: When did you find out Rebecca was dead?

SUSPECT: When the first officer arrested me. Maybe from the sheriff. I don't know, this whole thing is extremely upsetting. Why do you think I killed Beck?

DISTRICT ATTORNEY: Well, we're still learning the why. But here's where we are so far: We believe you drove up to the lake with Beck, and she rented a canoe that you got in together. You paddled out to a secluded area, and you hit her in the face with something, probably your paddle. You turned the canoe over and made sure she drowned. Then you swam to shore, walked through the woods back to your car, and from there drove up to Mammoth to go meet your boyfriend.

FRED HITE, COUNTY SHERIFF: That's when she went quiet. After a minute she said, "I have to call my uncle."

OWEN MASON, DISTRICT ATTORNEY: I told her, "You can talk to your uncle, no problem with that. But first we need to know the position you're taking here. Are you telling us you did or did not have anything to do with the death of Rebecca Alden?"

CLEO RAY: I told him I needed to talk to my uncle.

OWEN MASON, DISTRICT ATTORNEY: I checked my phone messages and saw one from Samson Griffith. I decided to call him back myself before putting him on with his niece.

SAMSON GRIFFITH: My phones were blowing up. Everyone from TMZ to *The New York Times* was calling. Yes, I was surprised. This wasn't like a mass shooting where a dozen people get gunned down. I mean, the victim was not well known. Cleo was on the rise, but she wasn't a big star. Sandy was a star. He and Cleo were an item. And we managed both of them.

It's that thing that hits the zeitgeist at the exact right moment. All of a sudden no one can get enough of the personal lives of these social media influencers. It was a titillating narrative with secret lesbian affairs, bisexual sex, hot young celebs.

And it came out of the gate at warp speed.

OWEN MASON, DISTRICT ATTORNEY: So I stepped out of the interview room and returned Mr. Griffith's call. He knew we had his niece in custody and asked if we'd begun to question her.

SAMSON GRIFFITH: He said they were in the process of *interviewing* her. I told him she should not answer any more questions without her attorney present.

OWEN MASON, DISTRICT ATTORNEY: I said, "Look, this does not have to be a five-alarm fire. We can take the heat down as long as Cleo tells us what happened on the lake."

SAMSON GRIFFITH: I'm familiar with high-stakes negotiations, and Mr. Mason sounded like he might not have the strongest hand. Maybe he didn't think he had enough to charge her yet and was trying to bluff me into giving up something.

OWEN MASON, DISTRICT ATTORNEY: I could see Mr. Griffith would be taking an adversarial position in the matter. Too bad. I ended the call and went back to the interview room.

CLEO RAY: He sat down, looked me in the eye, and said, "Two ways forward. One will be relatively smooth. We'll prepare a lesser charge, avoid a trial, and you'll spend some years in state prison."

OWEN MASON, DISTRICT ATTORNEY: "The other way this goes is your uncle sets you up with a fancy celebrity lawyer who'll take this to a painful, very public trial where there will be a good chance you'll be sentenced to life behind bars. So, Cleo, I am going to give you fifteen minutes to think about that, in here by yourself. Then you'll tell us which way you want to proceed."

JAKE CROWE, *INYO REGISTER*: Never seen a story from this part of the world blow up like that. Cleo Ray's Instagram gained hundreds of thousands of followers in the first twelve hours after her arrest.

DAVID KIM: When I got back to my phone, I had sixty texts and a full voice mail. A news crew from L.A. pulled up in front of our Mammoth house and started filming. They knocked at the door, but we didn't answer.

CLEO RAY: I was locked inside a room with no windows, no phone, no connection to the outside world. I laid down on the floor, shut my eyes, and focused everything on my breath.

OWEN MASON, DISTRICT ATTORNEY: She's a grown adult. If she wasn't book-educated, she's at least media smart. How else do you get all those people to follow you?

CLEO RAY: Mr. Mason came back in and I sat up. He said, "Have you made a decision?"
    I said, "I did not kill her. I am not a murderer."

OWEN MASON, DISTRICT ATTORNEY: That's the moment we began preparing for the biggest criminal trial in the history of Inyo County.

CLEO RAY: He set a landline on the table, plugged it in, and said, "One call. Let us know when you're done." Then he went out and shut the door. I was feeling so nervous and ashamed. When Uncle Samson picked up, I burst out, *"I'm so sorry."*

SAMSON GRIFFITH: I think I understand Cleo better than most. I knew what she'd come from, and there was no going back for her. She'd already achieved a lot. She was a striver and had the stuff to make something of herself. But below the surface she had an edge to her, a desperation she learned to keep well hidden.

CLEO RAY: I said I was sorry about five times. I hated involving him in this.

SAMSON GRIFFITH: I said, "You don't have to apologize. You shouldn't say any more until we can get a lawyer up there." She said, "But I have to tell you..."

CLEO RAY: "...I did not kill that girl, I swear to you, Uncle Samson, I did not kill her." For the first time since what happened at the lake, I let go. Totally fell to pieces.

SAMSON GRIFFITH: If that was a performance, it was extremely convincing. I said, "I understand. It's okay to cry, it's okay to be upset. We'll get it all worked out, Cleo. I promise you."

CLEO RAY: Whenever I was around my uncle I'd think, *He should have been my dad. My life would've turned out so much different.*

Sorry, Asa.

SAMSON GRIFFITH: I told her I'd have someone up there within twenty-four hours. "In the meantime, you have the constitutional right to remain silent, so exercise it. Do not answer any more questions."

CLEO RAY: I said I understood. I told him, "You've done so much for me, and I know this sucks for you, too, so please believe that I didn't do what they're saying I did."

SAMSON GRIFFITH: I believed her. I also knew all hell was breaking loose in the media. This was going to be a long walk on a tightrope—for all of us.

CLEO RAY: Before we hung up, Uncle Samson said, "By the way, I called your parents. I told them you'd been arrested."

That was a jolt. First time I'd stopped to consider how Elva and Asa would react. Worst thing that could happen was happening to me, and neither of my parents had entered my mind.

I guess that tells you something about me.

SANDY FINCH: The officers said they needed to get statements from everyone in the hiking party. They gave us forms and asked us to write out our recall of the events in Mammoth and on the trail and to submit the statements to them with our contact info before heading home.

The woman officer took me aside and said, "The D.A. wants to interview you in person."

I said, "If it'll help Cleo, sure."

David warned me. He said, "Why do you want to get mixed up in this?"

I said, "Because I don't believe it. Cleo's not a murderer. The idea is insane."

DAVID KIM: I told Sandy I agreed, it was crazy. But if they had evidence and it's enough to convict, do you really want to get involved in that? And if they don't have enough evidence and her uncle gets her released, fabulous. No need for you to go on the record here.

SANDY FINCH: He had a point. Except—I wanted Cleo to know I was stepping up for her.

OWEN MASON, DISTRICT ATTORNEY: Sandy Finch agreed to be interviewed and stopped by our office on the way back to L.A. I believe he truly cared about Cleo.

SANDY FINCH: He asked about our relationship. How we met, how long we'd known each other, how much we saw each other.

OWEN MASON, DISTRICT ATTORNEY: I asked if he'd ever met or heard of Rebecca Alden. He had no idea who she was.

SANDY FINCH: He asked where I'd been between noon and two P.M. on Thursday. Easy, I was in the company of seven other people. Then he asked if Cleo had talked to me about her past relationships. I said no. We hadn't had that talk yet.

OWEN MASON, DISTRICT ATTORNEY: I asked if he was aware that Cleo had been having a romantic relationship with a woman.

SANDY FINCH: I had no idea, none at all. He asked if knowing this would make a difference in my feelings toward her.

Look, if she had told me she was bi, I'd want to talk about it, sure. But I have no problem with a woman who is sexually attracted to other women. As long as she's honest about it.

OWEN MASON, DISTRICT ATTORNEY: I asked Mr. Finch if he was bisexual. He said it was none of my business. I couldn't disagree with him.

SANDY FINCH: He asked if I had any idea why Cleo would want to harm or silence another person. I thought, *Silence?* Interesting word choice.

I had no idea, none. I asked why *he* thought Cleo had killed this person.

OWEN MASON, DISTRICT ATTORNEY: We knew Cleo was not a random, compulsive killer. We believed there had to be a motive, something she feared about this woman. And the lesbian angle was compelling because

Ms. Griffith projected a wholesome personality in her fitness videos. She appealed to church girls.

SANDY FINCH: Our generation, whatever you call us, we're good with gay, straight, bi, transexual, pansexual, nonconforming, nonbinary. Would Cleo kill a female lover because she was afraid of being outed? I didn't see that.

OWEN MASON, DISTRICT ATTORNEY: My assistant D.A. calls it the Fear of Being Unfollowed Syndrome. Worst thing for one of these influencers is to lose followers. When it happens in large numbers, it's usually because someone is shown to be deceptive, acting privately in a way that contradicts their public brand. Cleo Ray's online persona was Southern California apple pie. A lot of her followers were teens, kids who did her workouts and meal plans and aspired to be her.

JILL TANAKA: (TikTok) "Friends, it's me, and yes, I was in the hiking party with Cleo Ray when she got arrested on Saturday. It was cray-cray *crazy*! I'm posting the group photo we took early Friday morning before we hit the trail. Zoom in on her face—she's smiling like she doesn't have a care in the world!"

HARLEY RAINES: (YouTube) "That was some wild shit going down with the hee-lo and cops on three-wheelers and I'm the only Black person there, so I was sure they were coming to get *me*. But no, they came to get the blond white girl. Mister officer's all smiling, asking am I okay, being chill. Like they got together before and said, 'Treat the Black dude extra nice. Don't want no problems there.'"

VIOLET GARCIA: (Twitter) "Trust me, I'm still in shock. I got caught in the middle of a scary real-life police action. It was terrifying. The honest truth is Cleo Ray is not one of my homegirls. I mean we're good, but we're like, *Hey, Cleo. Hey, Violet. You killin' it. Yeah, killin' it.* That's pretty much it."

ERIN NEWCOMB, CHIEF DEPUTY: The D.A. and the sheriff finished their initial questioning, so the next thing was to transport her to the county jail in Independence. The sheriff left the execution to me. Normally, this is no big deal. We secure the prisoner in the rear of the van, and there are two deputies in charge of the transfer, one driving, one monitoring. But we had media pouring in from all over, so I needed to assign six deputies to the transfer. Two in the van, two in a lead vehicle, two in a rear vehicle.

We headed south on the 395, and there was a caravan of twenty vehicles behind us. They kept driving up alongside and trying to shoot video of Cleo in the back. Which she didn't want, so she ducked below the windows. I thought, *This is someone whose livelihood depends on cameras being pointed at her, and now she's hiding from them.*

CLEO RAY: The infamous mug shot. When I get in front of a camera lens, my smile's automatic. No message to it. I wasn't communicating anything to social media or to anybody. Pure reflex.

ERIN NEWCOMB, CHIEF DEPUTY: The booking process at our jail is pretty extensive, and I stayed with Cleo throughout, keeping an eye on her, answering her questions, making sure the intake went smoothly. She passed the observation test. She appeared calm enough and emotionally stable, though clearly not happy to be there.

CLEO RAY: So many questions.
  "Do you have any sexually transmitted diseases?" No.
  "Do you have lice, crabs, or scabies?" No.

"Are you currently taking any prescribed medications?" No.

"Do you have any alcohol or drug use that may cause withdrawals?" No.

"Have you recently had a miscarriage or abortion?" No.

"Have you ever attempted or considered suicide?" Hmm. Attempted, no. Considered? Hasn't everyone?

"Are you thinking about killing yourself now?" Great question!

ERIN NEWCOMB, CHIEF DEPUTY: Cleo was maybe the healthiest, most vice-free incoming prisoner the Inyo County Jail had ever seen.

CLEO RAY: Strip search—not pleasant. And they made me take off Sandy's ring. I threw a fit and begged them to let me keep it, but that wasn't happening. I still get choked up when I think about taking it off.

ERIN NEWCOMB, CHIEF DEPUTY: She probably would not have used the ring to hurt herself or anyone else, but we couldn't make exceptions.

CLEO RAY: They gave me a uniform. One top, one pair of pants, one pair of shoes and socks. Black-and-white stripes, and they had nothing close to my size. I caught a glimpse of myself in a window and was physically ill.

ERIN NEWCOMB, CHIEF DEPUTY: Her intake score would have landed her in the general population, but we still assigned her an isolation cell. I told her it was only temporary and we'd move her to a pod after a period of observation.

CLEO RAY: I'd never seen the inside of a real jail cell. And then I was locked inside one. Metal mirror over a metal sink. Metal bed, no pillow. Toilet's a grate on the floor. No window.
Holy shit.

ERIN NEWCOMB, CHIEF DEPUTY: It's standard to put incoming prisoners on suicide watch for the first twenty-four hours. I didn't think there'd be an issue with Cleo, but we couldn't take any chances.

CLEO RAY: Social media wasn't just my job, it was my addiction. Sitting there alone, no phone, no way to connect—what were people saying about me? I had to believe a lot of my followers were being supportive. But maybe people were attacking me, shaming and blaming and hate-posting. I tried to focus on my breathing and shut down my brain because the complete disconnection from social media was making me feel insane.

I'd been working for years to create viral content. Now it was happening, but I was totally cut off from it.

OWEN MASON, DISTRICT ATTORNEY: Then the autopsy report came in. Blunt force injury to the bridge of the nose and right brow, likely resulting from a single blow—by an object such as a wooden canoe paddle. The cause of death was drowning. Rebecca was alive when she went into the water.

But there was a surprise. The autopsy revealed a second injury of blunt force trauma to Rebecca's head, behind the temple, toward the back of her skull. We hadn't seen it because the contusion was covered by her hair. This had also been caused by a blunt object, used with enough force to cause a moderate concussion.

These findings supported the theory that Rebecca had been attacked and struck violently—twice. Good chance she wasn't fully conscious, or was at least dazed, when the canoe turned over.

CLEO RAY: First night in jail I didn't sleep at all. That made three sleepless nights in a row. My brain was in a fog. After they turned the lights back on, an officer came in with breakfast. Styrofoam cup of black coffee, white toast, slice of boiled ham, and a hunk of scrambled egg coated with butterfat. That's when it hit me my diet would have to change or I'd starve to death.

Right then, starving to death didn't seem like the worst outcome.

JAKE CROWE, *INYO REGISTER*: My reporter's instinct was to focus on the victim. I got through to Rebecca's father and explained that as the number one news outlet in the area, the *Register* was deeply concerned with justice, whereas other news media might be more inclined to play up the sensational. I said I wanted to better understand his daughter so I could portray her as accurately as possible to our readers.

He agreed to see me the next day.

SAMSON GRIFFITH: I was rolling calls with reporters, crisis managers, my business partners. Gillian offered to go up and visit Cleo in jail. She thought she could get the straight story from her. But the smarter thing was to send an attorney first to assess the legal situation. Larry Smillie isn't a criminal lawyer, but we've worked together on a number of sensitive matters and I trusted him. We sent him to meet with the D.A. and then to go to the jail and talk to Cleo.

JAKE CROWE, *INYO REGISTER*: I arrived at the Alden home Monday morning. They live in Reseda, smack-dab in the middle of the San Fernando Valley. They bought the house before Rebecca was born, and because of neighborhood crime, they'd put security bars over the doors and windows.

News vans were parked up and down the block, and they filmed me going to the front door. They called out questions, but I said nothing and went straight inside.

Mr. Alden led me to a kitchen table where Mrs. Alden was sitting. She had a cat on her lap that she was stroking. It was their daughter's cat, which they'd adopted. Both parents expressed their distress over Rebecca being smeared in the media. They wanted to convey to me the true portrait of their daughter. They agreed to talk to me together, on the condition I quote only Titus, the dad. Mrs. Alden wanted nothing to do with the "mainstream media," which she very much distrusted.

TITUS ALDEN: Grace told the reporter, "She was such a good person, I could not have been prouder. She was so thoughtful, calling every other day, bringing over home-baked goody baskets for us, getting groceries, cooking meals on the holidays. She was naturally shy around people. She had the virtues of modesty and humility—rare for someone her age."

JAKE CROWE, *INYO REGISTER*: I asked if they'd ever heard of Cleo Ray, and did they know their daughter had been seeing someone?

TITUS ALDEN: Beck's mother and I had gone over and over this. We knew she was going out on dates, but she rarely mentioned names and never brought anyone home.

Beck had told her mother she was dating other women. She did not tell me. But she was going to. She said that in her text.

JAKE CROWE, *INYO REGISTER*: I asked how they would've felt about Rebecca getting married to another woman.

TITUS ALDEN: If this was her first real girlfriend, to my mind she was still experimenting. She was so young, had her whole life to work things out. Maybe she would've changed her mind. I don't know. How can you know?

JAKE CROWE, *INYO REGISTER*: As a parent, he still struggles with her not coming out to him. They did come to learn that Cleo was Rebecca's first intimate lesbian relationship.

TITUS ALDEN: My wife told Mr. Crowe that in recent weeks Beck seemed depressed. She was having a hard time with something, and on her last visit here, she put her arms around her mom and said, "I wish I was little again so I could crawl on your lap, curl up, and let you rock me to sleep."

Grace asked what was going on, and Beck said she was feeling blue, but she'd get over it. She came home to have dinner with us in late June. The next time we saw her, Thursday night, our daughter was lying dead on a steel table.

JAKE CROWE, *INYO REGISTER*: The Aldens wanted justice for their daughter. Titus swore he'd be at the trial every day to "stare that woman down" for what she'd done to their family.

OWEN MASON, DISTRICT ATTORNEY: The first attorney Griffith sent came to do reconnaissance. I told him we had a solid case and the best thing Cleo could do was take a ten-year minimum at the California Institution for Women. That would avoid a trial and eliminate the real possibility of his client's niece going away for a lot more time.

He said he'd take it under consideration. He wanted to interview Cleo, not with the intention of setting up any defense for her, because he wasn't a criminal counsel, but to get her side of things so he could go back and advise Mr. Griffith. I authorized this, and Mr. Smillie drove over to the jail.

CLEO RAY: I'd gone to a pretty dark place by the time they came to my cell and brought me to the meeting room where Mr. Smillie was waiting for me. He'd been sent by my uncle and saw I wasn't in good shape. He said he was sorry to see me like that. He acted sympathetic. Said my uncle would come up to see me soon, but first he wanted to be informed on the legalities of the case.

Mr. Smillie said, "You haven't been formally charged. There's still a chance you could get released. You didn't give much to the D.A., which is good. Have you told anyone else about what happened at the lake?"

"No. I did not kill Beck." He nodded. I started walking him through what happened. "When I asked Beck up to the mountains, my intention was to break up with her. I wanted to let her down easy. It was important to show her, even though I was moving on, that I still cared about her. A lot."

He asked, "Were you concerned she might not take it well?"

BRIAN BURLEIGH, ASSISTANT D.A.: Owen put me in charge of searching the lake and the surrounding area. We organized a group of volunteers to scour the woods from the point the suspect had come ashore and brought in local divers to check the lake bottom. We had a pretty good idea of where the canoe had tipped over, so it wasn't long before they found it.

Yeah, I knew it would be significant.

CLEO RAY: I was in the middle of telling what happened when Mr. Smillie got a text. He apologized for having to keep his phone on, then looked at his screen for longer than normal. I started imagining myself snatching it from him so I could check my Instagram. Then he set it on the table and said, "Cleo, I need you to be honest with me. When you paddled out on the lake with Rebecca, did you take a bottle of champagne?"

BRIAN BURLEIGH, ASSISTANT D.A.: My boss was very happy to receive that unopened bottle of Moët & Chandon. Best gift you can give a D.A.

CLEO RAY: I could see the doubt in Mr. Smillie's eyes. He listened to me all the way through, taking notes. Then he said he would meet with my uncle in the morning and present my side of the story.

Yeah. "My side" of the story.

He told me not to say anything to anybody until I heard back from him or my uncle. I kept asking questions, trying to stretch out the time as long as possible. Finally he had to head back and they took me to my cell.

I hadn't been convincing, I knew that. If I couldn't make that lawyer believe me, would Sandy, would my uncle, would my followers? Would a jury?

SAMSON GRIFFITH: I went to the firm's office in Century City and took Gillian with me. We sat down with the partners and Smillie. He took us through Cleo's story point by point. He brought up the text about the champagne bottle, and her reaction to that.

Still the question: Why? What was her motive? Fear of being outed as bisexual? From the beginning I thought the prosecution would have a hard time selling that.

GILLIAN GRIFFITH: Smillie did not paint a reassuring picture of Cleo's story. He had taken detailed notes and even quoted phrases she used.

SAMSON GRIFFITH: It's not the truth that wins in court, it's the best narrative. Cleo's narrative had weaknesses. The conversation broadened to include the other partners, and the consensus was, we needed a pro, someone with a proven track record at trial, who had a strong presence in front of cameras and microphones—there'd be a lot of those aimed at our lead defense attorney.

Given the circumstances, there was only one choice.

GILLIAN GRIFFITH: I had no problem with my dad making that call. But yeah, we knew bringing in someone that high profile would generate even more hype about the case. Already the hashtags were flying: #InfluencerMurder, #SocialMediaOnTrial, #InstagramVerdict.

SAMSON GRIFFITH: Could I have turned and walked away from Cleo at that point? It was an option. But she was more than a social media client, she was family. And I knew the universe would be watching how I handled this.

They dialed the number and handed me the phone. "It's Samson Griffith for Alana Belknap." The most famous female criminal lawyer in America picked right up, and the first words out of her mouth were "What took you so long to call?"

EPISODE THREE

GIRL CHARGED

Going LIVE today! Hey everyone, Cleo here, and there's still time to sign up for my "Tune Into You" fitness challenge with livestream trainings and coaching sessions. This course is about sweeping away obstacles and bad habits and programming a new relationship with your body and your mind. I am so excited about this content. It will help you unlock the badass fitness hero inside. And no one is more deserving of that gift than you.

YouTube, IGTV, and Facebook Live

CLEO RAY: Consistency is so important. I made sure to post something on one of my platforms every day. Not always big posts or big pieces of content. Sometimes it was "Hi, I'm here, this is where you can find me, this is my message."

Now this thing has happened, this huge life-changing event—and I have no way to put out a message. The Cleo Ray fitness planet is spinning off its axis and my channel's gone blank. I'm not even sure what I would have posted, probably something like: "Hey, everyone, it's me, and I'm okay. This is a problem that will take some time to work through, I so appreciate you hanging in there for me. Thank you, I can't wait to get back on track and be an even better person for this experience." That would've been good. I wish I could've posted that, just that.

SAMSON GRIFFITH: With Alana set to join the team, it was time for me to go visit Cleo at the Independence jail. Before I left, I checked her Instagram page. I wanted to look at her posts from before this happened. I found one from a few days earlier, where a follower had shared before and after photos. The before shot showed this woman overweight, out of shape, beaten down by life. After eight weeks of doing Cleo's exercise program and following her food guidelines, the woman had lost eighteen pounds. She was standing with her shoulders back, chin up, a gleam in her eye. Physically she looked healthier, but her caption on the after photo was about how her biggest transformations were mental and emotional. Cleo commented back, "Girl, I am so proud of you." And knowing Cleo, she meant that. She'd made a real difference in this person's life.

CLEO RAY: I was nervous he'd be angry, feeling blindsided, that I'd let him down.

SAMSON GRIFFITH: We don't own a vacation home in Mammoth, but we take a couple of ski trips up there every year. Independence is this tiny town—blink and you miss it. But it's got this classic old courthouse right in the middle of it. I'd glance over as we were passing by and think, *What a great place to set a murder trial.* Hah!

CLEO RAY: I needed my uncle to believe me. His support meant everything. I didn't care about anyone else. I just needed *him* to know I was telling the truth.
 Well, and Sandy.

SAMSON GRIFFITH: You can call to request a visit only on the day of, no reservations. Not the most convenient. I got on the 405 headed north at six A.M. and called from the car as I was driving through Mojave. When I said my name and who I was visiting, the deputy or correctional officer said she'd have to check with the sheriff first. I said, "Listen, I'm already halfway from L.A. and you're not going to deny me a visit with my niece." Yeah, I got hot. To the point this deputy person hung up on me.

I thought, you know, the reality here is the D.A. and the sheriff have the home-field advantage. Unless we got a change of venue, that was a circumstance we'd have to deal with. I needed to get control of myself. Making enemies of the Inyo County public servants would not be a good strategy.

So I went into my humble persona, not one that comes naturally, and called the jail again.

CLEO RAY: I thought he'd be there early, but they didn't come for me until three o'clock, which is the last visiting slot of the day. This time there were two officers escorting me, a man and a woman, and they seemed more tense than before. They told me we had thirty minutes, not a minute longer.

They put us in the private interview room next to the visitation cubicles, which wasn't normal procedure. Leave it to my uncle to get an upgrade.

When they opened the door and I saw him, I broke down. He hugged me and I cried—*sobbed* on his shoulder. He made one of the officers go get me tissues. I was a mess.

SAMSON GRIFFITH: Took her a few minutes to find her voice. First thing she said was "I didn't do it."

I said, "You haven't been charged yet, so that's a positive. And no matter what, you are going to be capably represented, be confident about that. Only thing I ask is this: you must be completely truthful with your lawyers. They can't do their job unless you are all the way honest with them."

CLEO RAY: He was very sympathetic. I told him how weird it felt not being able to post anything. He pulled up my Instagram on his phone and showed me some of the comments. My followers were being super supportive, and I felt a huge a wave of relief.

SAMSON GRIFFITH: I was forbidden from making any calls or handing Cleo my phone, so when I held it up for her to see what her followers were saying, the deputies got uptight. I said, "All I'm doing is letting her read a note. Nothing's going out from here."

CLEO RAY: Seeing those posts made me want to reply and tell everyone I was okay. I asked Samson if he would reply for me, but he said I shouldn't be posting anything until our attorney weighed in.

He put the phone away because there was business to discuss. My uncle is a practical man and great at communicating in high-pressure situations. I really respect that about him.

SAMSON GRIFFITH: Because of the media attention and the curiosity, Cleo was gaining thousands of new followers every hour. I spoke to the people at Instagram and YouTube and got them to leave her pages up while she was under arrest. I reminded them of the phrase in our Constitution, "innocent until proven guilty."

CLEO RAY: No, I didn't want my pages taken down. If I couldn't post new content, at least my old content could stay up and show people who I am.

SAMSON GRIFFITH: Cleo was popular with the right kind of audience. Her videos and posts were edgy without being controversial. Her image was pretty wholesome, she was Sister Super-Fit, the Ray-of-Sunshine Trainer. The public face she curated couldn't hurt her and would probably help in the court of public opinion.

CLEO RAY: He told me he'd received calls from my sponsors and had gotten them to hold steady for the moment.

SAMSON GRIFFITH: The police had already searched her condo and seized her laptop and other devices. I said to her, "This isn't going to be easy, but I know you're a fighter. You've come a long way on grit and hustle. I know you've got this. And I believe in you."

CLEO RAY: When he said, "I believe in you," I broke down again.

SAMSON GRIFFITH: "My believing in you is not the most important thing right now. It's you believing in yourself. I can see scenarios where you come back from this stronger than ever. Now that you're in it, it's up to you to turn it around and find the opportunity."

That was a fact. Millions more people knew the name Cleo Ray than did the day before.

CLEO RAY: He was like a dad to me and I wasn't going to lie to him. I started to tell him about what happened at the lake, but he stopped me. He didn't want to hear about that.

SAMSON GRIFFITH: I told Cleo I was hiring Alana Belknap. She knew who she was. I think it made the whole thing more real for her.

CLEO RAY: I'd seen a Netflix show about her, or about one of her cases. I could picture her being interviewed and questioning witnesses in court. Really sharp, totally on it. Which freaked me out, I got to say. Because Alana Belknap is a little scary. In a good way, if she's *your* attorney.

SAMSON GRIFFITH: I said, "Keep in mind, these investigators can dig up deleted emails and texts, things you thought were buried, that would embarrass you—or worse. You know now what they think you did, so ask yourself, are there things that could come back and hurt your side of the story?"

CLEO RAY: When you're in such a close emotional space with someone, like I was with Beck, you say and write emotional things. Yeah, I supposed there were texts and emails I'd sent that could probably be used against me. None I could recall offhand, because when I delete something, it's out of my mind permanently.

SAMSON GRIFFITH: I asked Cleo if she'd spoken to her parents. She said no, she didn't want to. I said, "Look, in these situations, you need everyone you can get on your team. And given where we are, their religious orientation might be helpful."

CLEO RAY: I looked away and nodded and didn't say anything. I asked how long it would be until we knew if charges were being filed.

SAMSON GRIFFITH: Personally, I felt there was no way this district attorney was going to let the case go. It was blowing up in the media, and he could leverage that kind of interest to his advantage politically. This was not a case where he needed a grand jury. The decision to prosecute was Owen Mason's alone.

I didn't tell Cleo that. I just said the maximum time someone could be detained without being charged was forty-eight hours, so the clock was ticking down.

And right then I got a text from my law firm.

CLEO RAY: Twenty minutes into our visit came breaking news—I was being charged with first-degree murder. Uncle Samson reached across the table and held my shoulders when he told me. But I didn't cry. I went numb, like when I first got arrested.

I realized the thing I wanted most was to hear Sandy's voice. Uncle Samson dialed him for me—the deputy stepped in and said no, the call was not allowed.

SAMSON GRIFFITH: Another deputy came in to escort Cleo back to her cell, and I put the phone on speaker. She could hear Sandy say, "Hello,

Samson?" Before they could get her out the door, she shouted, "I love you! I love you so much, Sandy!"

I admit it was a bit rash on my part, but I felt for her. Because no matter what happened from that moment on, her life was changed forever.

I was pretty sure Mason timed the announcement to coincide with my visit to the jail, knowing I'd be the one who had to tell her.

OWEN MASON, DISTRICT ATTORNEY: (Press Conference, Independence Courthouse) "Our office has long-standing policies for charging suspects with crimes. We have a thorough review process in place. Based on what we've discovered in the course of the preliminary investigation, we are satisfied the evidence shows the suspect guilty of the crime being charged. We have weighed factors such as the probability of conviction, the nature of the offense, and the deterrent value of prosecution to the offender and society in general.

"Regarding the financial expense to prosecute, the seriousness of the offense warrants it. This decision was made in consultation with my staff and the sheriff's office. We are unified, and we are confident this is the path toward justice."

JAKE CROWE, *INYO REGISTER*: Another reporter asked the question that needed to be asked. Given the suspect was a young woman with no prior arrest record or history of violence, why send the SWAT team after her? Wasn't that overkill?

Mason answered that the suspect's actions indicated she'd gone to great lengths to elude capture and he didn't want to take any chances. He took responsibility for making the call.

ERIN NEWCOMB, CHIEF DEPUTY: After the press conference, I went over to the jail to check on Cleo Ray. Did I think she'd be taking a plea deal? Not for one second.

BRIAN BURLEIGH, ASSISTANT D.A.: We knew they'd bring in a hotshot defense attorney, a seven-figure-retainer type. Were we intimidated? No, we were motivated. We knew we'd be the underdogs in the media, which only increased our desire to prosecute the case vigorously—fairly but *vigorously*.

And we knew something most of the world didn't—our D.A. was a superstar in the courtroom.

DUNCAN MCMILLAN: *As a criminal defense attorney, Alana Belknap is one of the most prominent and influential women in the legal profession. A frequent guest on cable news shows, she has won numerous awards and honors. Her high profile means the cases she takes on invariably come to national attention. For defendants, that can be a blessing and a curse.*

ALANA BELKNAP, DEFENSE COUNSEL: The fundamental question is: *Why represent this person?* Well, first I have to be asked. Next comes motivation: *Does the case and/or the client move me?*

I can tell you it's never about money or politics. I've got enough of the former and a strong aversion to the latter.

SAMSON GRIFFITH: I went from the jail in Independence straight to a meeting with Alana at the Beverly Hills Hotel. Smillie from my law firm and my daughter, Gillian, met us there. Our first big conference started at ten P.M. and lasted till two in the morning.

ALANA BELKNAP, DEFENSE COUNSEL: I'd spent a few hours on Cleo's Instagram and YouTube channel, and I saw someone who should come across sympathetically to a jury. That was my surface read. One never knows how a client will perform in the courtroom when their life is on the line.

GILLIAN GRIFFITH: Alana is brilliant, gorgeous, and wears Alexander McQueen suits and Gianvito pumps like no one's business. If she started an Instagram, she'd get a million followers in a day—and most of them would be women.

SAMSON GRIFFITH: I told her if she was ever looking for a social media agency, we'd be happy to discuss representation. She said she'd let me know.

ALANA BELKNAP, DEFENSE COUNSEL: My firm has a website, but I'm perfectly comfortable with what I do and who knows about it. I don't need Twitter and Instagram to raise my profile.

SAMSON GRIFFITH: We discussed change of venue. Alana told us it would be difficult to win the argument that Cleo couldn't get a fair trial in Inyo County.

GILLIAN GRIFFITH: Inyo County is white, rural, and Baptist. Like a slice of the Midwest, without the cornfields.

ERIN NEWCOMB, CHIEF DEPUTY: We're not all Baptists and we're not all conservative. We have a few liberal churches up here. Congregations that are inclusive, that collect food for the homeless and are environmentally conscious.

ALANA BELKNAP, DEFENSE COUNSEL: This could be a trial as much about the subject of sin as about the crime of murder. Only you'll never hear the word *sin* in the courtroom. It would never be uttered by the prosecutors or the jurors. It's not something you see or hear—it's something you feel.

SAMSON GRIFFITH: I knew this: as first-degree murder trials go, Alana and Cleo sitting next to each other at the defense table would be a pretty dazzling look.

ALANA BELKNAP, DEFENSE COUNSEL: I'd done my research on Owen Mason. Solid record, but there aren't many violent crime cases in Inyo County. A bar brawl now and then, but few murders go to trial. He may have good skills, but he doesn't get to practice them. That matters. He's never had a national spotlight on him. That matters, too.

If we couldn't get the venue changed, he'd have a home-field edge. But I've seen that work against a D.A. as many times as work in their favor. Juries have become hyperaware that their verdict is going to be dissected by a liberal-leaning media. Forensics aside, given a defendant who'd never been in trouble with the law and who appeared as all-American as Cleo, I thought a first-degree murder conviction would be a steep hill to climb for the prosecution.

SAMSON GRIFFITH: We were impressed with her. Because Alana is—impressive. I told her I'd wire the two-million-dollar retainer into her firm's account when the bank opened in the morning.

GILLIAN GRIFFITH: There were four of us in the meeting: me, my dad, Smillie, and Alana. We didn't leave the hotel until two in the morning. A little before seven A.M. our time, a tweet went out from a reporter on the East Coast saying Alana was on the case. I hadn't told anyone. Dad hadn't told anyone. We certainly didn't think it came from Larry Smillie.

It might have been someone from the hotel or a tabloid person staked out in the lobby. It's the Beverly Hills Hotel, after all. Neither Dad nor I wanted to believe the leak came from Alana.

OWEN MASON, DISTRICT ATTORNEY: I'd just poured my first cup of coffee when a call came in from Brian. "Alana Belknap," he said.

I smiled to myself and said, "The bigger they are, the harder they fall," or something like that. Then I had one of those defining-moment visions, a glimpse at my future obituary. The first line commemorated the one thing I would always be publicly remembered for.

I thought back to Rebecca on the autopsy table with her parents standing over her and my duty to the three of them. As long as I held that in my mind, I could look past the rest. Next thing I did was call my pastor and set up an appointment to see him one-on-one.

SAMSON GRIFFITH: By the time I got to the office, Twitter had exploded. One thing trending was #BiggerThanOJ. The O. J. Simpson trial happened back in the nineties, before the world went online. I tried to imagine the magnitude of something like that now. Yeah, I felt palpitations. But then I remembered Johnnie Cochrane and how he took someone who was flat guilty and got the jury to acquit him.

CLEO RAY: Every morning at six, my phone would be in my hand before my eyes were open. I'd look at my WhatsApp, my Twitter, my Instagram, my YouTube, my Facebook, my TikTok. I'd make a mental list of the must-responds before I was out of bed and budgeting that time against my morning workout and meal. Fitness tip: best to work out *before* a meal.

Waking up without my phone was like waking up without arms and legs. I've never had heroin withdrawal, but I've heard what it's like, and that's what I was feeling. For sixteen hours a day I'd been creating, watching, and listening to content nonstop. I hardly knew how to breathe without a phone in my hand.

At the jail, it's lights on at five A.M. every morning, and they make you clean your cell top to bottom. Every single morning.

OWEN MASON, DISTRICT ATTORNEY: And yes, we got our presiding judge, Roy Oberwaltzer, also known as Judge O. He's fair and strong. A good man.

ALANA BELKNAP, DEFENSE COUNSEL: First order of business was to find a co-defense attorney who practices in the county and knows the players. When I'm going into a remote jurisdiction, I like to bring an insider on the team. In my early days, I walked into a few traps that could have been avoided had I partnered up with someone familiar with the local courts.

After four or five hours online and on the phone, I narrowed in on Reuben and set a meeting.

DUNCAN MCMILLAN: *Reuben Jephson is a solo-practice attorney representing criminal defendants and family law clients, with over a decade of experience as a public defender. A graduate of the Lincoln Law School of Sacramento, he is a twenty-year resident of Bishop, California. A bachelor and a secular Democrat, he is in many ways an outlier in his community.*

REUBEN JEPHSON, CO-DEFENSE COUNSEL: I'd never been involved in a high-profile murder trial, nothing that got any further than *The Inyo Register*. Other than my law practice page, I'm not on social media. It felt like I was being plucked out of obscurity, and I was hesitant. Do I want to dive into that kind of media whirlwind?

Well, Alana Belknap is a more powerful force than any media whirlwind.

ALANA BELKNAP, DEFENSE COUNSEL: The best attorneys are like the best actors. Doesn't matter how many people are in the audience, they're going to perform to the highest level of their abilities. The stage is always the same, whether there are two eyes on you or ten million. Of course, there's more pressure when your face is popping up on everything from BuzzFeed to CNN, especially when you're not used to that kind of round-the-clock attention.

So my most important question to Reuben was, *Can you handle it?*

REUBEN JEPHSON, CO-DEFENSE COUNSEL: I had turned forty and been looking inward. I enjoy what I do, and I think I'm good at it. But once you step into the center ring, there's no turning back. I could walk down Main Street here and nobody would associate me with my job. If I took this case, that would likely change.

I could see it was going to be a complicated defense. And having argued against Owen on several occasions, I knew he'd be a formidable opponent. He's a hometown hero, so going against him in such a highly publicized case was not going to make me popular with a lot of my neighbors.

I asked Alana if I could give her my answer after we interviewed Cleo Ray. I wanted to have a face-to-face meeting before making a commitment.

ALANA BELKNAP, DEFENSE COUNSEL: The truth was, after Reuben I didn't have a Plan B. I called the jail and they slotted us in for two hours that afternoon.

CLEO RAY: When the deputy said who was there to visit me, I was like, "Okay, bring it." This was the biggest "interview" of my life. I would urge my followers to look in the mirror and tell themselves they were looking at the hero of their life story. I tried to look in my cell mirror, which was a metal plate bolted on the wall, and all I could see was a blur.

I put my failure with the other lawyer out of my mind. Here we go! Be strong, be myself, be the hero of my own story.

REUBEN JEPHSON, CO-DEFENSE COUNSEL: When we introduced ourselves, she obviously knew who Alana was, but she's looking at me like, "Who's this guy?"

ALANA BELKNAP, DEFENSE COUNSEL: Cleo started out nervous and talking the way she did in her videos. I said, "Relax. This is not an audition. We're here to have a real discussion with a real person, okay, not with the Instagram fitness queen."

CLEO RAY: If I'm not the Instagram fitness queen, who am I?

ALANA BELKNAP, DEFENSE COUNSEL: That first meeting is about getting the client comfortable with us and with the conversation. The ones who've never been in trouble are usually freaking out, and who can blame them? The first question is always "When can I get out on bail?"

CLEO RAY: Alana said she would never sugarcoat the truth. She'd tell me exactly what was going on. And she said, "Bail is not a sure thing in this case."

My stomach cramped. "Why not?"

She said, "You ran away from the scene of the drowning. The arresting officer observed you running away before you were arrested. We've got a judge who is not known for his compassion. I'm not saying he won't set bail, but there's a good chance he'll set an astronomic bail with tough conditions. We'll have to take these things as they come."

No bail? I'm stuck here until the trial? When could I start posting again?

ALANA BELKNAP, DEFENSE COUNSEL: I told her she shouldn't be posting anything on social media until this entire matter was behind her. I knew that would be hard for her, really hard, but it would help her get acquitted. That's our one and only goal here.

"Cleo," I said, "you and I are going to get along. I can already feel it. You'll be able to speak to me easily and truthfully. Everything you say to me is one hundred percent confidential under attorney-client privilege. If there is anything you don't want your uncle to know, I promise you I will not tell him."

REUBEN JEPHSON, CO-DEFENSE COUNSEL: I could see Alana was good at this.

CLEO RAY: At our first meeting, she brought me back from the edge. She said, "You're going to tell me everything I need to know, and I'm going to tell you everything you need to do. In every way you help me, you'll be helping yourself. And we are going to fight like hell to get you out of here and back into your life."

REUBEN JEPHSON, CO-DEFENSE COUNSEL: Alana pulls out a chocolate chip peanut crunch bar and a coconut Smartwater. Cleo looked like a kid at Christmas. Alana had found out her favorite energy snacks and took them out of her bag with the grace of a magician pulling roses from a hat. Oh yeah, I could learn a lot from this one.

CLEO RAY: I've had hundreds of those bars, but that one tasted the best of any before or since.

ALANA BELKNAP, DEFENSE COUNSEL: Cleo began to tell us her story, starting when she first met Beck Alden. She painted a vivid picture of their relationship, which lasted close to a year and a half. Cleo volunteered some details about the way they were together, about their sex life.

Because Beck wasn't out to her parents and Cleo was building her social media brand, they mutually decided to keep their relationship a secret.

REUBEN JEPHSON, CO-DEFENSE COUNSEL: It was awkward. But that was on me. I don't have any lesbian friends. Law school was the last time I remember being in close proximity to a gay woman. The subject was exotic to me. Made me feel guilty for living such a sheltered life.

CLEO RAY: Okay, the sexual *orientation* question. I'd been attracted to boys *and* girls from an early age—before puberty. It never felt weird or wrong, just normal. For me. I lost my virginity to a boy and to a girl within six months of each other.

Between guys and girls—it was about that particular person and experience. The difference was, with a guy it was going to be more physical, and with a girl it was more emotional. For me.

Keep in mind, I had two hyper-religious parents who condemned homosexuality and any kind of sex before marriage. I started thinking they were wacko by the time I was eight or nine, and pretty much stopped listening to them by my early teens.

Anyway, my big discovery was not that I loved boys more than girls or girls more than boys. I just knew I loved making love.

ALANA BELKNAP, DEFENSE COUNSEL: I know people who go both ways, who are *heteroflexible*. But I think most of them favor one gender or the other. In terms of the sex act, I believe Cleo had no preference. In my experience, that's unique.

If the case had been tried in Los Angeles or New York City, I wouldn't have given the issue a lot of thought. But in Inyo County, it had to be considered. If you rarely encounter alternative lifestyles, it's going to impact how you see the world.

ERIN NEWCOMB, CHIEF DEPUTY: It's a given, you're going to get stereotyped when your community is rural and largely Christian. Our attitude is accept it and move on.

CLEO RAY: I was attracted to Beck the moment I saw her. She was adorable. I could tell she was shy and kind of an introvert. Which made her more interesting. Most of the people I know are extroverts in the extreme. It was a change to meet someone sweet and quiet and—humble.

She was beautiful without selling it or even knowing it. And that appealed to me.

ALANA BELKNAP, DEFENSE COUNSEL: We were approaching the end of our time and the arraignment was scheduled for the next day. I had Cleo put a pin in her story, and we shifted into discussing what was coming next.

CLEO RAY: Alana laid out the possible consequences of guilty and not guilty. She said, "Cleo, this is one hundred percent your choice. The only thing I don't want is you coming back and saying you felt pressured to make one plea over another. You have to consider this independent of everyone and everything else—except for what you know in your heart is the truth."

REUBEN JEPHSON, CO-DEFENSE COUNSEL: After Alana explained the legal issues, Cleo took time to think about it. Which is what you want a client to do, no matter how guilty or innocent she feels. It's a choice she's going to have to live with the rest of her life.

> **BAILIFF:** All rise. The Superior Court of Inyo County, State of California, is now in session. The Honorable Judge Roy Oberwaltzer presiding. Please be seated.
> **THE COURT:** Good morning, ladies and gentlemen.
> **COURT CLERK:** Criminal cause for arraignment. Counsel, please state your appearances.
> **MR. MASON:** Owen Mason, district attorney for Inyo County.

MR. BURLEIGH: Brian Burleigh, assistant district attorney for Inyo County.
MS. BELKNAP: Alana Belknap, counsel for the defendant.
MR. JEPHSON: Reuben Jephson, co-counsel for the defendant.
THE COURT: Will the defendant please state her full legal name.
THE DEFENDANT: Mary Claire Griffith.

CLEO RAY: Shocker. I changed my name the day I turned eighteen. When I first came to L.A., my uncle and his family called me Claire—I never liked the name Mary. After graduating from high school, I wanted to make a change. Becoming Cleo Ray shut the door on one life and opened a door to the next. I was planning to legally change it—hadn't gotten around to it.

THE COURT: The charge is first-degree murder, defined as killing a human being in a way that is willful, deliberate, and premeditated. Ms. Belknap, have you discussed the charge carefully with your client?
MS. BELKNAP: We have, Your Honor.
THE COURT: Does your client wish to enter a plea at this time as to the charge?

CLEO RAY: *Willful, deliberate, premeditated.* Words I could never unhear.

MS. BELKNAP: She does, Your Honor.
THE COURT: Mary Claire Griffith, to the charge of first-degree murder, how do you plead?
THE DEFENDANT: Not guilty.

CLEO RAY: Because it was the truth.

REUBEN JEPHSON, CO-DEFENSE COUNSEL: I decided I wanted to work with Alana. And I wanted to help Cleo. Those beat out any concern over what consequences might come.

JAKE CROWE, *INYO REGISTER*: Her influencer name being different from her legal name shouldn't have surprised anyone, but a percentage of her followers hadn't suspected that Cleo Ray was anyone but Cleo Ray, or that she had spent the first eighteen years of her life as Mary Claire Griffith. Some saw it as a betrayal, that Cleo had been lying to them, when it's common for people to make up their social media names.

SANDY FINCH: I knew "Cleo Ray" was not the name she'd grown up with. But I never asked her birth name. It hadn't come up, I'm sure it would've eventually. To me she was Cleo. I'll always know her as Cleo.

SAMSON GRIFFITH: I had my staff monitoring Cleo's platforms. The comments on her pages between the arrest and her arraignment were almost all positive. The pro-Cleo sentiment was strong. But after it came out that Cleo Ray was not her legal name, there was a shift. Followers value being real over everything else.

CLEO RAY: Mary Claire Griffith was a stranger to me. But there she was, my shadow, right behind me the whole time. I'd tried to stuff her into a box, but it doesn't work that way with shadows.

SAMSON GRIFFITH: Alana and I had a bit of an issue early on. I hadn't caught in the agreement that her living expenses while on location were to be paid *in addition* to the retainer. She'd booked a suite at the Westin in Mammoth and rented a BMW X7. There were no accommodations in Lone Pine or Bishop that met her standards. I get it, she's a star, we're not putting her up at the Best Western. But the Luxury Suite is a grand a night and the car is a hundred fifty a day. If she's there six to eight weeks, I'm looking at an additional seventy grand to her fees.

I wasn't being a tightwad, I just asked her if we could talk about it.

ALANA BELKNAP, DEFENSE COUNSEL: Another thing I've learned in my career. If there's a snag in my daily routine caused by inadequate lodgings or transportation, that's an annoyance cost. I don't bring a personal assistant with me, and I need to be confident there will be no disruptions to my flow. This is not a diva thing. It's about the physical and mental space I need to devote one hundred percent of my time to defending a client.

Samson heard me. Rather, I let him know if he didn't hear me, I'd be on the next plane back to New York.

REUBEN JEPHSON, CO-DEFENSE COUNSEL: We went back to the jail for our second meeting with Cleo. After we got her on track, she came to the point where she and Beck made plans to go up to the lake. This was the critical part of her story, and it was the first time we were hearing the details. Alana and I took copious notes.

CLEO RAY: I'd never been questioned like that before. I mean, yes, at the sheriff's office after getting arrested, but that was different because I could avoid giving direct answers. Couldn't do that with Alana and Reuben.

ALANA BELKNAP, DEFENSE COUNSEL: Not telling Beck she was taking her up to the lake to break up with her made a certain amount of sense. So why the champagne? Cleo said it was their tradition to buy a bottle of Moët & Chandon for special occasions. But for *this* occasion?

CLEO RAY: If I'd said no to the champagne, Beck would have gotten suspicious and we would've had another fight. I was exhausted by all the fighting. I wanted to keep everything smooth until we got there.

REUBEN JEPHSON, CO-DEFENSE COUNSEL: I asked if there was a particular reason Cleo wanted to have the breakup talk while they were on the lake. She said because she thought it was a "safe" place to do it. Beck would be less likely to do anything reckless or violent.

ALANA BELKNAP, DEFENSE COUNSEL: Then came the obvious question. Had Beck gotten violent with her on other occasions? Cleo said yes, she had.

CLEO RAY: One time she threw a hairbrush at me in her apartment. I dodged it, but it hit a mirror and cracked it. The police found the crack and took a picture of it.

REUBEN JEPHSON, CO-DEFENSE COUNSEL: That's when she told us Beck came at her and slapped her when she found out Cleo had been lying about her and Sandy.

ALANA BELKNAP, DEFENSE COUNSEL: Had there been witnesses to these incidents? Cleo said not unless one of the neighbors heard something, because the only times Beck physically attacked her were in her apartment.

REUBEN JEPHSON, CO-DEFENSE COUNSEL: Alana asked if she ever got violent with Beck. Did Cleo hit her back, shove her, retaliate physically in any way?

CLEO RAY: That's not me. I'm a nonviolent person. I've never hit anyone in my life.

ALANA BELKNAP, DEFENSE COUNSEL: I asked the question the prosecution would surely seize on. If Cleo's reason for going up to the lake was to break up with her, why would Beck write a text to her mom that she was there to get engaged?

REUBEN JEPHSON, CO-DEFENSE COUNSEL: Cleo said she let Beck think whatever she wanted to think. And I asked, "Did you signal to Beck you were taking her up there for another reason? Something leading her to believe it was going to be a proposal?"

ALANA BELKNAP, DEFENSE COUNSEL: Cleo shook her head no.

CLEO RAY: I'd never been held that closely accountable for every word coming out of my mouth.

JAKE CROWE, *INYO REGISTER*: I was in court for the change of venue hearing. The defense argued that because of the lesbian relationship at the heart of the case, conservative jurors would prejudge Cleo.

Judge Oberwaltzer said that was the reason for a jury selection process. The defense would have the right to excuse anyone they felt could not objectively consider the evidence outside of their personal or religious moral standards.

The judge shot them down but opened the door for some battles once they got to selecting a jury.

OWEN MASON, DISTRICT ATTORNEY: Two significant developments happened before jury selection.

ERIN NEWCOMB, CHIEF DEPUTY: Along with the D.A.'s office, I went through the texts and emails on Rebecca's phone. There were bunches of texts, but no emails except for when they first started seeing each other. I know young people rarely use email. Everything is video chats and texting. But it did seem odd there were no further emails exchanged in their year and a half of being together. Then I noticed odd references in their texts, mentions of the names Liesl and Brigitta. My thought was, *Maybe they had a secret way of communicating, something that could have been copied to a place other than her phone or computer.*

Brian Burleigh was headed down again to Rebecca's apartment, and I said to look for a flash drive that she might have hidden. What do you know? He found one tucked inside a seam on the side of her bed mattress.

BRIAN BURLEIGH, ASSISTANT D.A.: On that same trip to L.A., I went to all the wine and liquor sellers within a mile radius of Rebecca's apartment. I showed the salespeople photos of the champagne bottle, of Cleo and Rebecca, and asked if they remembered either one making the purchase. Third store, guy at the register remembers them coming in together the prior Wednesday just before closing.

He said, "They seemed pretty giddy, all kissy-kissy with each other."

I asked, "Do you recall anything they said?"

He said, "When the blonde was turned away, the brunette leaned to me and whispered, 'We're getting engaged.'"

I asked, "Did the blonde hear her say that?"

He said, "I'm pretty sure she did, because she turned around and heard me say 'Congratulations.' She nodded to me and said thanks."

I said, "The blonde said, 'Thanks' after you said, 'Congratulations'?"

He said, "Yes. She said it softly, like she was downplaying it."

I got his contact information, and the moment I stepped outside, I called Owen. We had the bottle and the sales guy who remembered them. Score another witness for the prosecution.

REUBEN JEPHSON, CO-DEFENSE COUNSEL: Holding on to new evidence until the last possible moment is the oldest trick in the prosecutor's book. We didn't find out about the liquor store cashier until weeks later.

CLEO RAY: I was finally feeling strong enough to call Sandy. The phone situation is not great at the jail. It's on a wall in a public area and calls are monitored. I dropped my head down and spoke just above a whisper.

I was dying to hear his voice.

SANDY FINCH: I tried to call her at the jail, but they don't accept incoming calls. I had to wait until she called me. I was at a coffee shop checking my news feed when *Inyo County Jail* pops up on my phone. I walked out to the sidewalk. "Hey, Cleo," I said, trying to sound somewhat normal—good luck with that.

CLEO RAY: I had to lean against the wall to stay upright. Like, I wasn't going to cry? I got out a quivery "I love you. I'm sorry this is happening."

DUNCAN MCMILLAN: *Cleo Ray's outgoing call to Sandy Finch was recorded by Inyo County Jail officials.*

SANDY FINCH: You're okay?
CLEO RAY: So much better now that I hear your voice. Are you okay?
SANDY FINCH: Yeah, yes, I think about you all the time. You're safe there, right?
CLEO RAY: I'm safe. Physically, I guess. The guards have been decent so far. Where are you?
SANDY FINCH: Peet's on Montana. I stepped outside to talk to you.
CLEO RAY: Will you order a caramel macchiato for me and let it sit on the table across from you?
SANDY FINCH: I'll close my eyes, and when I open them, you'll be sitting there. How does that sound?
CLEO RAY: If I get one wish for the rest of my life, being there right now would be it.
SANDY FINCH: I want to come visit you.
CLEO RAY: I would love it.

SANDY FINCH: The jail website said no physical contact is allowed. I can't imagine seeing you and not being able to touch you. That would be torture.

CLEO RAY: I know, I know.

SANDY FINCH: I got a message from Alana Belknap. She wants to talk to me.

CLEO RAY: She's good, really good. You can trust her.

SANDY FINCH: Okay, I will.

CLEO RAY: I think about you every minute of the day and I dream about you at night.

SANDY FINCH: Me too, babe. Day and night.

SANDY FINCH: I said nothing about the case, about the insanity going on. I wanted to be normal with her. I think that's what she needed. We talked about how much we missed each other, how much we wanted to be together. There was a lot to say.

DUNCAN MCMILLAN, INTERVIEWER: How did things change for you in the aftermath of Cleo's arrest and indictment?

SANDY FINCH: You're referring to the backlash? I was getting pressured to publicly disown Cleo. Within those first days, a number of the companies I represent let me know that if I didn't make a statement about the situation, they'd have to reconsider their relationships with me.

What about being "presumed innocent"? Everyone is so freaked out now by the threat of boycotts and brand bashing. All I could do was ask them to hang in there, let it play out. But they wanted me to say something. Silence makes their customers go to the dark place. Trolls were posting that I helped her commit the murder, that I was an accessory.

DUNCAN MCMILLAN, INTERVIEWER: What were they saying your motive was?

SANDY FINCH: That I was terrified of people finding out my girlfriend was bisexual. They were saying we conspired on killing Beck to protect our brands. Didn't matter I had an alibi.

I had no playbook for that. I'd never known anyone accused of murder, never known anyone put on trial for a serious crime. Cleo and I had been dating about four months, and there were dozens of photos of us together online. Now people were photoshopping them in really ugly ways.

DAVID KIM: Our whole group was getting blowback for the Cleo thing. People said we'd been trying to hide her from the police. That was why we left our phones behind and took her into the wilderness. She had confessed to us, and we were accessories after the fact. I tell you, a lot of those conspiracy theories were generated by AI programs. When a news story breaks, it's fed into apps that spit out a hundred salacious variations designed to smear influencers with high engagements.

DAVID KIM: (IGTV) "Hey everybody. This is a special post to address the rumors and untruths circulating out there. Cleo Ray, @CleoRayFitness, did come to Mammoth to join our group for the hike. None of us had any idea what was going on with her. She said nothing and pretended like everything was normal. We were shocked when the officers caught up with us. We thought we were being punk'd. We couldn't believe it when we saw Cleo in handcuffs. The whole scene was mondo bizarro. The thing is, I'm not really friends with Cleo. I know her as the girlfriend of a friend. I didn't know anything about her background, only that she changed her name from Claire Griffith to something less white-bread."

DAVID KIM: I begged Sandy to post a video and say he was innocent, too. He thought it would look bad for Cleo. And I was like, "You're going to get sucked down into the vortex, dude!"

Someone started a Facebook page called Come Back Sandy Finch and posted photos of him with Cleo, and her face would be scratched out or photoshopped to look like a corpse—hideous. I called Samson Griffith and asked him to intervene. Sandy was his client, for God's sake.

SAMSON GRIFFITH: Look, Sandy's a grown man, he's smart, he's aware. I'm spending millions to defend my niece. I believe she's innocent. If he sticks by her and she's acquitted, this whole thing gets turned around. Then he'll be the loyal boyfriend who stood by his girl when everyone was telling him not to, and he'll shoot right back to the top again.

SANDY FINCH: Samson was in a tough spot. Some of his clients began leaving because of the negative media. I was doing back-to-back meetings with sponsors, trying to hold them in place. Thousands of people were unfollowing me, I was getting called out on Twitter, trolls were invading my platforms. The whole world watched me take a beating in real time. On social media there's nowhere to hide.

I was on a Zoom with a sports watch company when fifty texts hit my phone all at once.

The folder of secret emails between Cleo and Beck had been leaked online, and it set off this massive detonation.

OWEN MASON, DISTRICT ATTORNEY: The computer server for the Inyo County district attorney got hacked. Had it ever happened before? Not that we had any records of. Was there a prior concern it might happen? We took the normal precautions. It was disturbing, not only for our office but for the sheriff's office and all county offices.

Before you ask, I'll tell you, it was definitely not a leak from the inside. We had computer forensics people from the FBI come out, and they verified it. Someone from outside got into our system, found the folder, stole it, and posted it online. According to the FBI, from the moment they got into our system to the moment the emails were posted was under ten minutes. It was done by a person or by people who knew what they were looking for.

JAKE CROWE, *INYO REGISTER*: This was, like, over a year of emails between them. They used fictitious names to create accounts and only messaged each other. Cleo had deleted all the emails from her devices and shut down her account the day before they went up to the lake together. Beck said she'd done the same, and she had, but she also copied all the emails to a flash drive.

BRIAN BURLEIGH, ASSISTANT D.A.: Those emails. It was lovey-dovey for a long time. Then it got messy.

TITUS ALDEN: I read a few and couldn't read any more. It made us sick to see our daughter's private life exposed like that. Obviously if she deleted her account and hid the drive, she didn't want anyone seeing the emails. They were her personal property. She was being violated and couldn't defend herself. That's so wrong, taking a good person and tainting her after her death.

ERIN NEWCOMB, CHIEF DEPUTY: I knew those names sounded familiar. Liesl and Brigitta are from *The Sound of Music*. Remember when the von Trapp children introduce themselves to their new governess, Maria, and try to fool her by swapping names? Beck chose to be Liesl, the one hopelessly falling in love. I guess Cleo saw herself as the one not afraid to speak her mind, like Brigitta.

DUNCAN MCMILLAN, INTERVIEWER: Let's look at some of these secret emails between you and Beck. Would you provide a comment or some context and then read the email aloud?

CLEO RAY: This was our first Valentine's Day. We'd started seeing each other about three or four weeks earlier. And we decided to get new email addresses that only we knew about and wouldn't use with anyone else. It gave us permission to let loose with our feelings. This is Beck:

From: Liesl.DoReMi@gmail.com
Subject: Valentine's day earthquake
February 15, 2:36 AM

OMG, you just left and I'm still shaking from those 4 AMAZING Ogazzes. Your tongue is magic! I never thought it possible to feel the way you make me feel. I'm touching myself now and pretending it's you. Top myself off then a sweet deep sleep. You sleep deep too. LUV, your sister Liesl.

From: Brigitta.DoReMi@gmail.com
Re: Valentine's day earthquake
February 15, 11:05 AM

Totally sweaty after making a video, turning on shower, rubbing myself pretending you're standing behind me and it's your hand doing it. Thanks Liesl for another lovely Ogazz!

ERIN NEWCOMB, CHIEF DEPUTY: Within hours of the hack, the word *Ogazz* started trending across social media and has since become official sex slang for you know what.

CLEO RAY: This one's Beck writing to me after our first big fight. Maybe it should've been a red flag.

From: Liesl.DoReMi@gmail.com
Subject: Forgive me
June 23, 11:23 PM

I'm sorry I said what I said, that was mean and not at all how I really feel. It was the tequila, it messes with my brain and makes me say stupid stuff. I don't care if you look at other girls, I know what we have is totally solid and true. Please forgive me, Brigitta, it was the margaritas talking, not me. I'm not a jealous person I'm not! No more tequila for Liesl.

CLEO RAY: Things were nice around the holidays. We'd settled into a groove. My social media was growing. We still hadn't come out as a couple, but why rock the boat? Can't believe I just said that.

From: Brigitta.DoReMi@gmail.com
Subject: The Most Wonderful Time of the Year
December 20, 5:02 PM

How blessed am I to spend the holidays with the sweetest girl in the world. Can't wait to cuddle with my cutie and watch cheesy Christmas movies and do My Favorite Things. All I want for Christmas is to be with my Liesl. Love you so much, so excited to spend our first Christmas together. So long, farewell for now.

From: Liesl.DoReMi@gmail.com
Re: The Most Wonderful Time of the Year
December 20, 5:34 PM

I may be the sweetest but I am also the luckiest girl in the world to have you in my life. Who gets those adorable words said to them? Who gets to have her Velvet Cake and eat it too? Me me me! I've never felt so special or so completely adored. A tear of love just dropped on my screen, coming from the deepest place in my heart. Love isn't love till you give it away.

CLEO RAY: I met Sandy in mid-March. That's the context.

From: Liesl.DoReMi@gmail.com
Subject: Where are you?
March 25, 9:38 PM

I've been waiting for you for an hour and a half. I had to put our dinner back in the refrigerator and drink the wine I already poured. Where are you? Why aren't you responding to my texts? I'm worried and wondering if I should call the police. If you're out with your "friends," can't you take a minute to step away and text me back? It's horribly mean of you to leave me hanging like this. You didn't used to be this way. You used to reply within minutes. What changed? If something is changing for you, you should tell me.

From: Brigitta.DoReMi@gmail.com
RE: Where are you?
March 26, 7:41 AM

I am soooooo sorry I hurt your feelings but you've got to lighten up. You know I LUV you, only you, forever you, no one else ever! Please take that in and hold it. When I'm out with these people it's for my job, for the future, OUR future. We need F.U. money. I thought we were agreed on that. I love you, my sweet Liesl. You can relax.

CLEO RAY: This is when things were going downhill—for Liesl and Brigitta.

From: Liesl.DoReMi@gmail.com
Subject: Hello
June 1, 9:15 PM

I LUV U Brigitta Brigit Bri!

CLEO RAY: Less than ninety minutes later.

> From: Liesl.DoReMi@gmail.com
> RE: Hello
> June 1, 10:49 PM
>
> Why aren't you texting me back? And don't say you fell asleep, I know how late you stay up, and anyway you never turn your phone off. Are you talking to someone else? Are you ignoring me on purpose? That would make me so sad. You said we were good. Are we good? Are we? WHERE ARE U? God Dammit Bri!

SAMSON GRIFFITH: Beck was feeling the relationship slipping away, but Cleo kept reassuring her, which made Cleo come off as manipulative and deceitful. And Beck was the dumped girlfriend, left behind while Cleo was living it up with her new pals. That set off a wave of hating on Cleo. Especially by younger women, who made up the majority of her followers. It was a little scary to see how fast some of them turned on her.

Of course the D.A. leaked those emails. They spelled out the prosecution's narrative of Cleo the cad. Beck came off as both *pathetic* and *sympa*thetic. I tapped my phone and called Alana.

ALANA BELKNAP, DEFENSE COUNSEL: Before going back to talk to Cleo, I had to read and make notes on the emails. Sixty-three thousand words, a full-length novel. As I was reading, my dominant thought was *I am glad these are coming out now and not later.* We'd have time to develop a counternarrative to the surface story the emails told. They also portrayed Beck as volatile, needy, very insecure. Her instability reinforced everything that Cleo had been telling us.

CLEO RAY: The only clue that something had happened was when Alana and Reuben moved our meeting to the late afternoon. A voice inside told me something was up.

REUBEN JEPHSON, CO-DEFENSE COUNSEL: Alana and I met first to prepare a list of questions.

CLEO RAY: This one is pretty self-explanatory.

> From: Liesl.DoReMi@gmail.com
> Subject: do not deserve
> June 7, 1:18 AM
>
> I do NOT deserve to be treated like this. I've been sooooooo kind and giving and loving to you. My heart has been yours since the first time we got together. Why shouldn't I get the same from you? I'm incredibly upset and you constantly telling me to relax, to not be so intense is NOT helping. You told me that sometimes you feel like an impostor doing social media. That's not impostor syndrome, it's true! You ARE an impostor. You are NOT the person you pretended to be. How would you feel if I posted something on Instagram that PROVED you were an impostor? What would happen if your followers found out you were a LEZ? I deserve to be treated better! Stop hurting me!

ALANA BELKNAP, DEFENSE COUNSEL: We were looking at a relationship that's becoming more and more emotionally complicated. Because they were keeping it secret, they didn't have the usual support systems couples have. Girls need girlfriends they can talk to about their girlfriend problems. If the only person you can vent to is your partner, it puts more stress on the relationship.

CLEO RAY: This is me, losing my patience.

> From: Brigitta.DoReMi@gmail.com
> RE: do not deserve
> June 7, 3:50 PM
>
> You said you understood this is about raising my profile as an influencer. The more I get tagged, the more I'm out there with high-profile people, the higher my visibility. I thought you wanted me to succeed. I thought you supported my dreams. Now all I get from you are accusations and anger. It's really a turnoff.

REUBEN JEPHSON, CO-DEFENSE COUNSEL: Cleo swore to Beck she wasn't sleeping with Sandy. She was piling lies on top of lies and Beck was left to dangle.

CLEO RAY: What can I say? Love is weird.

> From: Liesl.DoReMi@gmail.com
> Subject: skycandy
> July 5, 1:10 PM
>
> Taking our beach chairs, skipping the beach scene, finding our own quiet place to sunbathe, the purr-fect afternoon. I should have rubbed more sunscreen on you, you were looking a little burned when we got up this morning. Or was that a rosy glow from our night of passion? Fireworks after the fireworks!! I LUV U.

ALANA BELKNAP, DEFENSE COUNSEL: And there was the email showing Cleo had outright lied to us.

CLEO RAY: Ugh. Really? Okay.

THE ANATOMY OF DESIRE

From: Brigitta.DoReMi@gmail.com
RE: skycandy
July 5, 1:12 PM

Yeah, love skycandy! Mind if I use it as a hashtag? You know what, I think we'll create some great content together in the future. OUR future. I'm having sooooooo much trouble concentrating on what to say in my next IG post. You do that to me, feeling crazy in love. Unplugging for now. Call you later LUV. #CleoBeckWedding

REUBEN JEPHSON, CO-DEFENSE COUNSEL: Cleo started sleeping with Sandy fairly frequently after they got together in March. She may have been drawn to him because of the visibility and higher engagement she desired, but then things turned more serious. She was looking for the right moment to break off with Beck. Cleo's someone who'll go to great lengths to avoid confrontation.

CLEO RAY: When the guard came to take me to Alana and Reuben, I was worried. When I walked in and saw their faces, I wanted to throw up.

Alana said, "So here's what's happened," and she told me about the emails being found on a drive at Beck's apartment and uploaded on the D.A.'s computer and then the D.A.'s computer getting hacked.

Ho-lee *shit*.

ALANA BELKNAP, DEFENSE COUNSEL: "And now the emails have been published by the major news outlets in this country and internationally." We put a pause there to let her absorb that. Outwardly Cleo kept it together, but I could see the upheaval behind her eyes.

REUBEN JEPHSON, CO-DEFENSE COUNSEL: Our first question was "Why didn't you tell us about the secret email accounts and the messaging between you?"

CLEO RAY: I'd thought they were permanently deleted. Oops.

ALANA BELKNAP, DEFENSE COUNSEL: We set a printed copy of the emails in front of Cleo. I said, "Only you know the real context of these. We've had a few hours to read through them, and we have general questions and questions regarding specific emails. Before we get into it, is there anything you want to say?"

CLEO RAY: Say it. Don't say it. Tell them. Don't tell them.

ALANA BELKNAP, DEFENSE COUNSEL: "The emails do confirm you telling us that Beck could be erratic."

CLEO RAY: The emails show how agitated she could get, and it was worse in person.

REUBEN JEPHSON, CO-DEFENSE COUNSEL: I asked, "Why did you keep lying to Beck about you and Sandy?" She said she was afraid Beck would lose it and make a scene on social media.

ALANA BELKNAP, DEFENSE COUNSEL: "Your intention was to protect your relationship with Sandy?"

CLEO RAY: They're trying to help, you know where this is going—tell them, tell them.

ALANA BELKNAP, DEFENSE COUNSEL: "#CleoBeckWedding"?

CLEO RAY: "All right," I said, and took a deep breath.

Beck was pressuring me hard to stop seeing Sandy. She was making threats, acting irrational, getting violent. Part of me wanted to go to Sandy and confess everything. But I didn't want to do anything to make him start rethinking our relationship. Those months we were together were the best in my life—and the most emotionally exhausting.

I'm scrolling down my feed one day and I see this headline:

COUPLE DROWNS WHILE KAYAKING IN NEW YORK LAKE.

And my very next thought is:

Beck can't swim.

EPISODE FOUR

GIRL
JUDGED

It's Taco Tuesday, and as part of my "Nourish to Flourish" campaign, I'm going to show you how to make your own tortillas. Then we'll top them with a delicious combo of roasted cauliflower, sautéed cherry tomatoes, pickled red onion, shredded cabbage, cilantro, and lime juice, drizzled with my special vegan mayo sauce. Nourishing food is the greatest gift we can give our bodies. It's easy to make healthy food taste fantastic and look pretty, too.

IGTV, CleoRayFitness

CLEO RAY: It started with physical sensations, my skin feeling like things were crawling on it, my scalp getting all tingly.

ALANA BELKNAP, DEFENSE COUNSEL: It was one of those times when you put your pad and pencil down and let the client talk.

CLEO RAY: Images would pop into my mind—Beck in the water flailing, Beck choking, Beck's head sinking under and not coming back up. They wouldn't stop, constant visions of her drowning. And then Sandy invited me up to Mammoth to go camping with him and David and a group of friends. I looked up the town online. It's called Mammoth *Lakes*. There are five lakes inside the town, but over a hundred and fifty in the county. I didn't know there were that many lakes in the whole state.

    This was when Beck was really after me, leaving angry voice mails and threatening messages, coming over to my place uninvited and trying to catch me with Sandy. "Stop seeing him! You have to stop seeing him!"

She was driving me insane. She could not detach from me. She'd say, "You're my first and only. I don't want anyone else. No one could make me feel the way you do."

We were still keeping our relationship a secret when she let me know she'd told her mom. Said she was dating another girl, without saying my name. Her mom was okay with it, I guess. But I'm thinking, *Now Beck will start telling everybody.* If it comes out that I'm a closet lesbian, that I haven't been authentic to who I say I am, that I'm a liar and a cheater, it could all come crashing down. The trolls start piling on and there's a massive unfollowing. Bye-bye, Cleo Ray.

Beck told me once her parents got her swimming lessons when she was young, but she had this kind of phobia about water, so she pretended she learned but never did. Not being able to swim was something she hid from people. She'd stay in the shallow end of the pool or at the beach go in only ankle-deep. She told me I was the only person on earth who knew this about her. She said it made her feel vulnerable, but it was a trust exercise and would create greater intimacy between us.

I'm having obsessive thoughts, panic attacks. What am I going to do? Then I see that headline about the canoers drowning in a lake.

Here's a way to put this craziness behind me.

My conscience is telling me, *Okay, I'll let you get away with this one thing, but from then on, you will be a saint. Just this one thing and then you'll only be good and only do good. You'll feed the homeless and volunteer at senior centers and be an activist for social justice.*

That was the deal.

And I made it.

So I went over to Beck's and told her I changed my mind. I was going to break up with Sandy and I wanted to marry her. I'd been meditating and putting it out to the universe and realized I wasn't into men after all. I was pursuing Sandy because of his status and how it could help me. I loved women and there was only one I wanted.

"You, Beck. And I am ready to make that commitment. I don't care if it hurts my influencer business. If people drop me, their loss. What's important to me is living the life I want to live. And that's with you, in the open—no more secrets, no more hiding."

I took her in my arms, and she cried. We made love and I said I wanted to propose to her the old-fashioned way, in a boat on a lake with a bottle of champagne. And I wanted to do it ASAP, so how about we drive up to the Sierras next Thursday morning? She said yes, and I held her and stroked her and swore I'd never lie to her or cheat on her again. All I wanted was to be with her and have fun and travel the world and grow old together.

And in my mind I'm saying, *I'm not this person. I am not.* I was in crisis, I was doing these things and standing outside myself, saying, *Stop! Don't do this. You can't do this.* But it was like I was overwhelmed by this dark energy. I had no control over it.

I found a lake six miles off the highway. At the end of an unpaved road, small boathouse, no motels or stores nearby. On the list of recreational lakes, Serene Lake was at the bottom.

On the drive up, it was like a second me was sitting in the back seat, watching and hearing myself saying these things to Beck, and I'm like, *Who is this person?* But I kept going, saying the things she wanted to hear. She was smiling and laughing and we were singing songs from a playlist I'd made: Janelle Monáe, Catey Shaw, Tracy Chapman. When we stopped at a rest area for a bathroom break, I kissed her and told her this was the happiest day of my life.

And in my head, I'm seeing her flail and thrash and go under. Only a psychopath can be thinking these things!

We drove past another bigger lake, and at the end of the road was a dirt parking lot with one or two other cars. I felt my cheeks getting hot and I asked Beck to go in and rent a canoe and said I'd wait for her at the dock with the champagne.

She was on such a high, I think she forgot about her fear of water or felt safe because she had a life vest. And I'm thinking, *I know exactly how I'm going to get it off her.*

We launched out, each with our own paddle, Beck in front, me behind. And Beck was saying, "This is so peaceful. We have the whole lake to ourselves. It's perfect!"

And I'm thinking, *Yes, perfect.*

I steered us to the cove I'd seen online. It was deserted, nobody around. I stopped paddling and said, "This looks like a good spot." I came forward and kneeled behind her and started kissing her neck. I put one hand under her life vest and stroked her breasts. She was the one who unhooked her straps and took off her life vest. I'm behind her with my arms around her, and I knew this was it, this was the moment. All I had to do was lunge to one side, the canoe would tip, and we would fall in the water, and it would be done. I'd be free, I'd go to Sandy, my life would be set.

REUBEN JEPHSON, CO-DEFENSE COUNSEL: I kept sneaking glances at Alana, but she wouldn't look at me. She was focused on Cleo's every word.

What am I thinking? *We're changing our plea.*

CLEO RAY: But then my mind starts flashing on all the sweet times we had together and how much she cared about me. And now I'm feeling this chill in my heart, this awful coldness, and it's spreading into my arms and my legs. Suddenly I'm hyperaware of the swaying pines, the cries of birds I couldn't see, the whispering breeze. Then I imagined Beck struggling in the water, reaching out to me, and the look on her face as she realizes I'm not going to help her, when she figures out the real reason I'd brought her here. And I knew her look of betrayal would haunt me day and night for the rest of my life.

I dropped my arms and Beck felt the change in me. She turned in her seat to face me. "Cleo," she said, "what's the matter? Are you sick? Should we go back to shore? What is it?"

I backed away and dropped into my seat. I looked at her and the words started gushing out. "I can't marry you. I can't be with you. I don't love you. I did, but I don't anymore. I love Sandy, he's the one I want to marry and be with. I'm sorry, I'm so, so sorry!"

Then Beck's face turned into this mask of rage and she lunged at me, claws out, and I lifted my paddle to protect myself, bracing it between my hands. And she stumbled forward and her face hit the shaft with her full weight, and she fell and smacked her head on the rim of the canoe and tumbled over into the water. The impact caused the canoe to turn over, and I tumbled in right after her. The lake was so cold it shocked my senses. I swallowed water and I made myself kick to the surface. My head broke through, and I gulped air and choked and grabbed for something to hold on to . . .

ALANA BELKNAP, DEFENSE COUNSEL: After hearing her story, we needed to meet with Samson, in person, pronto. Reuben and I drove directly from the jail down to his house in Brentwood.

SAMSON GRIFFITH: If they're coming from a meeting with Cleo to see me, driving the four and a half hours and not saying what it's about— yeah, I had a feeling they were not bringing great news.

REUBEN JEPHSON, CO-DEFENSE COUNSEL: It wasn't a confession of murder. But it was a substantial modification of the circumstances that brought those two women to that moment.

ALANA BELKNAP, DEFENSE COUNSEL: When a defendant changes her story—the one she told police, her family, her attorneys—it's a turning point. It was good she changed it before the trial started, but it's still problematic, because it puts a seed of doubt in the minds of those defending her.

As in, *What else hasn't she told us?*

SAMSON GRIFFITH: Cleo. Oh, Cleo.

Her story changed, but not the most critical part—she was still saying she did not *cause* Beck's death. No matter what she had in her mind driving up there and getting in that canoe, the actual drowning was not first-degree murder, it was an accident. Maybe negligent. But not willful.

REUBEN JEPHSON, CO-DEFENSE COUNSEL: It was our obligation to tell Samson we could go back to the D.A. and negotiate for a lesser murder charge. There was no guarantee the prosecution would accept that. But in light of this new information, the door was open to changing strategy.

SAMSON GRIFFITH: How's that going to play? After deny, deny, deny, she cops a plea before the trial starts? Okay, she did kill that girl, and her attorneys convinced her to take a deal before it was too late. In terms of Cleo being tainted the rest of her life, is it so different from a guilty verdict?

I asked Alana if she believed Cleo.

ALANA BELKNAP, DEFENSE COUNSEL: My fallback is usually "I believe in my client's right to the best defense possible." But in this case, Cleo's ability to tell the truth was becoming a major issue. I mean, she went forty-eight hours in a state of near pathological denial. She wasn't responsible in the sense she'd willfully caused Beck's death, but sure as hell responsible for not reporting what happened and pretending it hadn't happened.

I told Samson there was planning, malice aforethought—but did

Beck go into the water as the result of an intentional act on Cleo's part? I had plenty of reasonable doubt about that.

SAMSON GRIFFITH: Wasn't exactly the answer I was hoping for.

REUBEN JEPHSON, CO-DEFENSE COUNSEL: We left Samson's agreeing to think about it and get on the phone in a day or two. Which was a wise move, since we still had time before the trial.

ALANA BELKNAP, DEFENSE COUNSEL: The important thing was to keep Cleo's interests first. Before her uncle's, before her counsels'. The trial was shaping up to play out on a big stage. No trial, no chance for us attorneys to strut our stuff. But Cleo had a lot more at stake than we did.

ELVA GRIFFITH: We were given a time by a deputy and went to one of the booths where inmates can visit with friends and family. We sat there for half an hour waiting for Mary Claire. Then the guard came and said he apologized, but Mary Claire—he called her *Ms. Ray*—was refusing to see us.

Our feelings were hurt, we'd come all the way from Kansas City by bus. But we knew our daughter was under great stress. We prayed for the strength to endure her rejection and for Mary Claire to find forgiveness and talk to us. All we wanted was to see our daughter.

JAKE CROWE, *INYO REGISTER*: I got a tip from someone at the jail and drove to Independence. Cleo's parents weren't hard to find. A gaunt middle-aged couple dressed Salvation Army style walking the streets with a cloud of bewilderment over them.

I introduced myself and asked if I could buy them a lemonade and a taco.

SAMSON GRIFFITH: It was a matter of time before the media got their hooks into my brother and sister-in-law. Cleo's parents represented a part of her life she'd completely cut off and never talked about. From when Cleo first showed up at our door, through her working for the company and being represented by us, I think we spoke about Asa and Elva a total of four times. One of those times was on the day she was arrested.

ERIN NEWCOMB, CHIEF DEPUTY: We were still learning about Cleo's background. First we thought she was an L.A. kid. Turned out she grew up in the Midwest with missionary parents, traveling preachers. They were far from typical. They belonged to a poverty mission, a church that believed any kind of material wealth was a sign of the devil's work. They gave everything they earned to their home church and lived at a bare subsistence level.

Their daughter would have lived at that level until she was fifteen. And then she ran off to L.A. and disowned her parents and began striving to become a somebody. Most who knew her during those years agreed on one thing: she was driven.

OWEN MASON, DISTRICT ATTORNEY: The legal pundits were speculating that "fundamentalist" Christian parents would help the defendant's case in this jurisdiction. I disagreed. The fact she hadn't spoken to them in years and was refusing let them visit her showed how far she'd strayed from the path. Having Mr. and Mrs. Alden in the courtroom sitting behind the prosecution's table would be more powerful than Mr. and Mrs. Griffith sitting behind their estranged daughter.

I felt for them. And I wasn't the only one. Our pastor reached out, invited them to Sunday service and put them up for a few days. Mr. and Mrs. Griffith received only compassion from our community.

ELVA GRIFFITH: Mary Claire was a good child. She didn't give us much trouble growing up. We raised her to be independent, to be able to care for herself. Her father and I had heeded the Lord's calling together when we were first married. We spent a lot of time on the road for our ministry.

We could see she felt out of place, so we didn't require her to go with us every time we went on our missions. We prayed and believed she'd come around to the righteous life. The Lord's timetable is different with every individual.

One morning we got up and she was gone from her bed. When she didn't come back by dinnertime, we called the police. They told us this wasn't unusual. A lot of fifteen-year-old girls run away from home and return in a few days.

But Mary Claire didn't come back in a few days. We became frantic and our church friends helped us search for her. After six weeks we got a call from Samson, Asa's brother, who told us Mary Claire had come out to Los Angeles and wanted to stay there. I guess we could've legally forced her to come back to live with us, but that didn't seem right. Under Samson's watch, we knew she'd have resources. It made us sad, we missed her terribly, but we prayed our way through it.

CLEO RAY: I knew I had something to say, I just needed to find the right place to say it. Some people do it through the arts, some through teaching, some through public service. I saw these women speaking directly to other women through social media, and I said, *I can do that.* After I got my pages up and running, I realized it was not so much about my voice going out as it was about the voices coming back to me. These women I inspired to make a change, even a small one. They said, "You showed me the way to empowerment." And that's where I found my empowerment, through their stories and their voices replying back to mine. Any time I felt myself getting down, I went to my Instagram, and those beautiful, loving voices lifted me right up. They motivated me to meet my own challenges and do better. Because doing better is the best feeling there is.

JAKE CROWE, *INYO REGISTER*: After I posted my interview with Cleo Ray's parents, the story started trending on church message boards. Pastors began mentioning Cleo in their Sunday sermons. She was becoming both a protagonist and an antagonist in a national morality play, a dinner-table topic not only on the coasts but in the middle of the country, too. She was held up as a symbol of success and achievement, yet at the same time she represented all that was wrong with social media and the youth of America.

Her case turned into a cultural litmus test. If you sympathized with her, you were elitist, overeducated, godless. If you shamed her, you were embracing traditional values and Christian ideals.

The one person not getting to see any of this play out was the main character. She was cut off from social media because she was in jail, and she made a choice not to watch television. She had access to newspapers and print media but turned away. Cleo Ray deliberately walled herself off from the outside world. Out of fear, I guess. Fear of seeing everything she'd built come crumbling down.

DUNCAN MCMILLAN: *There are four small motels in town and one hotel in Independence, the old Winnedumah, across from the courthouse. Altogether, there are sixty available guest rooms. The nearest towns to handle an overflow of visitors are Lone Pine, sixteen miles south, and Bishop, forty miles north. Anticipating an onslaught of media and spectators for the trial, the locals began preparing their spare rooms to rent out.*

BRIAN BURLEIGH, ASSISTANT D.A.: Jury selection was scheduled for the Monday after Labor Day, meaning the trial would be underway by the time we hit the fall. The defense agreed to limit making motions that would cause delays—as long as we played heads-up with them. We were honoring the defendant's right to a speedy trial. And the speedier it was, the more money we'd be saving the county.

JAKE CROWE, *INYO REGISTER*: Sure, whatever. The truth was, the trial scheduling was at least partially driven by getting Mason up onstage and a guilty verdict before people voted in November.

REUBEN JEPHSON, CO-DEFENSE COUNSEL: The day before jury selection, the judge called us into his chambers for the pre-voir-dire conference. He wanted to get agreement on the scope of the questions we'd be asking prospective jurors. For us, there were two critical areas: social media and beliefs bias. The more someone participated in social media, the better for us...

ALANA BELKNAP, DEFENSE COUNSEL: ... and we favored those who were *less* religious rather than those who were *more* religious because of the inherent bias against homosexuality and bisexuality.

OWEN MASON, DISTRICT ATTORNEY: The law doesn't allow you to discriminate against a juror for their religious affiliation. The focus should be on a juror's ability to be impartial and follow the law. You can ask if a person's religion may cause them bias, but you should not be able to excuse a potential juror because he's a Christian who regularly attends church.

In our experience, religious jurors tend to be the most conscientious. You want people who take the issues of guilt and innocence seriously and have contemplated and discussed moral issues. To assume a religious person can't be fair-minded as a juror is itself prejudice.

ALANA BELKNAP, DEFENSE COUNSEL: The judge anticipated our concerns and tried to give us some leeway, but he was adamant about jury selection not becoming a debate on Christian values. He wanted to draw a line between asking if a person believed homosexuality was a sin and asking if they could find a sinful person innocent of murder.

REUBEN JEPHSON, CO-DEFENSE COUNSEL: The last thing we discussed was whether Cleo would be permitted to enter the court building through the rear door, because it was the most secure and would spare her from the media gauntlet. But Judge Oberwaltzer was inflexible—she would go through the front door like every other defendant who comes to his court.

ALANA BELKNAP, DEFENSE COUNSEL: Fine, the front door it is. We'll put Cleo in a semi-conservative suit, have her demonstrate humble confidence, and parade our perfectly imperfect client before the national media. If her way gets blocked by a microphone, she'll say, "All I want is a fair trial."

ERIN NEWCOMB, CHIEF DEPUTY: We knew the crowd would be big because the rooms in Independence and Lone Pine were all booked. What we didn't expect was how many people would be driving up from L.A. They started showing up two hours early, and by ten, the crowd went from top of the courthouse steps down to the sidewalk. And this was for jury selection!

FRED HITE, COUNTY SHERIFF: Usually it's one deputy per defendant, but for this defendant we assigned four, two running interference, two in rearguard position.

CLEO RAY: My second court appearance. Alana spent time prepping me, showing me videos of other women defendants around my age and how they acted in the courtroom. The dos and don'ts. I had trained myself to present in front of a camera, so I could flip a switch and appear pretty relaxed.

Navigate the fear, feel your feelings, but do not take off your mask.

GILLIAN GRIFFITH: On the first day of jury selection my dad and I were running late because of traffic, and oh my God. We hit a dead stop before we even got into town and had to park in a cow pasture. When we finally got to the courtroom, they told us the seats reserved for family had been given away and the court was full. The fire marshal was standing guard, and he wouldn't let anyone in unless someone came out. Dad managed to bribe a couple sitting in the gallery to give up their seats. A hundred bucks each, and we had to sit on folding chairs along the back wall.

ERIN NEWCOMB, CHIEF DEPUTY: I was in the courtroom assisting our bailiff with security. When Cleo came in and sat at the defense table, she and I met eyes. She smiled and waved at me. And despite the protocol, I waved back. Of course a camera recorded it, and when my waving to the defendant in a murder trial showed up online, I caught hell from Sheriff Hite.

CLEO RAY: I had a desire for attention—as a fitness influencer, not the defendant in a murder trial. Everyone was staring at me. I tried to keep my eyes down. A hand grazed my shoulder. I turned and there were Asa and Elva, eyes full of love and forgiveness. I said to myself, *If Jesus can rise from the dead, I can force myself not to implode.*

As I'm turning around, I catch sight of two more people staring at me. Beck's mom and dad. Their eyes were not full of love and forgiveness.

When I faced the front, it felt like people were shooting hate bullets at the back of my head. Welcome to the trial of your life, Cleo Ray!

TITUS ALDEN: It was the first time either of us had seen *the defendant* in person. I was mad enough to go up and slap her face, but my wife grabbed my arm and squeezed hard.

REUBEN JEPHSON, CO-DEFENSE COUNSEL: On the way inside the court I noticed local people recognizing me and frowning. I'd been reading the comments on *The Inyo Register*'s website. The consensus seemed to be that I was a traitor to the moral order. Up in Bishop I'd get maybe one or two cold shoulders a day, but I didn't feel true hostility until I took my place at the defense table.

> **BAILIFF:** Order in the court! All rise. The Superior Court of Inyo County, State of California, is now in session. The Honorable Judge Roy Oberwaltzer presiding. Please be seated.
>
> **THE COURT:** Good morning, ladies and gentlemen, and welcome. I see we have a full house today. What a surprise. I'm sure everyone here intends to be on their best behavior. That started with turning off your electronic devices and putting them away. I don't want to see anyone looking at or even holding a cell phone in my courtroom. If I do, I'll have you immediately escorted outside and you will be banned for the rest of the day. So we're clear, I don't give second chances. Are the prosecution and defense ready to begin jury selection in Case 73588–1, *The People v. Mary Claire Griffith*?
>
> **MR. MASON:** The People are ready, Your Honor.
>
> **MS. BELKNAP:** The defense is ready, Your Honor.

ALANA BELKNAP, DEFENSE COUNSEL: Smallest jury pool I've ever had to work with. The media age in the county is forty-seven years old. Did I say *media* age? I meant *median* age.

> **COURT CLERK:** Will the prospective jurors stand and raise their right hand? Do each of you understand and agree that you will accurately

and truthfully answer, under the penalty of perjury, all questions to you concerning your qualifications and competency to serve as a trial juror in the matter pending before this court?
PROSPECTIVE JURORS: I do.
THE COURT: Welcome to our panel of prospective jurors. Thank you for being here today. I am going to tell you a little about this case and introduce you to the prosecution, the defense, and the defendant, Mary Claire Griffith.

CLEO RAY: In the courtroom I'd be Mary Claire Griffith. Not even aka Cleo Ray. I thought that might help me get distance from the grim reality of what was happening in front of me. Cleo Ray wasn't on trial. Instead it was this Mary Claire person from the Midwest. Good luck, girl. I am so rooting for you.

REUBEN JEPHSON, CO-DEFENSE COUNSEL: First prospective juror was Asian, male, thirty-nine years old, master's in business administration. Regional manager at the Department of Water and Power, earning more than double the average salary in the county. We wanted him.

> **MR. MASON:** Sir, how many hours a week would you estimate you spend on the internet?
> **JUROR NO. 1:** I'd say between one and two hours a day, maybe ten hours a week.
> **MR. MASON:** Are you on Facebook?
> **JUROR NO. 1:** Yes.
> **MR. MASON:** Instagram?
> **JUROR NO. 1:** Yes.
> **MR. MASON:** Twitter?
> **JUROR NO. 1:** Yes.
> **MR. MASON:** Have you watched any of the defendant's videos on Instagram or YouTube?

JUROR NO.1: Not before I read about the case, but since then I have watched several, yes.

MR. MASON: And in watching those videos and seeing her posts, did you form an opinion about the defendant?

JUROR NO. 1: Just that she's appealing, in great shape, a good communicator. I could see why she has so many followers.

ALANA BELKNAP, DEFENSE COUNSEL: Mason tried to get the first juror dismissed for cause, saying the man had already formed an opinion about Cleo from watching her videos. We objected because a lot of people would have recently clicked on Cleo's videos out of curiosity, and the way she presented herself was designed to get likes and followers. Looking at her postings and acknowledging she's this cute, engaging twenty-five-year-old shouldn't be a valid cause for a challenge. The underlying reasons the prosecution didn't want him was his ethnicity made him more sensitive to bias and his education made him more broad-minded. Or, shall we say, liberal?

JAKE CROWE, *INYO REGISTER*: That first morning of voir dire they dove into one of the major themes of the trial—the distinction between the online Cleo Ray and the person off-line. Building a social media image is not the same as an actor playing a role, but the perky, likable character in her photos and videos is still a construct, a creation designed to engage a certain demographic. How could this person who exudes such authentic positivity be a stone-cold killer? That's the question the prosecution needed to answer.

REUBEN JEPHSON, CO-DEFENSE COUNSEL: The prosecution used one of its peremptory challenges for Juror 1, which we also objected to, but the judge allowed it and sent the man home. Too bad, we lost a good one there. One down, forty-nine prospects to go.

MS. BELKNAP: Madam, do you have any children who are close in age to the defendant?

JUROR NO. 6: I have two daughters, twenty-eight and twenty-three.

MS. BELKNAP: And how are your relationships with your daughters?

JUROR NO. 6: The older one and I don't speak. The younger one moved to the East Coast. I speak to her every few weeks.

MS. BELKNAP: Might the fact you're not close to your daughters influence your opinion of the defendant?

JUROR NO. 6: Well, I really can't say.

MS. BELKNAP: Can you try?

JUROR NO. 6: The defendant reminds me of my eldest. That might have an effect on me.

MS. BELKNAP: A positive or negative effect?

JUROR NO. 6: Negative. Mostly. I'm not sure.

MS. BELKNAP: Would you be able to put aside the comparison with your daughter and judge the defendant on the merits of the case?

JUROR NO. 6: I would certainly try to. I'd like to think I could.

ALANA BELKNAP, DEFENSE COUNSEL: We wanted Juror 6, and I'll tell you why. She had two daughters Cleo's age, one she didn't get along with and another who moved away from her, and that would make her more aware of not being biased against Cleo. Because of her experience with complicated family relationships, this woman would force herself to think things through and be more likely to question her instinctive judgments. These daughter issues seemed like they would bleed over into her opinion of Cleo, but actually the opposite is true. She would cut Cleo more slack.

OWEN MASON, DISTRICT ATTORNEY: A woman in her early fifties making forty thousand a year and struggling to give her daughters a decent life is going to see this successful young woman who makes five times her income and feel resentful. That's not bias, just natural human emotions.

We had a total of one juror by lunch. In most cases, we fill the whole box by the lunch break.

CLEO RAY: By midmorning on the first day, I'm thinking I cannot believe how much energy it takes to keep sitting up straight and not react to what's happening. When I'm creating content for my platforms, I control every detail. Nothing goes out I haven't triple-checked. There is no playback in court, I can't see that last bad picture and delete it. I can't tell when the pool camera is pointing at me or when someone is looking at me. There is not a single moment I can relax. I have to be "on" from when I walk into court until I walk out hours later.

GILLIAN GRIFFITH: At the first recess, they showed us to a room downstairs where Cleo's family could have privacy during the breaks. My dad took the initiative to greet Asa and Elva and ask them if they were doing okay.

I'd met my aunt and uncle once, years earlier, when they were passing through L.A. I remember how stiff and uncomfortable they seemed. I had no relationship with them. They were strangers to us.

ELVA GRIFFITH: Never had a problem with Samson or his family. We were grateful he'd taken in Mary Claire when he did. He and Asa took divergent paths in life and could not be more different. But there in court we were united on one goal—seeing Mary Claire exonerated.

SAMSON GRIFFITH: It was strained. But we shared a common cause. They mentioned how they wished they could visit Cleo at the jail. I hadn't known she was refusing to see them. I didn't think that was right.

Next chance I got, I sent Cleo a note basically saying: "I know there's a lot of unhappy history there, but it's breaking your parents' hearts that you won't see them. They love you and want what's best for you. This could be a chance to do some healing on both sides."

I added some Wikiquote about forgiveness. And Cleo went right on refusing to see them.

ALANA BELKNAP, DEFENSE COUNSEL: Then came the mountaineer guy who worked at The Sierra Adventure Shop in Lone Pine. Thirty-one, single. Healthy lifestyle, outdoors type, has a popular Instagram page. He and Cleo would be an instant hookup on match dot whatever.

> MS. BELKNAP: Do you belong to a local church?
> JUROR NO. 13: Yes, ma'am, High Sierra First Baptist. I actually lead the men's group there.
> MS. BELKNAP: You consider yourself an active member of the church?
> JUROR NO. 13: Yes, ma'am.
> MS. BELKNAP: Do you believe the Bible is the literal word of God?
> JUROR NO. 13: I do, yes.
> MS. BELKNAP: And what is your opinion of the church's stance on homosexuality?
> JUROR NO. 13: I believe homosexuality is wrong—but not irredeemable.

ALANA BELKNAP, DEFENSE COUNSEL: And he looks right at Cleo and smiles.

REUBEN JEPHSON, CO-DEFENSE COUNSEL: I caught that smile. It was brief. I don't think the prosecution saw it. And the camera hadn't recorded it.

ALANA BELKNAP, DEFENSE COUNSEL: It's kind of a given that a juror who is devoted to a church and believes in the inerrancy of the Bible will more likely benefit the prosecution and not the defense. However, do not underestimate the power of sex appeal. And it's a fundamental

Christian tenet that sinners can—must be—converted into followers of Jesus to find forgiveness.

BRIAN BURLEIGH, ASSISTANT D.A.: Jury selection was scheduled for one day, and at that rate it was looking more like five or six. Knowing Judge O, we figured he'd lose his patience sooner than later.

MR. MASON: Are you on social media?
JUROR NO. 22: I don't own a computer.
MR. MASON: Do you have a smartphone?
JUROR NO. 22: I have a cell phone. Not sure how smart it is.
MR. MASON: Do you use it to connect to the internet?
JUROR NO. 22: I use my phone for phone calls.
MR. MASON: Are you on Facebook or Instagram?
JUROR NO. 22: No.
MR. MASON: Have you ever used a social media site for anything?
JUROR NO. 22: Someone showed me Facebook once on their computer. Not interested.
MR. MASON: So, the defendant sitting there, have you ever seen her anywhere before?
JUROR NO. 22: Nope, never.
MR. MASON: Not even on TV?
JUROR NO. 22: Don't own a TV.

REUBEN JEPHSON, CO-DEFENSE COUNSEL: We'd used a number of our peremptory challenges, so the technophobe juror we wanted excused for cause.

BRIAN BURLEIGH, ASSISTANT D.A.: How does being disconnected from the internet make someone an unsuitable juror in a murder trial? Wouldn't common sense say a person like that would have zero bias because they hadn't been exposed to anything online?

REUBEN JEPHSON, CO-DEFENSE COUNSEL: If the juror hardly knows what social media is, beyond being disconnected from it, he's going to get lost during a lot of the testimony. It wouldn't be fair to him or the other jurors to have him sit on a case where a foreign language is spoken.

> **THE COURT:** Counsel, social media is not on trial here. It's tangential to the core issues of the charged crime. You haven't shown anything indicating Juror 22 would be biased against the defendant. Your "for cause" challenge is overruled.

REUBEN JEPHSON, CO-DEFENSE COUNSEL: Which meant we had to use another peremptory challenge. Advantage, the prosecution.

JAKE CROWE, *INYO REGISTER*: First full day of jury selection, two jurors impaneled. The next day as each new prospect took the hot seat, the antagonism between the prosecution and the defense intensified.

> **MS. BELKNAP:** What is your occupation?
> **JUROR NO. 33:** I'm the librarian at the Furnace Creek Branch of the Inyo County Free Library.
> **MS. BELKNAP:** Would it be fair to say you're a book lover?
> **JUROR NO. 33:** Yes, I love books.
> **MS. BELKNAP:** What kind of books do you like to read?
> **JUROR NO. 33:** I have to admit, I'm a bit of a true crime addict.
> **MS. BELKNAP:** What are some of your favorite true crime books?
> **JUROR NO. 33:** *Helter Skelter. In Cold Blood,* of course. *Fatal Vision.*
> **MS. BELKNAP:** I believe those are murder cases where trials figured prominently?
> **JUROR NO. 33:** That's true.
> **MS. BELKNAP:** And if memory serves, those cases ended with defendants being convicted of murder. Would that have an influence on you if you were a juror in this case?

JUROR NO. 33: I think it would make me a more discerning juror, knowing what I know about murder trials. I would be faster at processing the evidence.

MS. BELKNAP: More discerning and faster don't necessarily go together.

JUROR NO. 33: More efficient is what I meant.

BRIAN BURLEIGH, ASSISTANT D.A.: Turned out the librarian also watched a lot of true crime TV shows, like *Making a Murderer*, which depicts the prosecution in a negative light. We used a peremptory challenge on her. Nice lady, no hard feelings, but anything you read or watch is going to have an author bias—like the series you're making!

MR. MASON: You do a lot of fishing in the backcountry here?

JUROR NO. 41: I do. Since I retired, I go out five, six days a week during the season.

MR. MASON: Own your own boat?

JUROR NO. 41: Uh-huh, an eighteen-foot outboard Scout.

MR. MASON: Have you been out on the lakes in other types of boats?

JUROR NO. 41: All kinds. Rowboats, ski boats, sailboats.

MR. MASON: Canoes?

JUROR NO. 41: Absolutely.

MR. MASON: Do you know Serene Lake?

JUROR NO. 41: I do. The fishing's not great. I usually go to Rock Creek Lake next door.

MR. MASON: And have you been involved in a boating accident on any of these lakes?

JUROR NO. 41: Yeah, about four years ago I was up fishing Silver Pass Lake when a storm blew in and a wind gust swept me over the side. Damn near drowned.

ALANA BELKNAP, DEFENSE COUNSEL: An expert on boating—in lakes. Involved in an accident where he fell off his boat and almost drowned.

In the jury room, he'll be able to explain to them what we're portraying here is possible. Or "damn near" possible.

CLEO RAY: Reuben leaned over and whispered to me, "You can look the jurors in the eye. You've got a great smile, use it."

Look them in the eye and smile when they might be saying to themselves, *That evil murdering bitch.* Not easy. Takes practice.

JAKE CROWE, *INYO REGISTER*: This was the most intensive grilling of prospective jurors in Inyo County court history. The judge made it clear he wanted the process to be expeditious, but it dragged on to a third day and a fourth. I didn't blame the attorneys. They know the fate of the case is mostly determined the moment that twelfth juror is seated.

SAMSON GRIFFITH: The wrong jury means game over before the trial starts. Before a single witness had testified, both sides were fighting like they were in a cage match.

ALANA BELKNAP, DEFENSE COUNSEL: What happened as we left court on the fourth day was shameful.

CLEO RAY: I heard a voice shout, "Hey, Cleo!" I turned and splat. So disgusting.

JAKE CROWE, *INYO REGISTER*: The cameraman for KVME News was there and captured the moment in a 4K close-up. The first viral video from the trial. And by no means the last.

SAMSON GRIFFITH: A big wad of green phlegm landed right on her cheek. On Twitter it got Cleo a lot of sympathy. They said a woman did it, but it looked like a man's spit to me. Horrible.

FRED HITE, COUNTY SHERIFF: It was a mother with her two young daughters beside her. We confirmed she was not a resident of Inyo County.

SANDY FINCH: I had to shut my laptop and go for a long trail run. Stuff like that makes me lose faith in humanity.

ERIN NEWCOMB, CHIEF DEPUTY: It reflected poorly on our department. Judge O showed the wisdom to allow the defendant to enter the building through the rear, where we could keep the crowd away.

ALANA BELKNAP, DEFENSE COUNSEL: Cleo got pretty down after the spitting incident. Because she had no access to social media and refused to watch TV or read the newspaper, she wasn't aware of the polarizing figure she'd become. I had a talk with the sheriff, let him know our concerns, and asked them to put her on watch at least until the end of the trial.

She's in the bloom of her youth, a rising star, attached to one of the most desirable bachelors on the planet. And suddenly she's locked in a tiny jail cell, on trial for her life, and has random people literally spewing hate at her. That's a harsh reality to wake up to every morning.

SANDY FINCH: I was on the list of prosecution witnesses and had given a deposition for them. I got a call from Alana Belknap asking if I'd come up and meet with her. I'd been intending to go visit Cleo, but I was slammed with keeping my business on track and the visiting hours were very limited. That's not an excuse, but I guess it sort of is. We scheduled my meeting with her lawyers and my visit to the jail on the same Saturday.

REUBEN JEPHSON, CO-DEFENSE COUNSEL: Most of our out-of-court meetings took place at Alana's suite up at the Westin. She'd have room service deliver a platter with European cheeses, bruschetta, ceviche, fresh baked bread. Not only is she a brilliant lawyer, she's first class all the way.

Sometimes after work we'd have a glass of wine and stare out her floor-to-ceiling windows at the mountains. I never get tired of looking at the Eastern Sierra. That view restores my sense of perspective. Alana grew up in Denver and has a vacation home in Vail. She's a mountain person, too. We'd talk about all different things, but somehow the conversation, no matter how far afield, would come back to the case. So many layers, so many angles of approach.

SANDY FINCH: It was the first time I'd been back to Mammoth since that weekend. I drove by myself, turned off my phone, and blasted the new Harry Styles album. Yeah, I passed the courthouse in Independence. Weird to think that in a few days I'd be inside there testifying at my girlfriend's murder trial.

ALANA BELKNAP, DEFENSE COUNSEL: We'd interviewed Sandy over the phone, closely went over his deposition, but we needed to meet him in person to prepare him for what to expect on the witness stand. I felt a lot of sympathy for him. A classic case of collateral damage. Here he's carved out this successful niche in the world, has this incredibly bright future, and out of nowhere gets T-boned by a speeding train he never saw coming.

SANDY FINCH: I knew why the prosecution was calling me to testify. I was with Cleo during the time between the drowning and her arrest. She never mentioned anything about being up at that lake or this other girl. It showed her lack of remorse, right? That she had ice water in her veins? I'm not a psychologist, I can only tell you what I saw when I looked in her eyes.

REUBEN JEPHSON, CO-DEFENSE COUNSEL: They were going to destroy her credibility by showing Cleo had been lying to Sandy all along.

ALANA BELKNAP, DEFENSE COUNSEL: They were going to ask about the sexual interactions between Sandy and Cleo. They wanted the jury to see Sandy react.

SANDY FINCH: If helping Cleo meant I had to be nonreactive on the stand, I would do that.

ALANA BELKNAP, DEFENSE COUNSEL: We did some role-playing. I'm the prosecutor. "Mr. Finch, when you went into the tent that last night and were alone with the defendant, did you go to sleep? No? What did you do? You said in your deposition the defendant was 'amorous.' What did you mean by that? Did she seem at all sad to you? Upset? Troubled? In your deposition you also used the word *frisky* to describe the defendant's behavior. Can you explain that more? You said in regard to your lovemaking, 'She took charge.' What did you mean by that?"

SANDY FINCH: My answer to every question would be transcribed, recorded, broadcast, streamed, printed—and follow me the rest of my life. It didn't matter what I said, it would be taken out of context, edited to make me look however someone wanted me to look. Might as well tell the truth, right?

ALANA BELKNAP, DEFENSE COUNSEL: Sandy asked, "When I'm on the stand, is it okay to look at her?" I said, "You can glance, smile, whatever feels natural, but avoid looking at her right after the prosecutor points out a lie she's told you. I'd also ask you not to hold eye contact with her. That's where you risk getting derailed."

SANDY FINCH: I didn't want to look like I was avoiding saying certain things to make her look better to the jury. I just had to answer their questions, briefly and truthfully.

I needed to forgive her for the lies she told me before I took the stand. I needed to take the charge out of that. When it was Alana and Reuben's turn to ask questions, they would lead me through "the Cleo redemption narrative."

ALANA BELKNAP, DEFENSE COUNSEL: On cross we'd be treating him as a character witness for Cleo, to steer the impression of her back to her simple humanity, to show how much Sandy adored her.

REUBEN JEPHSON, CO-DEFENSE COUNSEL: We told him not to volunteer explanations, to be respectful to the judge and the prosecutors, and not to be afraid to the look jurors in the eyes. He came across as very genuine. His feelings for Cleo were sincere.

ALANA BELKNAP, DEFENSE COUNSEL: I knew it had been eight weeks and this was Sandy's first visit to the jail. He and Cleo spoke by phone, he sent her letters, but they hadn't seen each other in person since the arrest. I knew his coming there was a big deal to her, and I asked him to be encouraging. The best way to help her was to keep it positive.

SANDY FINCH: I felt more confident about the case after that meeting. Seemed like Cleo was in excellent hands with those two.

Next stop, the county jail. Eighty-five miles for me to think through my half of the visit. I could feel my hands sweating on the steering wheel.

CLEO RAY: Nervous? Are you kidding? This was our first face-to-face since you know when. Two months had gone by. I'm wearing this ugly prison uniform, I'm all pale, my hair's greasy.

Would I see a flicker of uncertainty in his eyes? A flash of rejection? Would I crumble then and there, knowing I was losing the love of my life?

SANDY FINCH: Never visited anyone in jail, never been inside a jail. But as the guy whose brand is about leaning in to new experiences, I'd just lean in to this one, too.

CLEO RAY: There would be a glass partition between us, and we'd be using wall phones to talk. I'd be in shackles until I was inside the booth ready to be seated. And we had half an hour. Thirty minutes. One thousand eight hundred seconds.

SANDY FINCH: First words out of her mouth were an apology for how she looked. I smiled and said, "You look beautiful." I meant it.

CLEO RAY: "Do these stripes make me look fat?" He laughed. He put his hand against the glass and I covered it with mine. "I can feel your touch," I said.

He said, "I've been feeling your touch this whole time."

DUNCAN MCMILLAN: *The Inyo County Jail recorded the visit between Cleo Ray and Sandy Finch on the afternoon of September twelfth. By arrangement with the sheriff's office and permissions from the persons involved, what follows is the actual audio from their visit.*

CLEO RAY: Can you tell my arms are still pretty toned? I've been doing incline push-ups on the bunk in my cell.
SANDY FINCH: You're amazing. Sorry it's taken me so long to get up here.
CLEO RAY: You're here now, that's all I care about. You met with Alana and Reuben?
SANDY FINCH: I did. They're on top of this. You're going to get out of here,

Cleo, I know it. And on that day I'll be right outside to pick you up, and we'll drive straight to the airport and go somewhere far away together.
CLEO RAY: Really far away. Where?
SANDY FINCH: Remember the resort we looked at in Bali?
CLEO RAY: With the sea-cliff villas and private infinity pools?
SANDY FINCH: First thing we'll do is turn off the Wi-Fi.
CLEO RAY: We'll lock our phones in the safe, bring stuff to read.
SANDY FINCH: I don't think we'll have much time for reading.
CLEO RAY: Why not?
SANDY FINCH: Because we'll be in bed making love day and night.
CLEO RAY: Not only in bed. In the pools. On the deck lounges.
SANDY FINCH: In the shower, in the steam bath, in the jungle.
CLEO RAY: Sorry, I'm losing it. I miss you so much.
SANDY FINCH: I miss waking up with you. Going for trail runs up Temescal. Hitting the farmers' market, making breakfast together.
CLEO RAY: My asparagus hash. Two eggs on top, sunny side up.
SANDY FINCH: Mmm, so good.
CLEO RAY: Do you know how sorry I am?
SANDY FINCH: Babe, my job is to cheer you up, not make you cry.
CLEO RAY: Right now, this is what me cheered up looks like.

SANDY FINCH: The time went by too fast. We'd just started and then it was over.

CLEO RAY: The guard knocked to let me know the visit was up and I was like, "Noooo!"

SANDY FINCH: Dull fluorescent lights, cinder-block walls, no way to even touch her. That is cruel and unusual punishment.

CLEO RAY: The guard came in and started putting my shackles back on.

I said, "Wait a second." I turned to Sandy and said, "Go, please, go now. I don't want you to see me like this."

SANDY FINCH: I was about to say I didn't care, but instead I left. I was shook up, man. I went out, got in my car, and had to sit a while before I felt able to drive. To see this person I cared about in that situation—it was really freaking hard. That was one long trip back to L.A.

OWEN MASON, DISTRICT ATTORNEY: Before court started that Friday, the judge calls us and defense counsel into chambers. We'd had to bring in a second jury pool and were into our fifth day of selection. The judge made it clear he wanted a jury seated by the end of the day. He confronted the defense.

ALANA BELKNAP, DEFENSE COUNSEL: The judge said, "You are not going to find your perfect jury here. This is not L.A. or New York. We have what we have, and you will work with what we have."

I said, "Your Honor, we are not hoping for a perfect jury. Our perfect jury doesn't exist in this county. But we have to find a fair jury."

He said, "If today does not move along expeditiously, I'll take over the questioning and decide who's qualified to sit and who is not. Are we clear?"

This was a glimpse into our future. We're seeing a judge who can get cranky and doesn't have much patience. Sure, let's have a mistrial. Set us up for the appeal. In the meantime, you have a presumed-innocent defendant who's getting spat on in front of your courthouse.

JAKE CROWE, *INYO REGISTER*: They struck out in the morning session. Now it's Friday afternoon, and the attorneys start questioning a Native

THE ANATOMY OF DESIRE

American man from the Paiute tribe who's a co-owner of the big casino in Bishop. He's a proud, broad-bodied fellow in his late forties who wears thousand-dollar snakeskin boots and a turquoise bolo tie.

MS. BELKNAP: You were convicted of a crime when you were a younger man?
JUROR NO. 94: Yes. When I was twenty, I pled guilty to a battery charge and served two years in county jail.
MS. BELKNAP: Did you feel the sentence was fair?
JUROR NO. 94: Maybe not at the time, but looking back I do, yes.
MS. BELKNAP: Do you think that experience with the judicial system and being incarcerated would affect your ability to be fair and impartial in this case?
JUROR NO. 94: I think I'd be able to see both sides more realistically. I understand the process, I understand the stakes. Yeah, having gone through that would make me see the big picture more clearly.
MS. BELKNAP: Do you feel any bitterness toward the courts?
JUROR NO. 94: I don't. In fact, I tell people the experience made me a better person, possibly even saved my life.

BRIAN BURLEIGH, ASSISTANT D.A.: Tough one for us. He's one of the most respected businessmen in the county, an activist and a philanthropist for the people of his tribe and for all the California tribes. We believed him when he said he didn't feel bitter toward the prosecutors or the court for his earlier conviction and jail time. But we knew he championed causes for people in trouble with the law. In other words, he's going to consider the defendant's background and the hard knocks she's taken. Even if it's not conscious, his instinct will be to give her a break.

The defense wanted him, so we'd be the ones to go on record with a challenge. Judge O was spitting mad about how long jury selection was taking. The man's a first-class citizen, a supporter of the Inyo County political establishment. We had to take him and hope for the best.

ALANA BELKNAP, DEFENSE COUNSEL: Nine men and three women were sworn and seated. Juror 1, female, a fifty-three-year-old owner of a skin care salon, white. Juror 2, male, a thirty-one-year-old mountaineering guide, white . . .

REUBEN JEPHSON, CO-DEFENSE COUNSEL: Juror 3, male, a sixty-six-year-old retired Park Services ranger, white. Juror 4, male, a thirty-five-year-old pharmacy assistant, white . . .

ALANA BELKNAP, DEFENSE COUNSEL: Juror 5, female, a sixty-two-year-old high school algebra teacher, Hispanic. Juror 6, male, a forty-one-year-old car sales associate, white . . .

REUBEN JEPHSON, CO-DEFENSE COUNSEL: Juror 7, female, a forty-six-year-old bank branch manager, white. Juror 8, male, a thirty-seven-year-old independent computer consultant, white . . .

ALANA BELKNAP, DEFENSE COUNSEL: Juror 9, male, a sixty-eight-year-old retired archaeological field technician, white. Juror 10, male, a forty-four-year-old restaurant fry cook, Hispanic . . .

REUBEN JEPHSON, CO-DEFENSE COUNSEL: Juror 11, male, a seventy-two-year-old landscape painter, white. Juror 12, male, a forty-nine-year-old casino owner, Native American.

ALANA BELKNAP, DEFENSE COUNSEL: We'd had to fight tooth and nail for that jury. It wasn't great, but it could have been a lot worse.

SAMSON GRIFFITH: Alana and Reuben were working long hours, taking depositions, examining evidence, interviewing expert witnesses. One thing they weren't doing, to my dismay, was going out to the media and promoting our side of the story.

ALANA BELKNAP, DEFENSE COUNSEL: With all the noise on the news and social media, your messaging can get lost if it comes too early. The most opportune time to make your arguments is as the trial is starting. That's when the headlines rise to the top of people's feeds, and you can create the strongest impressions.

SAMSON GRIFFITH: I'm a specialist in media messaging, been doing this a long time. The reason you go out early is to get feedback and have the time to shape your message.

REUBEN JEPHSON, CO-DEFENSE COUNSEL: We held our first press conference at the hotel across the street from the courthouse after jury selection had been completed.

JAKE CROWE, *INYO REGISTER*: Like everything else connected to the trial, that event broke the record for the largest press conference ever held in Inyo County.

BRIAN BURLEIGH, ASSISTANT D.A.: I went across the street and slipped into the hotel lobby, which was packed with media and spectators. The defense attorneys had set up a platform at the north end of the room and brought their own PA system.

Owen decided he should stay away, and I agreed. We knew Reuben personally and Alana by reputation, and we weren't expecting any serious shenanigans from them.

ALANA BELKNAP, DEFENSE COUNSEL: I know Samson fancies himself the expert, but I've been doing this a long time, too. Our message was the drowning of Rebecca Alden had been a tragic accident and the county sheriff and district attorney had overreacted. They sent out a SWAT team and a highway patrol helicopter to capture an unarmed social media influencer who had no criminal record and posed no threat to public safety. Their whole approach was over the top from the start. They got caught up in their own zeal to *pursue justice* and painted themselves into a corner where they had no choice but to charge murder one. The other option was to admit their mistakes and back off, but that's a rare occurrence in these rural jurisdictions.

REUBEN JEPHSON, CO-DEFENSE COUNSEL: It was more or less a dress rehearsal for our opening statement. On that last thing, right, it may have been a bit too aggressive on our part.

ALANA BELKNAP, DEFENSE COUNSEL: (KVME-TV) ". . . and lastly it must be asked *why* the district attorney made a rush to judgment. It's been reported in the local news that an election is coming up, and Mr. Mason is in a tight race to keep his job. Mr. Mason has not tried a significant criminal case in some time. His election campaign seems premised on his demonstrating his effectiveness at taking on a powerful celebrity culture and punishing transgressors in plain sight. It's a show written and produced for his home audience, and Mr. Mason has cast himself as a law-and-order hero who rides to the rescue of the victimized and the politically underrepresented."

BRIAN BURLEIGH, ASSISTANT D.A.: *Really?* They were going there? Impugning the integrity of the prosecutor? I'm sorry, that's a slimy move, especially right before the trial starts. Criticize the evidence, complain about our tactics, but attack the *character* of our district attorney?

I didn't wait to get back to the office. I phoned the boss as I was crossing the street.

JAKE CROWE, *INYO REGISTER*: The defense based their attack on my reporting. Now, I never made an evidentiary connection between Mason's maneuvers and the upcoming election. We published his denials in full. I'd pointed out the prosecution's ambitious timeline vis-à-vis the November vote. I didn't see that as coincidence, but even the district attorney deserves the presumption of innocence.

SAMSON GRIFFITH: Major I-told-you-so moment. Even though it was probably true, making it about the political aspirations of the D.A. got slammed across the board. Over 60 percent of the tweets and comments were negative. Had this message been put out two weeks earlier, we would've been able to pivot and focus on the law enforcement overreaction. But no, the defense would be starting the trial now with a scarlet A for *Asshole* on their foreheads.

OWEN MASON, DISTRICT ATTORNEY: Didn't bother me at all. I have to say, I expected more from the greatest female criminal lawyer in America. Whatever she was trying to accomplish, it backfired.

CLEO RAY: After Sandy's visit, I was inspired to do everything I could to get acquitted so we could be together. I'd stay totally focused on the trial and keep visualizing us at that resort in Bali.

At the evening meal, two inmates I didn't know were sitting across from me. They knew who I was from the TV news. They were talking louder than normal for my benefit—saying my defense team had totally screwed up at the press conference. I just shut them out. Whatever that was about, it was out of my control.

That night I had this dream I was making love to Sandy in the tent. Suddenly I realized it wasn't Sandy, it was Beck. I froze and stared at her and she said, "Don't stop."

I said, "So you're not mad at me?"

She said, "I hate you. But I still want you."

I jumped up and left the tent to look for Sandy, and I found Beck sitting next to him at the campfire. He said, "Beck loves you more than I do, so I'm out." Then he stepped into the flames and caught on fire. Beck started laughing. She got up and led me back into the tent and we started having sex again. I could hear Sandy screaming, but Beck was on top of me and I couldn't move.

ERIN NEWCOMB, CHIEF DEPUTY: The conference room in the D.A.'s office had been turned into a war room, with empty pizza boxes piled in the corner. Every wall had deposition pages, photos, reports, and diagrams taped to them. The timeline moved chronologically left to right, so you could see each advance in the investigation.

I cleared my mind and started at the beginning. The story that the evidence told was epic.

BRIAN BURLEIGH, ASSISTANT D.A.: We were never better prepared than we were for *The People v. Mary Claire Griffith*.

OWEN MASON, DISTRICT ATTORNEY: I read a murder trial book written by another prosecutor, and I highlighted this quote: "Justice rarely feels like you expect it to."

What he meant was, you can never predict exactly how a trial will go, no matter how airtight your case. Something unexpected always happens. And what separates the good attorneys from the great ones is how they deal with surprises.

Motive was not the strongest part of our case. Not that the defendant didn't have one. But Sandy Finch said he would not have had a problem finding out Cleo Ray was bisexual. Her uncle had lectured me on the prevalence of *pansexuality* among young people. We firmly believed we could win the case on the evidence, but the defendant's fear of being outed as a lesbian wasn't as compelling as it could be.

As we were going through the event chain one more time, the receptionist buzzed in and said there was a call for me from the Western Missouri Correctional Center, an inmate named William Sparser. I didn't know the name and thought it must be either a prank or someone I'd met through my law career calling to wish me luck. I almost didn't take it.

I accepted the charges, and Mr. Sparser's voice came on the line. His first words were "I know the real reason that Claire Griffith killed Rebecca Alden."

ALANA BELKNAP, DEFENSE COUNSEL: I was on the treadmill at the Westin fitness center getting my cardio work in. I see my phone light up with the name *Owen Mason*, which meant it was coming from his private line. And some intuition told me he wasn't calling just to say hi.

EPISODE FIVE

GIRL PROSECUTED

Here's a question for you. What do you do when you're at a crossroads? Do you go to your best friend and ask advice? Do you talk to a trusted family member, hike up to a mountaintop and ask God? Do you make a vision board, pour a glass of wine, and think it through yourself? When you come to a fork in the road, how do you choose which path to take? Let me know at CleoRayFitness.com. I'm really curious.

Podcast, CleoRayFitness

CLEO RAY: They say fight or flight is triggered in your lizard brain. It can be overridden by the more evolved parts of your brain. But once you've crossed into that survival zone, it's nearly impossible to pull yourself back. That I can verify.

REUBEN JEPHSON, CO-DEFENSE COUNSEL: When the request came for a closed-door meeting with Mason and Burleigh, we were caught off guard. This is the night before opening statements, and we're ready to hit the field. Alana came down from Mammoth and I met her in front of the D.A.'s Bishop office. They were holding it there so as not to draw media attention, given reporters were camped out at the Independence Courthouse.

BRIAN BURLEIGH, ASSISTANT D.A.: We weren't gloating. Okay, maybe the tiniest bit. I'm kidding, no, this was serious business and we were obligated to disclose it anyway. With this kind of last-minute bombshell, the right thing to do is to have the attorneys all sit down and hash it out face-to-face.

OWEN MASON, DISTRICT ATTORNEY: The corrections officials in Missouri were very helpful and within a day had turned over their records to us. They also set up a video call between William Sparser and our office so he could give us his account and we could question him. By the time we summoned the defense to a meeting, we had a lot of information.

The first thing I said to Alana and Reuben was "All gamesmanship aside, something's come up that we need to deal with. We are approaching you as colleagues in the law, not adversaries, and we'd like to come out of this with mutual agreement on next steps."

ALANA BELKNAP, DEFENSE COUNSEL: On the night before a trial starts, when an opposing counsel begins a meeting that way, it means he's drawn a pair of aces to go with the pair he's already holding.

OWEN MASON, DISTRICT ATTORNEY: William Dean Sparser was serving a term of twenty-five years for multiple felony offenses including vehicular manslaughter and evading arrest. He'd already served ten years. And one day in mid-June he was surprised to receive a visitation request from a woman in California named Rebecca Alden. He had no idea who she was.

BRIAN BURLEIGH, ASSISTANT D.A.: Rebecca had a story to tell about her girlfriend Cleo Ray. See, Cleo has these scars on her right hip and upper thigh, and during an intimate moment Rebecca asked about them. Cleo revealed that as a teenager she'd been the passenger in a car that got into a police chase. The car ended up running off the road and flipping over, and she got pretty banged up.

OWEN MASON, DISTRICT ATTORNEY: Rebecca did some detective work on her own and traced the incident to Kansas City, Missouri, and a

THE ANATOMY OF DESIRE

convicted felon named William Sparser. And she found out a piece of information Cleo had omitted. What set off the police chase was the hit-and-run killing of a nine-year-old girl. Sparser, who'd been under the influence, had accidentally run the girl down but then raced away with police in pursuit. He lost control around a curve and ran off the highway. His car flipped over and landed upside down. He was knocked unconscious and critically injured. But according to news reports and court records, he was the only one inside the car. There was no mention of a passenger.

Rebecca went to visit Mr. Sparser in prison to confirm that Cleo Ray, the former Mary Claire Griffith, had been his passenger during the police chase. Rebecca brought photos of Cleo, and Sparser didn't hesitate. That was the girl he'd known as Claire Griffith ten years earlier, and yes, she had been in the passenger seat through the entire sequence of events.

BRIAN BURLEIGH, ASSISTANT D.A.: Sparser asked Rebecca why she would go to such lengths to investigate her girlfriend's story. She told him she'd been considering whether to marry Cleo and was checking to see how truthful she'd been about her past.

OWEN MASON, DISTRICT ATTORNEY: That's where it stayed until a couple of months later, when Sparser is watching cable news in the rec room and sees Claire Griffith going into a courthouse—only to find out she's on trial for Rebecca's murder. He thought about it for a few days, and then, according to this man who pled guilty to the killing of a child, his conscience got the best of him and he placed a call to the prosecuting attorney.

Of course, it didn't matter what motivated him to reach out to us. His entire visit with Rebecca was recorded on prison video cameras and confirmed everything he said.

ALANA BELKNAP, DEFENSE COUNSEL: One of the weakest points of the prosecution's case suddenly became its strongest. Those emails with their veiled and not-so-veiled threats were put into a new perspective. Beck hadn't merely been threatening to reveal their affair. She'd been holding the hit-and-run murder of that girl over Cleo.

BRIAN BURLEIGH, ASSISTANT D.A.: Sparser had nothing to gain by outing Cleo as a passenger in the car. He wasn't pinning any responsibility on her. He wasn't on social media but was aware if she got connected to the hit-and-run, it could hurt her. Especially because she'd fled the scene and not told anyone.

Sound familiar?

ALANA BELKNAP, DEFENSE COUNSEL: Mason wanted to take it straight to the judge, but we needed to talk to our client first. The sheriff made arrangements for us to meet with Cleo in the interview room at five-thirty A.M.

CLEO RAY: When the guard came so early and said my attorneys were there to see me, I knew it wasn't going to be good.

ALANA BELKNAP, DEFENSE COUNSEL: We had a large coffee waiting for her. She took one look at our faces and sat down with this heavy sigh. I said, "The D.A. got a call from a man named William Sparser who's serving time at a prison in Western Missouri. Sparser told them Beck had visited him there a few weeks before she died. We need to hear from you about this. Once again, the only way we can help you is if you are completely truthful and transparent with us. *Completely.*"

REUBEN JEPHSON, CO-DEFENSE COUNSEL: She'd tell us a little, we'd ask questions, and then she'd tell us a little more.

CLEO RAY: I was fifteen, my hormones were kicking in, and I was in full rebellion mode. Every communication with my parents turned into a screaming match. I was cutting school most days, dodging truant officers, hanging with my fellow dropouts. These weren't street kids. They were middle class, in homes with a single parent who worked during the day, or they had a basement room where they could lock out the grown-ups. As a group, we were aware enough to know opioids were deadly, so we smoked weed and drank beer and played video games.

I never had my friends over to where we lived. I was too embarrassed. I never talked about my family, and my friends never asked.

REUBEN JEPHSON, CO-DEFENSE COUNSEL: And then it all started tumbling out.

CLEO RAY: One day this guy Will showed up, a friend of someone's older brother. Nineteen, had a job at a fancy hotel downtown, had money, seemed like a step up from everyone else. I started fantasizing he might be the guy who could show me the way out of my life. I wanted what he had. Freedom!

I set my sights on Will Sparser, did the flirting thing, and made plans to see him the next night. No way was I telling Asa and Elva, so I pretended to go to bed, made it look like a body was sleeping there, and climbed out the window. Wasn't the first time I'd done that.

I had Will meet me at an intersection a few blocks away. He was driving a really nice car. He didn't tell me he was borrowing it from a friend and hadn't told his friend he was borrowing it. Technically it was stolen. He'd already been drinking and held out a bottle of tequila. I took one drink, but it tasted awful and I didn't have any more.

He said, "What's your deal? You got a boyfriend?"

"No," I said. "You got a girlfriend?"

He said, "Nope, we broke up. Want to be my girlfriend?"

"I'm too young for you, right?"

"I don't know," he said. "Have you had sex yet?"

"Maybe," I said.

He said, "Lean over and kiss me."

"Why should I?"

He took another drink and said, "Because I can help you out. You want to get a job and start making your own money, right?"

I said, "I want to get away from my parents, and that means having my own money."

He said, "The Marriott downtown is looking to hire. That's where I work. You'd have to get fake ID to prove you're eighteen. I could help you out there, too."

I could see where this was going.

"Wouldn't ask much in return," he said. "A blow job once in a while. Maybe starting now."

"How do I know you'll follow through?"

"How do I know you give good head?"

"I'm good at whatever I set my mind to."

Then he unzipped and pulled it out and said, "Stroke it so I can see what you got." I thought, *That's not real sex, I can do that.*

I reached over and he started getting excited and I said, "Watch where you're going," and he opened his eyes but shut them again and I looked ahead and saw some girls waiting to cross at the corner. The car started drifting and I pulled my hand away and he turned to me and didn't see them and he hit one of the girls. And the car kept going and I could feel her getting dragged under the wheels and the other girls started screaming. I ducked under the dashboard, but Will kept driving. He was speeding away and I heard a siren start up behind us. I screamed, "Stop!" but he kept going faster. I stayed under the dash crying and begging him to stop, but he said he couldn't go to jail and he kept racing and swerving and then skidding. I felt the car lift up and it came down hard on its side, glass shattering, and it flipped over and over. Finally everything came to a dead stop.

I thought I was dying, at least paralyzed. But I started moving my arms and legs. There was broken glass everywhere and a small opening in the passenger window and I squeezed through it. I was able to stand up. We'd crashed into an open field and it was all dark. In one direction I could see hills and in the other direction a line of flashing police car lights coming. My instinct was to run away from the sirens. I made my legs carry me, but they were bleeding and hurting bad. I kept falling and getting up and my head was throbbing. I kept going and made it to the hill and slid down the other side and hit the bottom. No one could see me. To stay out of sight I had to crawl through a gravel lot littered with empty cans and broken bottles. When I felt safe enough, I got up and ran until I came to the next highway. I had some money, so I found a bus stop and got on one and rode it as far as I could.

I wasn't going back home, that was for sure.

DUNCAN MCMILLAN, INTERVIEWER: The question on everyone's mind was, in the moment Beck confronted you about Sparser, what were you thinking?

CLEO RAY: Nothing good.

SAMSON GRIFFITH: I was driving up from L.A. for the first day of the trial when Alana called. She'd come out of the meeting with Cleo and told me her story. I listened. When she was finished, I asked, "So what's changed?"

She said, "That's what we need to talk about."

I said, "Is Cleo still saying she didn't kill Beck?"

She said, "Her story about what happened on the lake is the same."

I said, "And you still believe her?"

She said, "It only matters what the jury will believe. And this new information makes Cleo look more guilty."

Then I said something like, *That's why you get paid the big bucks—to manage our narrative in the face of curve balls like this.*

ALANA BELKNAP, DEFENSE COUNSEL: There it was, the last decision point, the last moment we could have avoided trial. I said to Cleo, "We need you to know this: you could be a hundred percent innocent of causing Beck's death and not be acquitted. In fact, an acquittal just got harder. We won't make you change your plea. If you know in your soul you're not guilty of the charge, then our job is to guide the jury toward finding sufficient reasonable doubt."

Cleo said, "If I changed my plea, it would be a lie. I'd be saying I'm guilty when I know it's not true. I can't base the rest of my life on a lie, I just can't do that. You understand, right?"

I may not have agreed, but I did understand.

GILLIAN GRIFFITH: I said to my dad we should cut our losses. Cleo had lied about the real reason she went to the lake with Beck, she lied about what Beck had on her, and I knew of many other things she'd lied about. How could we trust anything she said? That redneck prosecutor was going to kick our asses. Dad got pissed when I said that. But someone had to tell the truth. And it sure as hell wasn't going to be my cousin Cleo.

ERIN NEWCOMB, CHIEF DEPUTY: They were calling Judge O but kept getting his voice mail. I was drafted to go to his house and knock on his door at six-thirty in the morning. "Sorry to intrude on you at this hour, sir, but Mr. Mason has received significant new information on the Mary Claire Griffith case and is asking to postpone the morning session so he and defense counsel can meet with you about it."

He mumbled, "Fine," and shut the door. I'm guessing I caught him before his first cup of coffee.

OWEN MASON, DISTRICT ATTORNEY: The issue was not a legal one. It was about messaging. We made a full disclosure to opposing counsel, gave them time to speak with their client. We'd even made arrangements for the defense to depose the new witness before we called him to the stand.

We had to agree on the most benign way to put this information out and explain why the start of the trial was being delayed until the afternoon. How do we communicate this piece of *breaking news* as neutrally as possible?

JAKE CROWE, *INYO REGISTER*: First surprise was seeing *Inyo County Prosecutor* on my incoming call screen as I'm having a pretrial breakfast burrito in the lobby of the Winnedumah. Second surprise was hearing it's Burleigh and Jephson wanting to phone-conference with me. Took a breath, stepped out to the sidewalk, and said, "Good morning, fellas. What can I do for you?"

I was the first reporter to learn about the Sparser situation. They asked me to report it on our website and provide the news release to the other reporters there in the hotel lobby. Burleigh said, "Try not to overplay this. The only thing extraordinary here is the timing, which we had no control over. The judge and both sides agree it's important to keep moving forward, so court will start promptly at two o'clock this afternoon."

First time in my career I got to be in a press conference where I was answering the questions instead of asking them.

SAMSON GRIFFITH: Took Twitter about five minutes to explode into a mushroom cloud: #CleoLiarLiar, #PsychoBitchKilledaKid, #ChildKillerInfluencer. YouTube finally took down Cleo's channel, and within minutes Instagram did the same. The way the news was spinning it, you'd have thought Cleo had been the one driving the car.

The Cleo-Beck email leak had been damaging, but it was nothing compared to the meltdown caused by #TheSparserReveal.

SANDY FINCH: I'd held on to two-thirds of my sponsors and my clothing and accessory line was still on track. But when #TheSparserReveal happened, I got calls from my business partners asking me to publicly back away from Cleo. I had no way to communicate with her to find out the real story.

I needed help, so it was time to have a serious talk with my agent.

SAMSON GRIFFITH: What am I going to tell him, *Go ahead, denounce my niece to save your clothing line?* I had to be frank with him.

"Sandy, I've got a clear conflict of interest here. I'm not the person to advise you on this."

SANDY FINCH: He told me to go with my conscience. So I did. No matter what, I knew I couldn't sell out Cleo. I'd have to take the hit.

I composed one email and sent it to my partners. "I will be supporting my friend Cleo Ray through the end of her trial. I believe she's not guilty." By the end of day, I'd lost another third of my sponsors and it wasn't looking good for my clothing line. Five years of building up my social media business, and in the span of a few hours it was practically gone.

JAKE CROWE, *INYO REGISTER*: Incidentally, that was the first day of fall, and the daytime temperature dropped from the seventies to the fifties. The internet was burning up, but there was a chill inside the courthouse. They had to fire up those old floor radiators, another way the building exists in a time warp.

THE ANATOMY OF DESIRE

DUNCAN MCMILLAN: *There are sixty fixed wooden seats in the gallery section of the Superior Court of Inyo County, and it's possible they are the originals installed back in 1922. Evidence for this can be found on the undersides, where metal racks are attached, designed for male spectators to place their Stetsons. In addition, there are twenty-five folding chairs set up along the back wall and down the sides of the gallery. Eighty-five gallery seats total, and there were three hundred people a day trying to get in to watch the trial.*

The bailiff and the judge devised a plan that allowed a single press pool camera and operator; eight seats rotated daily for print and other media; six reserved for friends and family of the victim, six for friends and family of the defendant. Courthouse personnel got five seats. Residents of the county got twenty-five seats and had to register on the day prior to the court session; people from outside the county got twenty seats and had to sign up on the prior day for a lottery. Spectators were required to arrive one hour early and pass through a security screening. Any preregistered spectator not seated twenty minutes before the proceedings forfeited their seat to the next person on the list. All weapons were prohibited, including any sharp objects, aerosol cans, and flammable liquids. All electronic devices had to be turned off and put away prior to entering the courtroom.

REUBEN JEPHSON, CO-DEFENSE COUNSEL: I knew the case was a media sensation, but I was not prepared for the experience of walking into the courthouse, a walk I'd taken hundreds of times, through a gauntlet of the public and press and hearing my name shouted out by strangers.

One time when I stepped outside for a breath of air, a Japanese tour guide approached to ask if I would take a photo with his tour group. They'd been visiting Manzanar and heard about the social media murder trial happening up the road. So I posed with these twenty visitors from Japan, none of whom spoke English. I could see in their eyes they considered me a celebrity. I felt kind of foolish, but they seemed really grateful to be getting selfies with me.

CLEO RAY: Alana and I had planned my wardrobe and look. She had experience "presenting" female clients to their juries, and I trusted her judgment. I was limited to one outfit at a time, to be put on just before leaving for the courthouse and taken off immediately after returning. No jewelry was allowed, neat hair was a must. Mine would be tied back in a low ponytail. For makeup, I could use only foundation, blush, and lip gloss. Eye makeup was out. For my trial debut, I wore a heather-gray skirt, knee-length, a pale yellow blouse with a skinny belt, and black leather flats. Alana requested "softly feminine and moderately conservative." It was a long way from my public image of skintight leggings and sports bras, but I think I pulled it off.

DUNCAN MCMILLAN: *The interior of the Independence courtroom looks like a touring company set for Inherit the Wind. It was built three years before the Scopes Monkey Trial, and has hardwood ceiling fans and neoclassical plaster designs along the tops of the walls and ceiling. Encircling the gallery are framed black-and-white photos of past superior court judges going back to the frontier days of the nineteenth century, stern-looking men with upright-sounding names like George Monroe Gill, John Allen Hannah, and Walter Anderson Lamar.*

JAKE CROWE, *INYO REGISTER*: When I take a seat in that courtroom, it's like I'm sitting in the laps of ghosts, a century's worth of people who've sat in these chairs to witness our criminal justice system in action. Through the Roaring Twenties, the Depression, World War Two, the Cold War, the Vietnam War—Charles Manson came here in 1969 to be arraigned for stealing a car. This was after his arrest for the Tate-LaBianca murders. A half dozen of his girls followed him up here and stayed overnight in a motel down the street.

BRIAN BURLEIGH, ASSISTANT D.A.: You could hear a pin drop, like everyone was afraid of breathing too loud. Through the windows we could hear the low rumble of the crowd outside. Which became the background sound for the whole trial.

BAILIFF: Order in the court. All rise. The Superior Court of Inyo County, State of California, is now in session, Honorable Judge Roy Oberwaltzer presiding. Please be seated.

ERIN NEWCOMB, CHIEF DEPUTY: Sheriff Hite and I sat in on Mason's opening statement. He was the quarterback of our hometown team, so in our minds we were cheering for him.

MR. MASON: May it please the court. Ladies and gentlemen of the jury. I would like to personally thank you for hanging in there during the longer than normal selection process. Some of you may have been surprised by the exceeding care that the state and the defense took to choose the twelve of you to sit and judge this case. We're a smaller county in population, and it was important we find twelve individuals who could see and hear the facts of this case and weigh them with all the fairness and understanding the law and our Constitution demands. For the prosecution's part, our exceeding care has been driven by an incredibly strong motive—that the victim, Rebecca Grace Alden, and her family, and the People shall see that justice is served.

SAMSON GRIFFITH: I'm no fan of the district attorney, but he's a gifted public speaker. He has a talent for modulating his voice so he sounds spontaneous while hitting the right notes. A sense of cadence and phrasing without a lot of distracting body language. He'd make a great master of ceremonies. Or audiobook narrator.

MR. MASON: You twelve citizens have been summoned and chosen to take on a truly awesome responsibility. You are the ones who will decide whether justice is achieved in this case. Your call to action is to hear the testimony, see the evidence, separate fact from fiction, and deliver your verdict. As I learned the facts here starting back in July, I had no doubt it was my duty to prosecute this action on behalf of the People. Now it will be your duty to learn the facts and apply the law with unwavering rigor. At times you may find yourselves challenged to interpret those facts and weigh them against the concept of reasonable doubt. Picture that blindfolded figure holding up the scales, balancing the cause of justice on one side and reasonable doubt on the other. You are the embodiment of that figure. Those scales will be held in your hands. You and you alone will determine to which side they tilt.

TITUS ALDEN: When Mr. Mason was making his opening statement, my wife and I started feeling hopeful. And grateful to have a man like him on our side.

MR. MASON: The facts here will take you inside the lives of two young women. One of those women is dead. The other sits before you at the defense table, very much alive. The People of the State of California charge that the crime of murder in the first degree has been committed by this woman, Mary Claire Griffith, against the victim, Rebecca Grace Alden. The People charge that Ms. Griffith, the defendant, conceived, planned, and carried out the murder of Rebecca Alden. The People will show the defendant deceived Rebecca for the purpose of getting her up to a remote lake in Inyo County, and with malice aforethought and in cold blood, struck her in the face and head, then turned over their canoe. While Rebecca struggled in the deep water without a life vest, the defendant pushed the canoe away and treaded water as she watched her "girlfriend" sink below the surface and not come back up.

CLEO RAY: As he was speaking, those moments after the canoe tipped over came back to me in a rush. Under the table, I clenched my fists so tightly my fingernails dug into my palms.

MR. MASON: And after she was sure her mission to silence Rebecca had been accomplished, the woman sitting before you swam ashore, walked back to where her car was parked, got inside, and drove away to go meet her boyfriend for a romantic camping weekend. Over the next forty-eight hours, the defendant acted as though nothing had happened, showing no guilt or remorse, just hiking through nature with friends, laughing at their jokes, making love to her boyfriend, behaving as though she didn't have a care in the world. Ladies and gentlemen, over the next weeks you will be hearing about secrets and lies and betrayal and deceit. You will be exposed to uncomfortably intimate revelations. Though the drama of it may seem complex and convoluted, I simply ask you keep coming back to what will be these undisputed facts: the defendant was present alone at the drowning death of the victim, then fled from the scene, told no one, and pretended as though nothing had happened. Holding the scales of justice in your hands, in full possession of the facts and the law, you must judge Mary Claire Griffith based on her known and irrefutable actions.

ALANA BELKNAP, DEFENSE COUNSEL: If Owen Mason moved to the big city and joined a private firm, he'd be billing several million dollars a year. I do admire people who aren't in it for the money.

MR. MASON: The People will acquaint you with Rebecca Alden, whose life ended in terror and shock as she realized the murderous intentions of her beloved, the woman sitting before you. Rebecca had not quite reached her twenty-second birthday and worked as a hair and makeup artist for videos, commercials, and TV shows. She was the only daughter of Titus and Grace Alden, raised in their two-bedroom home on a modest residential street in Reseda, California, a modest community in the middle of the San Fernando Valley. She'd moved out of her parents' home to live on her own in a small apartment a few miles away. Rebecca was happy and proud to have a place of her own, and after moving in, she went to a shelter and adopted a kitten. She named it Mary Lennox after a character in her favorite childhood book. Her parents and friends described Rebecca as socially reserved. She went on dates now and then, enjoyed going to the movies or playing miniature golf, but according to those who knew her best, while she had friends who were boys, she never had a boyfriend. Some assumed she'd be a late bloomer to the world of romance and relationships.

JAKE CROWE, *INYO REGISTER*: Mason used the word *modest* to describe Rebecca at least half a dozen times. Modest meaning simple, humble, free of pretension. In contrast, he characterized Cleo Ray as ambitious, aggressive, always looking to climb the next rung.

MR. MASON: While working hair and makeup on a shoot for the Griffith All Media company, Rebecca caught the eye of Cleo Ray, a young woman who'd begun her rise as a successful social media influencer. Cleo Ray was the made-up name of Mary Claire Griffith, which is her legal name and the name under which she is being prosecuted here. Ms. Griffith had been raised in economic poverty. Her parents, Asa and Elva, traveling missionaries affiliated with a small church in the Midwest, didn't have a permanent home or even a bank account. For food and shelter, they often had to rely on the charity of the people they recruited to their faith. This is not the history Ms. Griffith told Rebecca. To Rebecca, she reflected back the person Rebecca most wanted her to be. Ms. Griffith professed a goddess-centered spirituality and a deep sensitivity to Rebecca's emotional needs. She portrayed herself as someone who could lead Rebecca to her most authentic self. You see, Ms. Griffith perceived something in Rebecca others had not. Romantically, Rebecca leaned toward women.

ALANA BELKNAP, DEFENSE COUNSEL: *"Leaned* toward women." The prosecution never once used the word *lesbian* to describe Beck. She was *inclined* toward women, *favored* women; her *preference* was women. They were afraid using the word *lesbian* would taint the jury's impression of her.

On the other hand, they consistently labeled Cleo as lesbian and bisexual.

REUBEN JEPHSON, CO-DEFENSE COUNSEL: It was what we expected. Mason was painting Cleo as a predator and Rebecca as her prey.

MR. MASON: We will show the defendant positioned herself as the dominant partner in the relationship. She opened up Rebecca to a new dimension of her sexuality and introduced her to physical pleasures she'd never experienced before. She surely and systematically led Rebecca into the deepest of infatuations. The defendant was Rebecca's first real love, and she thrived on Rebecca's passionate attachment to her. And then—and then the defendant became involved with another, higher-profile social media influencer, a man named Sandy Finch.

JAKE CROWE, *INYO REGISTER*: Mason described Sandy as Cleo's social media climbing dream come true. The best-looking, most popular, highest-earning influencer she'd hooked up with yet. And as Beck had fallen hard for her, Cleo fell hard for Sandy Finch.

MR. MASON: The defendant found someone to help her achieve her ambitions in a way Rebecca would never be able to. And so the defendant began to detach herself from Rebecca, and Rebecca could feel her slipping away. And as the defendant broke dates and would be unreachable for days and absent from her own apartment night after night, Rebecca's heartache turned into emotional desperation.

JAKE CROWE, *INYO REGISTER*: There was no denying that at the end Beck had turned aggressive and threatening. So they set it in the context of being two-timed by Cleo Ray, with Cleo lying to her, betraying her, driving Beck to extreme behaviors—like tracking down William Sparser.

MR. MASON: We will show the defendant's pattern of manipulation and deception, and you will see behaviors that cross over into a form of "sexual gaslighting." She would sleep with Rebecca to placate her, then go missing for forty-eight hours. When Rebecca would question her or complain, the defendant would tell her she was inventing problems, she herself was sabotaging their relationship, while at the same time the defendant's relationship with Sandy Finch was growing more serious. The defendant began looking for an opportunity to break off with Rebecca—and that's when Rebecca dramatically turned the tables on her.

JAKE CROWE, *INYO REGISTER*: Since the news had just broken that morning, a lot of people still hadn't heard and were taken by surprise by what Mason said next.

MR. MASON: There was more, much more the defendant had been hiding. The People will call a witness named William Sparser, currently incarcerated in a Missouri prison serving twenty-five years for the hit-

and-run killing of a nine-year-old girl. He will testify that Mary Claire Griffith was a passenger in the car when the girl was hit. He will testify that Mary Claire Griffith ran away from the scene out of fear of getting in trouble with the law. He will testify that Rebecca Alden visited him in prison and he told her of Ms. Griffith's involvement in the nine-year-old's death. And we will show that Rebecca attempted to use this knowledge to pressure the defendant into giving up her relationship with Sandy Finch and compel her to recommit to their relationship. The defendant was backed into a corner. Rebecca threatened to reveal her darkest secret, to publicly disclose a shameful crime that could destroy the defendant's relationship with Sandy Finch and wipe out her social media success.

CLEO RAY: It took every ounce of my self-control to be still. This man didn't know me or Sandy, and he never met Beck. It was unreal. At one point I leaned to Reuben and whispered, "Can I object?"

JAKE CROWE, *INYO REGISTER*: Mason concluded his opening statement at five minutes to five and the judge put the court in recess until nine the next morning. I tried to hear what people were saying as they left the court. Cleo's side, her parents and uncle and cousin, stayed quiet and neutral. Beck's side, the majority, were vocal about how well they thought Mason did.

REUBEN JEPHSON, CO-DEFENSE COUNSEL: After court we caravanned up to Mammoth. Samson and Gillian had booked rooms at the Westin, and we met with them in Alana's suite.

ALANA BELKNAP, DEFENSE COUNSEL: I didn't need to look at the news or social media to see how Mason's opening had played. He'd been strong across the board. Now, selling your narrative to a passive audience without interruption doesn't equate to how you'll be at examining and cross-examining witnesses. But I told Samson and Gillian to expect Mason to be good at that, too.

SAMSON GRIFFITH: I said, "Round one to the prosecution."
Alana said, "Round one is only halfway over."
I said, "And your thoughts about how to counter the Sparser reveal?"

ALANA BELKNAP, DEFENSE COUNSEL: "When he's in the witness chair on cross-examination."

SAMSON GRIFFITH: "You're going to concede this to Mason in your opening statement?"

ALANA BELKNAP, DEFENSE COUNSEL: "I'm not conceding anything. In fact, what we need to do is tell the truth and position Cleo as someone who is ready to tell it all and tell it from her heart."
Samson squinted and turned a shade paler. "What does that mean?"
It was time to have *the conversation*.

REUBEN JEPHSON, CO-DEFENSE COUNSEL: Alana and I had been discussing it privately. Would it be a gamble? Yes. But the bigger gamble would've been to build our narrative on a premise we knew was false.

ALANA BELKNAP, DEFENSE COUNSEL: The truth defense, what a novel idea. Yes, Cleo took Beck up to the mountains and found a remote lake to take a boat out on. Not to propose and get engaged. Not to gently let her down and say she was moving on. Beck had threatened Cleo with real harm.

Beck was committing emotional extortion against Cleo. The prosecution had painted her as a modest and sweet and socially shy late bloomer who rescued kittens. But the truth was she'd become abusive. She was threatening Cleo. "Either be with me or I will hurt you." That's called blackmail.

SAMSON GRIFFITH: I looked at Alana. "Are you going to say Beck got what she deserved?"

ALANA BELKNAP, DEFENSE COUNSEL: See, there were two victims here. Two young women in the throes of a dying love affair, one of them refusing to let go. Beck was threatening to kill everything Cleo had worked so hard for. And to kill Cleo's new relationship. Cleo was justifiably afraid of Beck. Out of desperation, she made a choice to preserve her reputation and her new love.

SAMSON GRIFFITH: "You mean you want Cleo to testify?" I said, raising my eyebrows.

ALANA BELKNAP, DEFENSE COUNSEL: Who better to tell her story? Absolutely, Fifth Amendment, the right not to self-incriminate. And I've had cases where under no circumstances would I have put my client on the stand. But in this case, because of all the emotional nuances, all those gray areas of love and passion and intimacy, Cleo was the only witness who could effectively convey her experience of what happened.

GILLIAN GRIFFITH: My dad was not sold. He thought it was too risky to change strategies at the last minute. He wanted Alana to reconsider.

SAMSON GRIFFITH: It's, like, twelve hours before the defense's opening statement, and she's pivoting to a whole new strategy. My assets, the reputation of my family, my twenty-five-year-old niece's future, it's all on the line.

REUBEN JEPHSON, CO-DEFENSE COUNSEL: They went back and forth, and it got heated. Finally Alana said, "Let me do my job and decide the best strategy to get an acquittal—or I'll walk."

Samson's eyes popped open. "You can't walk now. It's too late. That would be legal malpractice."

She picked up her phone and started booking the next flight out of the Mammoth airport.

SAMSON GRIFFITH: It's a rare and unpleasant feeling to get my balls crushed like that. I said to Alana, "In front of two witnesses, I'm saying to you this feels fraught with risk. But because I can't have our lead counsel quit the night before we go in front of the jury, I am agreeing, under protest, to let you do it your way."

REUBEN JEPHSON, CO-DEFENSE COUNSEL: I wasn't blind to Samson's argument. But having gotten to know Cleo as I had, I believed she would make the strongest case on her behalf. And by the way, that's not something you announce up front. You want to keep the prosecution off-balance and not telegraph your moves, especially one of that magnitude. That way we could also change our minds up to the last minute.

So we swore an oath this would go no further than the four of us in the room.

ALANA BELKNAP, DEFENSE COUNSEL: I asked them to excuse me, because I wanted to get plenty of rest before the next morning.

Samson said, "You're not going to do any more practicing?"

I told him what I tell all my clients. "I've been practicing for this my entire life."

THE ANATOMY OF DESIRE

CLEO RAY: Alana and Reuben arrived at the jail that morning for another visit before court started. They told me they wanted to change our strategy.

BAILIFF: All rise. The Superior Court of Inyo County, State of California, is now in session, Honorable Judge Roy Oberwaltzer presiding. Please be seated.

JAKE CROWE, *INYO REGISTER*: As a lady of the big city and a nationally known advocate for women's and defendant's rights, Alana Belknap was stepping into a different arena than she was used to.

MS. BELKNAP: May it please the court. Ladies and gentlemen of the jury, good morning. I am going to make a prediction. After hearing from all the witnesses and viewing all the evidence and being given explicit instructions on how to apply the law, I predict the main question you'll keep returning to in your deliberation will simply be this: Was it first-degree murder? First-degree murder is defined as the willful, deliberate, and premeditated taking of a human life. First-degree murder requires a person to take direct or "willful" action against another person. It can result only from a conscious cause-and-effect sequence. I pull a trigger, you are shot. I plunge a knife, you are stabbed. I push you off a cliff, you fall. Now, if I intend to kill you but I do not pull the trigger or plunge the knife or push you, but you die anyway because the gun accidentally fires or you accidentally fall onto the knife blade or you accidentally fall off the cliff, did I commit a willful and deliberate action that caused your death? Intention that does not result in a willful act cannot equal first-degree murder.

BRIAN BURLEIGH, ASSISTANT D.A.: I'm hearing these words *intent* and *intention*, and I'm thinking, *Wait a minute,* the defendant's claim is she *did not* intend to kill Rebecca. She'd taken her up to the lake to break up with her. I traded a glance with Owen and saw the same question in his eyes.

MS. BELKNAP: The prosecution was right about one thing: this will largely be the story of two women and the most intimate details of their relationship. From the outset, for reasons that will become apparent, both women agreed theirs would be a secret relationship. Quick note. The defense will refer to the defendant, known on the record as Mary Claire Griffith, as Cleo Ray, the name she adopted seven years ago and by which she is known to family, friends, and the public. We will also refer to Rebecca Alden as Beck, the name she is known by family, friends, and the principals in this case.

JAKE CROWE, *INYO REGISTER*: It would be a murder trial with two defendants: Mary Claire Griffith and Cleo Ray.

MS. BELKNAP: This secrecy resulted in Cleo and Beck conducting their relationship with conscious discretion, behind closed doors. They didn't have the usual outlet of talking to friends and family about their relationship. This caused a pressure to build up from the inside. It also means we have no witnesses who can testify to directly observing them together. We have emails, texts, phone messages, and cards they exchanged, but how they treated each other, how they laughed and cried with each other, how they fought with each other, how they loved each other—these things were experienced solely by the two people involved. One of them is gone. The other sits at the defense table.

CLEO RAY: Alana and Reuben wanted to go with the truth defense. They said Uncle Samson had been doubtful but was willing to go with it.

They wanted me to testify and tell *my* story. That gave me this amazing surge of hope. The earworm I took into court that day was "the truth shall set me free." *The truth shall set me free.*

MS. BELKNAP: Have you ever known a couple, be they married or dating, and thought, *They seem perfect together*, only to discover that one is having an affair or they're abusive to each other or getting a divorce? Even in publicly declared relationships, it's hard to know what goes on in the privacy of a couple's bedroom. The prosecution will try to convince you only one partner in this secret relationship was unfaithful, destructive, toxic. But you know from your own lives that "it takes two to tango," that both parties share responsibility for the emotional health of a relationship. The love tango involves two individuals coming together, and the chemistry they create becomes unique to that coupling, like a fingerprint. If you put either one of them with another partner, the fingerprint changes. The chemistry of Cleo and Beck's relationship was created by each of them equally as they brought to it their individual life traumas, fears, and desires.

JAKE CROWE, *INYO REGISTER*: There seemed to be a fascination with the intimate details of a relationship between two young women. The LGBTQ community found an opportunity to publicize general misperceptions and fallacies about gay relationships. They sent representatives to Inyo and set up an information booth outside the courthouse. Then church groups began confronting them and the sheriff had to post an officer next to the booth to keep the peace.

MS. BELKNAP: Reams of poetry have been written about the agonies and emotional madness of romantic love. We will show you the printed cards Cleo and Beck exchanged. In one that dates from later in their relationship, Beck quotes the Greek poet Sappho:

> O Venus beauty of the skies,
> To whom a thousand temples rise,

Gaily false in gentle smiles,
Full of love-perplexing wiles;
O goddess from my heart remove
The wasting cares and pains of love.

BRIAN BURLEIGH, ASSISTANT D.A.: I'm not embarrassed to say I had to look up Sappho on Wikipedia. An ancient Greek erotica writer from the island of Lesbos. An appropriate reference for this jury? *Okay.*

MS. BELKNAP: The evidence will show that Beck is speaking here about her own "wasting cares" and "pains of love." You will come to see that she is crying out to express the "perplexing" longings of her own heart. We will detail for you the intensity of feeling these two women shared, and how their feelings transformed from loving and mutual to toxic and obsessive. Moments of ugliness will be revealed, and you will plainly see how things spiraled down further and further, headed toward a catastrophic outcome. And when you've heard all the testimony and seen all the evidence, you will be left with this: Did the prosecution prove the drowning of Rebecca Alden resulted from a willful act by the defendant? Did Cleo Ray consciously and deliberately pull a trigger, plunge a knife, push her off a cliff? Has the prosecution sufficiently demonstrated that Cleo Ray took the action that must have occurred—beyond a reasonable doubt—to justify a finding of first-degree murder? I'll make another prediction: the prosecution will fail. Because that is not what happened.

SAMSON GRIFFITH: Alana proved she was the real deal. People were tweeting out her words in real time. The reaction was massive: #BlissToAbyss, #FrolicTurnsDiabolic, #InfatuationObliteration. One of the headlines was ALLIES TO ENEMIES ON LOVE'S BATTLEFIELD. Maybe our lead counsel's last-minute pivot would pan out.

REUBEN JEPHSON, CO-DEFENSE COUNSEL: When they go for the head, we go for the heart.

> **BAILIFF:** Please raise your right hand. Do you solemnly state that the testimony you may give in the case now pending before this court is the truth, the whole truth, and nothing but the truth, so help you God?
> **MS. GRACE ALDEN:** I do.
> **MR. MASON:** Good morning. Will you please state your name and relationship to the victim?
> **MS. GRACE ALDEN:** Grace Alden, and I'm Rebecca Alden's mother.
> **MR. MASON:** I imagine you may find some of these memories upsetting, Ms. Alden, so if you need to slow down or take a break, let us know, okay?
> **MS. GRACE ALDEN:** Okay. Thank you.

JAKE CROWE, *INYO REGISTER*: Turned out Beck's mom remembered a lot more on the stand than she had during my interview. Maybe she was saving the details for when she was called as the prosecution's first witness.

> **MR. MASON:** Your daughter took you aside to share something personal with you?
> **MS. GRACE ALDEN:** Yes, she said she was afraid I would judge her, and I said whatever it was, I would still love her, and I knew her father would feel the same.
> **MR. MASON:** What did she share with you?
> **MS. GRACE ALDEN:** That she had met a woman—actually she said *girl*—who had swept her off her feet.
> **MR. MASON:** She used those words, this woman—girl—had swept her off her feet?
> **MS. GRACE ALDEN:** Yes. Beck said the girl had made her realize that she

was—that she liked girls, in the romantic sense.

MR. MASON: So this other girl was the aggressor?

MS. BELKNAP: Objection. Leading.

MR. MASON: I'll rephrase. Did Rebecca tell you about how the relationship got initiated?

MS. GRACE ALDEN: She said the other girl made the first move. And that she guided Beck into how to be with other girls.

REUBEN JEPHSON, CO-DEFENSE COUNSEL: It's delicate cross-examining a victim's family, especially the mother. Between us, Alana and I felt I might have the lighter touch.

MR. JEPHSON: You said Beck told you this woman guided her into how to be with other girls. That wasn't against your daughter's will, was it?

MS. GRACE ALDEN: No, it wasn't.

MR. JEPHSON: Did Beck introduce you to the woman she was having the relationship with?

MS. GRACE ALDEN: She did not.

MR. JEPHSON: Did Beck tell you the name of the woman she was having the relationship with?

MS. GRACE ALDEN: No, they'd agreed to keep it a secret.

MR. JEPHSON: Did Beck ever show you a video or photo of the woman she was having the relationship with?

MS. GRACE ALDEN: I saw a photo of a blond girl taped to the mirror in Beck's bedroom that I believe is the defendant.

MR. JEPHSON: Did Beck identify the blond girl in the photo as the woman she was having the relationship with?

MS. GRACE ALDEN: I just assumed.

MR. JEPHSON: You never observed Beck and her girlfriend together?

MS. GRACE ALDEN: No.

MR. JEPHSON: And did Beck ever mention they were having problems in their relationship?

MS. GRACE ALDEN: Not directly.

MR. JEPHSON: Did Beck verbalize to you that she and her girlfriend were having problems?

MS. GRACE ALDEN: No.

REUBEN JEPHSON, CO-DEFENSE COUNSEL: The second prosecution witness was a woman who lived in the apartment next to Beck's. Tina Jordan had noticed Beck looking upset as she was coming and going from her apartment and had heard Beck crying on the outside deck, which was adjacent to hers. Being a good neighbor, Ms. Jordan asked Beck if she'd like someone to talk to. Ms. Jordan's college major had been psychology, and a few weeks before her death, Beck accepted her invitation to come over.

MR. BURLEIGH: And what did Rebecca say to you?
MS. TINA JORDAN: Well, first she said she was upset that her "boyfriend" was breaking up with her. But I hadn't seen a man anywhere near her place. She saw I was doubtful, because she corrected herself: "My girlfriend is breaking up with me."
MR. BURLEIGH: Did she say why her girlfriend was breaking up with her?
MS. TINA JORDAN: It was because her girlfriend had found a new guy—*guy*—who was really successful and could help her career.
MR. BURLEIGH: What else did she say to you about her girlfriend?
MS. TINA JORDAN: That she only cared about getting more followers for her Instagram. And Beck was feeling like a fool for not seeing how ruthless she was.
MR. BURLEIGH: Rebecca used the word *ruthless* to describe her girlfriend?
MS. TINA JORDAN: Yes, that stuck in my mind. She called her "a ruthless bitch."

ALANA BELKNAP, DEFENSE COUNSEL: We had deposed Tina Jordan and were ready for cross.

MS. BELKNAP: Having considered starting your own therapy practice, are you aware that people in the throes of a breakup may be prone to exaggeration and extremes of behavior?

MS. TINA JORDAN: They may be.

MS. BELKNAP: Have you ever met the defendant, Cleo Ray?

MS. TINA JORDAN: I have not.

MS. BELKNAP: Did you ever see the defendant at your apartment building?

MS. TINA JORDAN: No, but I didn't move in until May first.

MS. BELKNAP: So, not having met or seen the defendant, you couldn't know whether Beck was telling the truth or misrepresenting things because of her distress over the breakup?

MS. TINA JORDAN: I was only hearing one side, but I believed Beck was telling me the truth.

MS. BELKNAP: We're talking about exaggerations and distortions by a woman in a state of deep emotional anguish. Would it be fair to say that when Beck came over to your apartment that day, she was in the throes of an emotional trauma?

MS. TINA JORDAN: Well, yes.

OWEN MASON, DISTRICT ATTORNEY: The great email-reading debacle? Clearly, I hadn't thought it through. I take full responsibility for that.

BRIAN BURLEIGH, ASSISTANT D.A.: We had the emails from their secret accounts put up on a projection screen and had Sheriff Hite read them out loud, because he was the first to see what was on the flash drive and wrote the evidence report. He's this manly guy with side whiskers and a gravelly voice.

SHERIFF HITE: "OMG, you just left and I'm still shaking from those 4 AMAZING Ogazzes. Your tongue is magic! I never thought it possible to feel the way you make me feel. I'm touching myself now and pretending it's you. Top myself off then a sweet deep sleep. You sleep deep too. LUV, your sister Liesl."

BRIAN BURLEIGH, ASSISTANT D.A.: People started giggling, including jurors. The judge gave a warning, but then came people outright laughing. Owen tried doing the reading, and that wasn't working. I tried reading and same thing. Our male voices were distracting from the content.

OWEN MASON, DISTRICT ATTORNEY: I asked for a sidebar and said to the judge, "We need to have a woman read these emails because they sound ludicrous coming from men." Defense counsel pointed out we had no women on the prosecution team and the bailiff and court clerk were men. The court reporter was a woman, but she was needed to keep the record. They would object if we tried to bring in an outside female reader.

BRIAN BURLEIGH, ASSISTANT D.A.: "How about the chief deputy? She's been on the investigation team from day one. We'll excuse the sheriff and call her."

ERIN NEWCOMB, CHIEF DEPUTY: That's how I got the job. Granted, it was not easy. There was a lot of graphic language and emotional stuff in there. And the judge warned me not use any inflection, so I had to read everything in a deadpan tone of voice.

Some of those words and phrases had never come out of my mouth.

MR. MASON: Thank you for helping us out here. Will you read the email on the screen, dated June eighteenth, from Rebecca to the defendant?
CHIEF DEPUTY NEWCOMB: "You are driving me insane with your lies and broken promises. You sold yourself as the most kind and sensitive and

caring woman I'd ever meet. Then you come back after being gone and act all sorry and stroke me like your little dog and tell me you still care when you don't mean a single word. You told me there was no one else who made you feel the way I do. Now you're like, PSYCH, just kidding."

MS. BELKNAP: Objection, the witness is inflecting her voice.

MR. MASON: Excuse me, Your Honor, the word *psych* is capitalized in the text. The writer herself was giving it emphasis.

MS. BELKNAP: Your Honor, Mr. Mason has interrupted me again and talked over me to make his point. He's using his own form of capital letters here, and it shouts disrespect.

THE COURT: All right, let's relax. Chief Deputy Newcomb, I know it is tempting to emphasize words written in caps or given an exclamation point. But I have to ask you to try reading all the words with the same tone.

CHIEF DEPUTY NEWCOMB: Yes, Your Honor, I understand. I'll try harder.

THE COURT: Proceed.

MR. MASON: Please read the next email on the screen, dated June nineteenth, with the subject *payback*.

CHIEF DEPUTY NEWCOMB: "Maybe there's a way I can pay you back for how you've destroyed us. One little message posted on the right page that would show up on hundreds of thousands of feeds within an hour and trigger a chain reaction and cause the fake person Cleo Ray and her fake brand CleoRayFitness to explode into a million pieces. Is that what you want?"

CLEO RAY: The deputy was doing the reading, but all I could hear was Beck's voice. And I sat there wondering how long her voice would live inside my head.

Forever.

MR. MASON: The People call William Sparser.

JAKE CROWE, *INYO REGISTER*: They flew the guy out from a maximum security prison in Missouri at Inyo County's expense. It was legally complicated, and a lot of officials in both states had to sign off, but Mason got it done. William Sparser was someone they needed to nail down their motive theory. But it happened so fast neither the prosecution nor the defense had much time to prepare. Sparser entered in shackles, surrounded by four Missouri state policemen who were the size of the Kansas City Chiefs' defensive line. Our sheriff's department tripled its security detail. It felt like there were more armed officers than spectators in court that morning.

CLEO RAY: I looked at him, thinking, *I have no idea who this man is*. I'd so completely cut myself off from that life. He's a stranger, and the "Claire" he was talking about was also a stranger. I was able to emotionally detach while he was testifying, because nothing he was saying applied to Cleo Ray.

> MR. MASON: Please state your name and current residence.
> MR. WILLIAM SPARSER: William K. Sparser, Western Missouri Correctional Center in Cameron, Missouri.
> MR. MASON: Do you know the defendant, Mary Claire Griffith?

ALANA BELKNAP, DEFENSE COUNSEL: Shaved head, enormous arms and shoulders from pumping iron every day, thick neck all tatted up. But he had this boyish face and a smooth, resonant voice. Uh-huh, worst nightmare for every mother of a teenage daughter.

> MR. MASON: Were you and the defendant dating?
> MR. WILLIAM SPARSER: Oh, no, sir. I'd seen her at the Odin dance club downtown. We danced a few times there. Then I saw her at a friend's house. She came up to me and said she wanted to go out with me.
> MR. MASON: To be clear, your "first date" was the next time you saw each other, the night of May sixteenth, ten years ago?

MR. WILLIAM SPARSER: Yes, sir. I was going to take her to a party over in Westport. She set a meeting place, because her parents were strict and she had to sneak out of the house.

MR. MASON: Her parents did not approve of her going out with you?

MR. WILLIAM SPARSER: I was nineteen and she was fifteen, I think. I was already out of school and on my own. If it was my daughter, I wouldn't have let her go out with me.

ELVA GRIFFITH: Hard to listen to. There was so much we'd never known.

BRIAN BURLEIGH, ASSISTANT D.A.: I glanced back at Cleo's parents. They were like stone statues. But they kept showing up every day, I'll give them that.

ELVA GRIFFITH: Of course I wish we'd kept a closer eye on Mary Claire. Doesn't every parent wish that after your daughter gets in trouble?

MR. MASON: What was Ms. Griffith doing while you were driving the car?

MR. WILLIAM SPARSER: Well, she leaned over and started rubbing my crotch.

MR. MASON: Did you ask her to do that?

MR. WILLIAM SPARSER: No, sir.

MR. MASON: Were you surprised?

MR. WILLIAM SPARSER: No, sir. She had a reputation.

MR. MASON: You're saying the defendant began to masturbate you while you were driving?

MR. WILLIAM SPARSER: Yes, sir.

MR. MASON: And then what happened?

MR. WILLIAM SPARSER: Well, it was feeling good, and, you know, I took my eyes off the road for a few seconds and suddenly I hit something.

MR. MASON: You hit a nine-year-old girl named Jeanine Jefferson?

MR. WILLIAM SPARSER: Yes, sir. I didn't see her, but Claire did right before it happened because she screamed. I remember hearing that scream.

THE ANATOMY OF DESIRE

MR. MASON: Ms. Griffith saw the girl before you hit her?

MR. WILLIAM SPARSER: Yes, she screamed, "Stop!" or "Look out!" or something.

MR. MASON: And what did you do?

MR. WILLIAM SPARSER: I freaked out. Drove away as fast as I could.

MR. MASON: Why did you drive away?

MR. WILLIAM SPARSER: Because I was drinking, because it wasn't my car, because I didn't want to go to jail. And as Jesus Christ is my witness, I'll never regret anything more than making that choice.

CLEO RAY: He had this incredibly detailed tattoo covering the front of his neck. I stared at it and could see this collage of wavy overlapping lines. And then there it was. Right in the middle was an eye, a single human eye staring out. I just fixated on it.

MR. MASON: Did Rebecca tell you her reason for coming out to visit to you?

MR. WILLIAM SPARSER: She said "her friend Cleo Ray" had told her about what happened the night of the police chase. And she wanted to know if she was telling the truth.

MR. MASON: Did Rebecca show you a photo of Cleo Ray?

MR. WILLIAM SPARSER: She did. It was Claire Griffith. No doubt about it.

MR. MASON: Did Rebecca say whether Ms. Griffith knew she was going to visit you?

MR. WILLIAM SPARSER: Rebecca said she hadn't told her.

MR. MASON: Did she say why she hadn't told her she was going to see you?

MR. WILLIAM SPARSER: She said it was because she didn't trust her.

MR. MASON: Why didn't she trust her?

MR. WILLIAM SPARSER: She said Claire had told her a bunch of other lies. She wanted to hear my side of what happened before she confronted her about it.

MR. MASON: Rebecca said the defendant had told her about what happened that night?

MR. WILLIAM SPARSER: Yes, but she hadn't told her the part about the girl getting killed.

BRIAN BURLEIGH, ASSISTANT D.A.: It's a risk to bring in a witness who's a convicted felon and currently incarcerated, but Sparser was respectful and responsive and convincing. I was watching the jury carefully. They were hanging on every word.

MR. MASON: Did Rebecca seem like she was afraid of Cleo?
MR. WILLIAM SPARSER: Yes, sir, I did get that impression.

ALANA BELKNAP, DEFENSE COUNSEL: The prison had recorded the whole visit between Beck and Sparser, and we were given a copy. Which we watched twice, with a lot of pauses and rewinds.

MS. BELKNAP: Mr. Sparser, you testified you got the impression from Rebecca that she was afraid of Cleo?
MR. WILLIAM SPARSER: Yes, ma'am.
MS. BELKNAP: Rebecca never said those words, did she?
MR. WILLIAM SPARSER: Not those exact words.
MS. BELKNAP: Rebecca never said any words indicating she was afraid of or scared of or feeling threatened by Cleo, did she?
MR. WILLIAM SPARSER: I didn't say she did.
MS. BELKNAP: What gave you the impression Rebecca was afraid of her?
MR. WILLIAM SPARSER: The way she was talking about her.

REUBEN JEPHSON, CO-DEFENSE COUNSEL: Knock down his credibility, piece by piece.

MS. BELKNAP: Mr. Sparser, would you describe for us the car crash you got into as a result of running away from the police?

THE ANATOMY OF DESIRE

MR. WILLIAM SPARSER: It was real serious, ma'am. The car was totaled. I got messed up.

MS. BELKNAP: The highway patrol report stated the vehicle was traveling between eighty and ninety miles an hour, driver lost control, and multiple rollovers occurred. You had to be extracted from the wreck by the Jaws of Life. The medical report from the hospital stated you had several broken bones, including a fractured skull. It further says that you were in a coma. At what point did you come out of the coma?

MR. WILLIAM SPARSER: I was in and out of consciousness for almost a month.

MS. BELKNAP: And when you became conscious enough to answer questions from the police, did you tell them you couldn't remember the hit-and-run and crash incident?

MR. WILLIAM SPARSER: I did.

MS. BELKNAP: And when they asked if someone else had been in the car with you, you said?

MR. WILLIAM SPARSER: That I couldn't remember.

MS. BELKNAP: And when did you tell the authorities there had been a passenger in the car during the hit-and-run and the police chase?

MR. WILLIAM SPARSER: I didn't. But I did remember after a while. I remembered everything.

MS. BELKNAP: Who did you tell about there being a passenger in the car, other than Rebecca Alden during her prison visit?

MR. WILLIAM SPARSER: No one. What's the point? It wouldn't get me a lighter sentence.

MS. BELKNAP: Did you testify that your passenger was masturbating you while you were driving, and that's why you took your eyes off the road?

MR. WILLIAM SPARSER: I didn't say she caused the accident.

MS. BELKNAP: You claimed to have amnesia after the crash, true?

MR. WILLIAM SPARSER: And that was true—until it came back to me.

MS. BELKNAP: You never told anyone there was a passenger in the car because you didn't remember until Rebecca Alden came to visit you, isn't that true?

MR. WILLIAM SPARSER: No, it's not.

MS. BELKNAP: You have a parole hearing coming up. And if you could show the board that you cooperated with the prosecution in a murder trial, that would help your case for early parole, would it not, Mr. Sparser?

MR. WILLIAM SPARSER: It couldn't hurt. But that's not why I'm here. I have a conscience.

BRIAN BURLEIGH, ASSISTANT D.A.: Didn't matter whether Sparser was telling the truth about remembering Cleo being in the car. He'd told Rebecca she was in the car, Rebecca believed it, and she used that against Cleo. That was the point. If Rebecca goes on social media and outs Cleo Ray for being involved in the killing of a nine-year-old girl, how can Cleo prove she wasn't in the car?

CLEO RAY: They excused him, and he looked at me as he was heading out. I looked right back. Damn, you know what? I wanted to thank him. Getting into his car that night was ultimately what led me to coming out to California and becoming Cleo Ray. It was tragic for that girl and her family, but for me it was the first step toward a new life.

CLEO RAY: I was in a daze and I heard the prosecutor say, "The People call Sandy Finch." I knew it was coming, but I still felt a jolt.

SANDY FINCH: I prepared the way I would for when I immerse myself in a new sport. Clear my mind of prejudgments, open my senses to the unexpected, become a vessel for observation.

Mentally, I was good to go for my first ever experience as a witness in a murder trial. Emotionally, with Cleo sitting ten feet away, that would be the real test.

REUBEN JEPHSON, CO-DEFENSE COUNSEL: The prosecution planned it for the greatest contrast possible. Here they had Maximum-Security Convict Guy: shaved head, tattoos everywhere, looks like his idea of a good time is stabbing you in the heart with a screwdriver. Now comes Mr. Stylish Sweetheart Guy: clean-cut, soulful, and gorgeous. It was a graphic depiction of how Cleo's life had progressed over those ten years, going from a troll to a prince. It wasn't subtle, but for the jury, I'm guessing it was effective.

> **MR. MASON:** Mr. Finch, please tell us what you do for a living.
> **MR. SANDY FINCH:** I produce content for my social media brand, the Professional Amateur.
> **MR. MASON:** What kind of brand is the Professional Amateur?
> **MR. SANDY FINCH:** I go out and embed myself in different sporting and gaming endeavors, then report on my experiences over my platforms.
> **MR. MASON:** And what are your top platforms and how many followers do you have on each?
> **MR. SANDY FINCH:** Primarily my YouTube channel, with around eighteen million subscribers, and my Instagram, with around five million followers.
> **MR. MASON:** And if you had to estimate your annual income from all revenue sources, what would it be? Ballpark.
> **MR. SANDY FINCH:** Close to two million dollars.

SAMSON GRIFFITH: He was looking at his earnings from the past year. The first six months of the current year, his numbers had been skyrocketing. Had it not been for the scandal and the loss of his deals, he was on track to make five million. Of which Griffith All Media would get 15 percent.

> MR. MASON: Mr. Finch, can you tell us about how you first met the defendant?
>
> MR. SANDY FINCH: We met at a birthday party for a friend of mine, at a restaurant in Santa Monica Canyon. I'd heard of Cleo because we have the same social media agent, Samson Griffith. I knew she was his niece, I knew she was a fitness influencer, and that's about all. We were sitting next to each other at this dinner and started talking. Next thing I knew they were closing the restaurant and we were still sitting there talking.

CLEO RAY: Memory. That first dinner, he leans over to refill my wineglass. I get my first inhale of him. It's not a cologne or aftershave scent, it's like something in nature, a garden by the sea with a breeze blowing, fragrant with a hint of—something masculine.

> MR. MASON: And tell us about how your relationship with the defendant progressed.
>
> MR. SANDY FINCH: We saw each other the next day, and the next. Then I had to go to Tokyo for sponsor meetings and a promotional shoot, but we stayed in touch on WhatsApp.
>
> MR. MASON: And when you returned from your trip?
>
> MR. SANDY FINCH: We started seeing each other almost every day.
>
> MR. MASON: When did you first sleep together?
>
> MS. BELKNAP: Objection. Relevance.
>
> MR. MASON: Your Honor, the timeline of how the relationship progressed sexually had direct impact on the defendant's relationship with the victim. The highly charged sexuality between the defendant and this

witness was the catalyst for the breakdown of her relationship with the victim.
THE COURT: Objection overruled. You may answer.
MR. SANDY FINCH: I'm a little uncomfortable, because a man never tells . . .

CLEO RAY: Memory. Our first kiss. It was like every kiss before that never happened, and every kiss after would be measured against this one.

MR. SANDY FINCH: . . . we had sex that first night when we met at the restaurant. In my car. In the parking lot.

CLEO RAY: From the stand he looked at me, apologizing with his eyes. I replied silently, *It's okay.*

MR. MASON: Now, that first night or any of the subsequent time you spent together, did the defendant tell you she was already in a committed relationship?
MR. SANDY FINCH: No.
MR. MASON: Did you ask her if she was attached to anyone?
MR. SANDY FINCH: Yes. She said she wasn't.
MR. MASON: Did you ask about her prior relationships?
MR. SANDY FINCH: She told me she'd never been serious with anyone before.
MR. MASON: Did she disclose she'd been involved in a lesbian relationship?
MR. SANDY FINCH: No. But I never asked her that specifically, so she didn't lie.

SAMSON GRIFFITH: Mason went through the timeline of the Cleo/Beck emails, showing how Cleo had lied to Sandy over and over. She was living two different lives. She'd been trying to extricate herself from Beck as gently as possible because she was afraid of what Beck might do if she just walked away. In hindsight, she should've walked and let the cards fall wherever.

> **MR. MASON:** And on that occasion, were you aware the defendant had come to you after seeing Rebecca and engaging with her in sexual contact?
>
> **MR. SANDY FINCH:** I was not.

JAKE CROWE, *INYO REGISTER*: The weather had been cooling, but the temperature in the courtroom was sizzling. By then the trial was livestreaming with no content warnings. Anyone of any age could follow it. The court got a wave of calls and emails demanding the proceedings be censored during explicit testimony. Judge Oberwaltzer wanted to show openness so he wouldn't be accused of censorship in his court, only it backfired. Moms and dads were shouting, "Too much! Protect our community from those shameless media celebrities!"

Things got more X-rated as the trial went on.

SANDY FINCH: I get that Cleo was afraid of losing me. The irony is, I would've forgiven her for everything. Even running away from the car crash. That's how much I loved her.

> **MR. MASON:** And had the defendant ever said anything to you about being involved in a hit-and-run where a young girl was killed?
>
> **MR. SANDY FINCH:** No.

CLEO RAY: Memory. Waking up in Sandy's bed and he's not there. I hear him in the kitchen and I smell food cooking. I put on one of his shirts, go out, and he's making this breakfast he learned to make in Argentina.

Scrambled eggs, salmon, fried potatoes, green peas, grilled onions. It tasted like love—pure, sweet, delicious.

> MR. MASON: Thank you, Mr. Finch, that's all I have.
> THE COURT: Ms. Belknap.

REUBEN JEPHSON, CO-DEFENSE COUNSEL: I don't think there was anyone in the courtroom who didn't believe him. We were confident he'd go a long way to helping us rehab Cleo.

> MS. BELKNAP: Mr. Finch, from the first time you met Cleo Ray, did she ever ask you for help with her social media engagement?
> MR. SANDY FINCH: No.
> MS. BELKNAP: Did Cleo Ray ever ask you to contact a brand or a business and help her to get an endorsement deal?
> MR. SANDY FINCH: No.
> MS. BELKNAP: Did Cleo Ray ever ask you to share any of her content on your platforms?
> MR. SANDY FINCH: No.
> MS. BELKNAP: Did Cleo Ray ever ask you to help her network at launches or promotional events?
> MR. SANDY FINCH: No.
> MS. BELKNAP: Was there ever a moment that you suspected she was with you because it would positively impact her own popularity on social media?
> MR. SANDY FINCH: Not once.

JAKE CROWE, *INYO REGISTER*: In her emails, Beck accused Cleo of being with Sandy because he could help her build her social media following. The defense attacked that theory from multiple angles.

> MS. BELKNAP: Did Cleo ever tell you about her early life or upbringing?
> MR. SANDY FINCH: She avoided it. She would talk about her uncle

Samson and how grateful she was to him. But in terms of her own parents or childhood, she either didn't talk about it or would change the subject.

MS. BELKNAP: Based on what you've subsequently learned about her upbringing, was anything she told you about that period in her life untruthful or a lie?

MR. SANDY FINCH: What little she did tell me, like her parents being extremely religious, turned out to be true.

SAMSON GRIFFITH: I know that sticking with Cleo cost him, professionally and personally. But what he said on the stand endeared him to masses of women from age ten to a hundred and ten. His heart was wide open, he was a hundred percent real, and he was standing with his woman no matter what.

MS. BELKNAP: Did you ever tell Cleo you disapproved of lesbians or bisexual women?

MR. SANDY FINCH: No way. Early on, I even told her I found two women making love a beautiful thing.

MS. BELKNAP: So then, after Cleo's arrest, when you learned about her bisexuality, did it change your feelings toward her?

MR. SANDY FINCH: Not the slightest bit.

REUBEN JEPHSON, CO-DEFENSE COUNSEL: The prosecution's motive for Cleo was partly built on the premise that her lover Sandy would have rejected her if he found out about her relationship with Beck. We proved that wasn't the case.

MS. BELKNAP: And learning that Cleo had not been truthful about still being with Beck as she was developing her relationship with you, has that changed your feelings toward her?

THE ANATOMY OF DESIRE

MR. MASON: Objection. The witness's current feelings about the defendant are irrelevant.

MS. BELKNAP: It goes to the issue of motive, Your Honor.

MR. MASON: How he feels about her today has no bearing on her motive at the time.

MS. BELKNAP: Mr. Finch can speak to the defendant's character with more personal knowledge than anyone else in this proceeding.

THE COURT: I'll allow it.

MR. SANDY FINCH: My feelings toward her haven't changed because I understand the situation she was in, and I don't consider what she was doing was unfaithful to me. Breakups can be complicated, sometimes they don't end cleanly. That's not criminal, it's just life.

MR. MASON: Objection. Your Honor, it's not proper for him to go on and on like that.

MS. BELKNAP: May I suggest the prosecutor show a little patience and quit trying to hurry this proceeding so he can have it wrapped up by the first Tuesday in November.

MR. MASON: I beg your pardon? What are you insinuating?

THE COURT: I'll have none of that in my courtroom, Ms. Belknap. And if you try it again, I'll hold you in contempt.

MS. BELKNAP: I apologize, Your Honor. And to you, Mr. Mason. Now can we allow the witness to speak in a whole paragraph, if that's what he needs, to tell the jury what he knows about the defendant's character?

THE COURT: Proceed, Ms. Belknap.

MS. BELKNAP: Mr. Finch, were you here in the courtroom for Mr. Sparser's testimony?

MR. SANDY FINCH: Yes, I was.

MS. BELKNAP: And was there anything Mr. Sparser revealed about Cleo that has caused you to change your feelings toward her?

MR. SANDY FINCH: No. Cleo has made mistakes. She's tried to cover them by telling lies, some of them big lies. But she is not a violent or cruel person in any way.

MR. MASON: Your Honor, begging your pardon, Mr. Finch is giving his opinion now.

THE COURT: The jury will disregard the witness's last answer.

CLEO RAY: Memory. Sandy leaving the witness stand. I had tears streaming down my face, and he reached into his pocket, pulled out a pack of tissues, and handed it to me as he went by. No words were exchanged. It was just a spontaneous thing. Everyone in the courtroom saw it. I can't tell you how grateful I was for those tissues.

JAKE CROWE, *INYO REGISTER*: The prosecution's case took eight days. They'd brought on the boathouse attendant who rented them the canoe; the fishermen who ran into Cleo near the crime scene; the sheriff and deputy who were first to arrive; the medical examiner who determined the cause of death and what caused the injuries to Beck's face and head; other medical experts to testify to how the injuries occurred; Beck's mom, friends, and coworkers; the clerk that sold them the champagne; other influencers who were in the hiking party; William Sparser; and Sandy Finch. Their case was that Cleo had lured Beck up to the lake with an intent to kill, and once she got her out on the water Cleo struck her in the face with the paddle, smashed her on the head for good measure, tipped the canoe over, and watched her drown. They did not have an eyewitness to the actual murder, so technically their case was circumstantial, but they'd dotted their *i*'s and crossed their *t*'s. Mason had done his job, and most legal pundits agreed the prosecution had presented a compelling case.

Now it was time for Big City Lawyer Belknap and Local Defender Jephson to present their counternarrative. And coming off that opening statement, anticipation was sky-high.

CLEO RAY: That Friday, they moved me from a single cell into a double with an inmate on the other side. At first I was nervous. But having someone to talk to turned out to be a good thing, and my "pod partner" was this really great Native American woman in her mid-thirties. She was serving three months for theft, and it wasn't her first time in there. Her name's Leti, spelled L-E-T-I. Smart. Funny. Self-taught like me. We just clicked.

Sandy had stayed overnight in Mammoth and was set to visit me on Saturday. We still wouldn't be able to touch, but I was dying to personally connect with him after he testified. He'd been only a few feet away in the courtroom, but it felt like miles. Leti let me borrow her lavender shampoo and conditioner, and then showed me how to do a twisted side braid and loosen it up to look stylish but relaxed. I still didn't have a real mirror to see myself, but Leti gave me a double thumbs-up. I wanted to surprise Sandy and look pretty for him.

We agreed he'd come at two o'clock, and he called the jail ahead to make the appointment. About a quarter till, I got a case of raging butterflies. Steady, girl, you've got this!

Two o'clock, the guards didn't come for me. Two-fifteen, two-thirty, no Sandy. I'm pacing the floor, my stomach hurts, and Leti is trying to be encouraging, saying, *He'll be here, he'll be here.*

At three o'clock the guard opened the door and I'm thinking I must've gotten the hour wrong. But he handed me a folded note and shut the door again. I sat down on my bunk and saw it was Sandy's handwriting. And it was like I could hear his voice:

> *Dear Cleo, I am so sorry. I'm not sure what's wrong with me, but I'm not up for a visit after all. I wish I could give you a good excuse, but the truth is, I don't have one. I feel terrible doing this to you. Please find it in your heart to forgive me. I'll be in touch soon. Love, Sandy.*

It just flattened me. I fell back and couldn't move. Leti got angry on my behalf and offered to put a curse on him.

"No," I said, undoing my braid. "He's the best man I've ever known. Nothing can change that. Nothing." Then I turned to the wall and cried my eyes out.

EPISODE SIX

GIRL DEFENDED

I'm sharing this post of a poodle and an African wild dog playing with each other, #InThisTogether. First it made me laugh, then I got tears in my eyes. It's true and it's crazy, and what it means to me is that true things can look crazy and crazy things can be true. Plus, I'm terrified of African wild dogs but also find them incredibly cute, and that's like in life, when we're afraid of and attracted to something at the same time. If we can be okay with having both those feelings at once, that gives us more room to breathe.

Instagram post, CleoRayFitness

DUNCAN MCMILLAN: *I'd just come back from a long shoot and post in Europe and was planning a little R and R at my home on Maui. I'm kicking back on the lanai with a rum punch and my phone pings. I think about ignoring it but succumb to the urge and click on the message. It was an ex-girlfriend sending me a link to a site with a collection of Cleo Ray videos that had been taken down from Instagram. One of her superfans had posted them and asked people to rate them. I started watching this endearingly cheery person urging and encouraging her followers, superficially aware of what had been emerging at her trial. Up until then I'd mostly bypassed the story, considering it another reality show soap opera. But now I became fascinated by the chasm between who this person had been as Mary Claire Griffith at fifteen and who she'd become as Cleo Ray at twenty-five.*

And then it clicked. This was about more than a young social media influencer on trial for murder. It was a striking metaphor for this moment in our culture. So I called my producer, pitched the idea, and she said, "Go. I can set this up in twenty-four hours, but this thing is happening right now. Go."

I pulled together a bare-bones crew and had them meet me in Independence. The court was in recess when I pulled in, and I started walking the residential streets. You can walk the whole town in under an hour. I came upon this great old clapboard church, Pioneer Memorial. It's like out of a John Ford Western, a Methodist house of worship established in 1871.

Then I found the Eastern California Museum, a charming repository that houses a collection of historic artifacts inside and out, including the ruins of an old mining town in its backyard. The museum is run by a volunteer staff working "to preserve the diverse heritage of Inyo County, the Eastern Sierra, and the backcountry from Mono Lake to Death Valley." I began hearing from locals about the Owens Valley Water Wars and the long, contentious history between Inyo County and the city of Los Angeles. The agriculture business in this part of the state, which given its geography should be flourishing, has literally been dried up by the money and power of Los Angeles hijacking its water resources. Litigation between this David and Goliath has been going on for decades. Inyo County was forced to shift to a tourism economy and has suffered through many a downturn. If you look closely, you can see the edges fraying.

I went in search of a bite to eat, and it was pointed out to me that the best lunch in town comes from a taco truck at the south end of the main drag. As I approached, I could see a line extending down the block. After a twenty-minute wait, I ordered two shrimp tacos, which turned out to be the most delicious I've ever had—and I've had a lot of taco truck tacos.

MS. BELKNAP: The defense calls Rose McGloughlin.

JAKE CROWE, *INYO REGISTER*: Rose was a video production costumer and occasional coworker of Beck's. She kicked off a group who became known as the "anti" character witnesses.

> MS. BELKNAP: And what did you notice about Beck on that day you worked with her?
>
> MS. ROSE MCGLOUGHLIN: She was fixated on weddings. She'd cut photos out of magazines, had a bunch on her phone. I said, "You need a groom

before you can have a wedding." She said, "There's a groom. Only he doesn't know about the wedding yet."

MS. BELKNAP: What did you take that to mean?

MS. ROSE MCGLOUGHLIN: That she was trapping someone into marrying her.

MR. MASON: Objection. The witness is offering her opinion, move to strike it.

THE COURT: The jury will disregard the witness's last remark.

MS. BELKNAP: What else did Beck say about a wedding or the groom?

MS. ROSE MCGLOUGHLIN: She said, "I have a plan for getting her to the altar." Then she said, "Did I say *her*? I meant *him*." But it was clear she meant *her*.

BRIAN BURLEIGH, ASSISTANT D.A.: It's a risky strategy to defame and blame the victim. Juries can be uncomfortable with that. Because what are you saying? She deserved it?

JAKE CROWE, *INYO REGISTER*: With each new witness you could see the argument building. Not that Beck deserved it, but that she was a full contributor to the growing toxicity of the relationship.

MR. JEPHSON: Can you give examples of what you describe as Beck's quick temper?

MS. MELIA TORRES: Well, we were in class learning about how to diminish an actor's facial wrinkles. The instructor came over and gave her a critique. Beck picked up her makeup kit and turned it over on the floor. Another time she found out someone else got a job she'd been counting on, and she backhanded half a cup of coffee off the table. She said she was sorry and cleaned it up. But she could be temperamental like that.

BRIAN BURLEIGH, ASSISTANT D.A.: Let's just say the prosecution examined these people vigorously on cross. "Ms. Torres, have you ever expressed anger by slamming your fist or stomping your foot?" "Well, yeah." "Did you ever see Rebecca's anger directed at another person?" "Well, no."

MS. BELKNAP: Describe these photos of Cleo you found on Beck's phone.

JAKE CROWE, *INYO REGISTER*: The questioning of the computer forensics expert who'd examined Beck's laptop and smartphone went on for several hours.

MR. EUGENE ZIMMER: It was apparent to me they'd been taken while Cleo wasn't looking. She shows no awareness of being photographed.
MS. BELKNAP: How so?
MR. EUGENE ZIMMER: Well, there were several of Cleo showering. Mostly taken from behind, or a side shot in the mirror.
MS. BELKNAP: Can you give us other examples?
MR. EUGENE ZIMMER: Cleo hooking her bra strap, Cleo pulling on her underwear, Cleo working on her laptop.
MS. BELKNAP: So these photos are characterized by Cleo not looking, turned away, involved in solo activities. How many of these types of photos were on Beck's phone?
MR. EUGENE ZIMMER: Hundreds.
MS. BELKNAP: Could you see them grouped by date? Were more of these photos taken on later dates than earlier ones?
MR. EUGENE ZIMMER: Yes. In January this year, there were two or three on a given day. In June, there were dozens taken on each day.
MS. BELKNAP: What would be an example of these later photos?
MR. EUGENE ZIMMER: Cleo sleeping in bed. Lying on her side, head on pillow, eyes closed, naked from the waist up. I counted thirty-three single click photos of her in that position, taken in a span of twelve minutes, between 4:15 and 4:27 A.M.

SAMSON GRIFFITH: Thirty-three photos of my half-naked niece up on the projection screen. One of many moments I should have been allowed to take out my phone and check my messages.

ERIN NEWCOMB, CHIEF DEPUTY: During my nonworking hours I went over to where they set up the LGBTQ information booth. I took time to talk to the volunteers and hear what they had to say. They came from all across the state, north and south, from colleges and nonprofit groups. Nice people, decent people, just looking to support and inform. I learned some things. Beyond all the noise of the trial, there were issues being talked about that needed to be talked about.

JAKE CROWE, *INYO REGISTER*: The defense called a psychologist who specialized in LGBTQ therapy and had interviewed Cleo while she was in jail. She took the stand and the whole gallery leaned forward.

> **MS. BELKNAP:** Dr. Rosen, given your research and clinical experience, would you tell us the definition of bisexuality?
> **DR. KAREN ROSEN:** A bisexual person is someone who is able to form a physical, emotional, and/or romantic relationship with a person of the same gender or a different gender.
> **MS. BELKNAP:** And how prevalent is bisexuality in the United States?
> **DR. KAREN ROSEN:** The current research shows 5.5 percent of women and 2 percent of men identify as bisexual. Some studies suggest that social context, including level of education and an emphasis on physical appearance, may play a bigger role in determining a woman's sexual fluidity than a man's.

SAMSON GRIFFITH: What was being said are things *we* take for granted. But for a lot of the country these are exotic lifestyles. The defense felt it needed to educate the jury. I have to admit, at times I felt like standing up in court and declaring, "This is normal. This is the way people are, so get with it." I ended up not doing that.

MS. BELKNAP: Can you speak to the stereotyping of bisexual women?

DR. KAREN ROSEN: Bisexual women who have come out to family and friends are more likely to get responses like "You're just going through a phase" or "You must be a sex addict" or "You're only doing this because you know it's a turn-on for straight men."

MS. BELKNAP: Dr. Rosen, have you interviewed the defendant and discussed her sexual identity with her to the extent you can render a professional opinion?

DR. KAREN ROSEN: I conducted five one-hour interviews with Cleo Ray at the Inyo Jail and followed up with fifteen pages of written questions and answers. So yes, I've had enough input to form an opinion.

MS. BELKNAP: And where do you find Cleo Ray on the sexuality spectrum?

DR. KAREN ROSEN: Cleo derives pleasure from and is responsive to both traditional genders. Sexual attraction is not gender-driven for her, it's about the attraction that gets reflected back to her. In that sense, she's gender blind.

MS. BELKNAP: The more Cleo feels desired, the more desire she feels in response?

DR. KAREN ROSEN: Yes. Her sexual desire is triggered less by the gender of the person she's getting the attention from than the magnitude of that attention.

GILLIAN GRIFFITH: When Cleo looked in your eyes, she tried to locate herself in your gaze. If you signaled attraction, she would match whatever intensity you expressed. That's not bisexuality, that's emotional insecurity.

MS. BELKNAP: Tell us your impressions of Cleo Ray and Beck Alden's relationship, starting when they first got together.

DR. KAREN ROSEN: Cleo was the initiator, but Beck was immediately responsive to her. Cleo came to the relationship having had other lesbian sex experiences. Beck had no lesbian sexual experiences prior to meeting Cleo.
MS. BELKNAP: How did that shape their early relationship?
DR. KAREN ROSEN: Cleo took the role of the dominant partner. She mentored Beck in lesbian lovemaking.

CLEO RAY: Proud of that. I was patient and sensitive and funny and wise—me, wise! We'd get up late on Sundays, go to the drive-thru Starbucks, get nonfat lattes and chocolate chip muffins, come back and spend the afternoon in bed fooling around.

MS. BELKNAP: In terms of emotional stability, how would you characterize the first year of their relationship?
DR. KAREN ROSEN: Mostly happy and mutually fulfilling.
MS. BELKNAP: Did that begin to change?
DR. KAREN ROSEN: Yes. After Cleo met Sandy Finch.

JAKE CROWE, *INYO REGISTER*: Alana and Dr. Rosen had worked together on other trials, and they had their act down. When they shifted gears, you could feel the atmosphere change in the courtroom.

MS. BELKNAP: Dr. Rosen, have you seen situations in your clinical practice where one partner in a lesbian couple is unfaithful with a man?
DR. KAREN ROSEN: I have.
MS. BELKNAP: What is that like for the other partner, the one who's cheated on?
DR. KAREN ROSEN: Infidelity in any monogamous relationship is painful for the partner betrayed. But when a lesbian lover cheats on her partner with a man, there is greater intensity to the betrayal. The rejection is amplified by the messaging "I wasn't truly gay when

I was with you," and the emotional wounding is complicated by psychological disorientation.

MS. BELKNAP: And the fact this was Beck's first lesbian relationship, might that lead to further emotional complications?

DR. KAREN ROSEN: The bonding involved in that first love experience is critical to the defining of a person's sexual identity. So the trauma of rejection is all the more devastating, the hit to one's self-worth is harder to work through. Beck had no emotional reference point beyond that one relationship.

MS. BELKNAP: And this kind of betrayal leads to what types of psychological issues in the person betrayed?

DR. KAREN ROSEN: Depression, certainly. Flares of anger. Anxiety.

MS. BELKNAP: Obsessive thoughts?

DR. KAREN ROSEN: Yes.

MS. BELKNAP: Revenge fantasies?

DR. KAREN ROSEN: Yes.

MS. BELKNAP: You saw the photos from Beck's phone of Cleo that were secretly taken. What do those tell you about Beck's psychological state?

DR. KAREN ROSEN: As she felt Cleo slipping further away, Beck became more compulsive.

BRIAN BURLEIGH, ASSISTANT D.A.: The defense was trying to portray Rebecca as a *Fatal Attraction*. Even if that was true, which there's no absolute proof of except for a few emails, it is not a justification for the defendant plotting to murder her.

MS. BELKNAP: Dr. Rosen, did you talk to Cleo about her childhood?

DR. KAREN ROSEN: I did.

SAMSON GRIFFITH: I also found that testimony memorable because in court that day I happened to be seated right next to my sister-in-law.

DR. KAREN ROSEN: Cleo felt emotionally neglected by her parents because of their obsession with their religion—to the point of experiencing it as abuse.

MS. BELKNAP: How did that emotional abuse impact Cleo?

DR. KAREN ROSEN: She learned to compartmentalize her feelings. To keep dissonant emotions—they love me, they abuse me—locked off from each other.

MS. BELKNAP: And did this way of coping show up at other times in Cleo's life?

DR. KAREN ROSEN: Yes. For example, the way she isolated her relationship with Sandy from her ongoing involvement with Beck.

MS. BELKNAP: Did this coping mechanism affect Cleo's behavior following the accident on the lake?

DR. KAREN ROSEN: Yes, for Cleo to carry on with any semblance of normality, she had to put a mental wall between her negative feelings about what happened to Beck and her positive feelings about being with Sandy and her friends. She was in a pathological state of denial.

GILLIAN GRIFFITH: Karen Rosen lives in the East Village, wears a nose ring, and has platinum pixie-cut hair. Owen Mason wears blue button-downs and dark gray ties, and parts his hair on the side. When Mason began to cross-examine her and came toward the witness stand, the visual contrast was conspicuous.

MR. MASON: Good afternoon, Dr. Rosen.

DR. KAREN ROSEN: Good afternoon.

MR. MASON: Now, did you ever meet the victim in this case, Rebecca Alden?

DR. KAREN ROSEN: I did not.

MR. MASON: Never spoke to her, never interviewed her. You are forming your opinions based on what the defendant told you about her?

DR. KAREN ROSEN: I also read the email correspondence, the cards, the discovery.

MR. MASON: But you never personally observed the defendant and Rebecca together.

DR. KAREN ROSEN: Emails are a form of conversation.

MR. MASON: Answer the question, please.

DR. KAREN ROSEN: No, I did not personally observe Cleo and Beck together.

MR. MASON: And did you interview Rebecca's parents?

DR. KAREN ROSEN: I did not.

MR. MASON: Did you interview any of Rebecca's friends or coworkers?

DR. KAREN ROSEN: I did not.

MR. MASON: Other than what you learned from the defendant and from written correspondence between victim and defendant, you consulted no other sources who were personally connected with Rebecca Alden?

DR. KAREN ROSEN: No.

JAKE CROWE, *INYO REGISTER*: The prosecution hadn't objected much during direct. Then we found out that was because they were confident they could score their points on cross.

MR. MASON: And on what did you base your opinion that Rebecca Alden was a virgin to lesbian sex when she first got involved with the defendant?

DR. KAREN ROSEN: On what Beck personally told Cleo and then reaffirmed in her emails.

MR. MASON: How do you know Beck was telling Cleo the truth?

DR. KAREN ROSEN: I don't.

MR. MASON: Dr. Rosen, isn't it true your theories about Rebecca's extreme behavior in regard to Cleo are in large part founded on this assumption? I can read back your testimony if you like.

DR. KAREN ROSEN: You know that Beck did have prior experience with lesbian sex?

THE ANATOMY OF DESIRE

MR. MASON: Thank you for asking. I would direct you and the jury to please look at the projection screen. You will see posts from the Facebook account of a woman named Lia Passarelli. Can you tell me what you see in the photos?

DR. KAREN ROSEN: I see Beck kissing a girl, which in no way proves she had sex with her.

MR. MASON: Kissing indicates intimacy, romantic involvement.

DR. KAREN ROSEN: They could have kissed on a dare.

JAKE CROWE, *INYO REGISTER*: Soon as she said it could have been a dare, Mason put up four photos taken at different times of Beck making out with Lia. Dr. Rosen walked right into that one.

MR. MASON: Dr. Rosen, are you aware of studies that show the prevalence of intimate partner violence in LGBTQ relationships as high or higher than the general population?

DR. KAREN ROSEN: Different studies require different assessments.

MR. MASON: Here is a list of forty-two studies that address the prevalence of intimate partner violence in LGBTQ relationships. Do you have a reason to discount any of those findings?

DR. KAREN ROSEN: I would have to take the time to read these to offer a judgment.

MR. MASON: What are the established risk factors involved in intimate partner violence? Is one of the factors the desire for dominance in a relationship?

DR. KAREN ROSEN: Yes.

MR. MASON: And is another risk factor the experience of parental neglect as a child?

DR. KAREN ROSEN: Well, yes.

MR. MASON: And isn't one of the strongest predictors of intimate partner violence found in someone who experiences emotional or psychological abuse from their partner?

DR. KAREN ROSEN: It is.

MR. MASON: You testified that you read the emails between Rebecca and the defendant, and you interviewed the defendant over five hours. Did the defendant experience Rebecca's messages and behavior toward her as emotionally abusive?

DR. KAREN ROSEN: She did.

MR. MASON: No further questions.

CLEO RAY: Self-help books, podcasts, emotional IQ tests online, did them all, but I'd never had a therapy session. I thought I had to be the type who could power through any problem. You can get over any obstacle if you don't give up. That mindset helped me get a lot of Instagram followers. Now I had Karen Rosen's voice in my head telling me to see the obstacles inside and not worry so much about the ones outside.

ALANA BELKNAP, DEFENSE COUNSEL: As we were putting on our defense, Cleo's parents approached me after court one day. I was aware of them sitting there day after day and of the tension because Cleo wanted nothing to do with them. I felt I shouldn't interfere. But they came to me and asked if I would talk to her about allowing them to visit her at the jail. I felt bad for them. They were in such a tough position. So I said to Cleo, "Listen, in matters of family, you make your own choices. But if you grant your parents a visit, I think it may alleviate some stress. On both sides."

She looked away and was quiet. Then she said, "I'm worried it would break me." I asked how. She said, "I've kept them out of my heart for so long, if I even start to let them back in, I don't know what would happen. I might fall apart. I'm scared."

I put a hand on her shoulder and said, "I get it. I didn't have a great relationship with my parents. Sometimes I have to fight hard not to be consumed by those resentments. But if you let go of any expectation for how it'll affect you and stay focused on how it will help them, so they can maybe heal a little, you can come away knowing you did a kind thing. And they'll come away with a sense of connection that will ease their burdens. My two cents. Your call."

ELVA GRIFFITH: We know our daughter is embarrassed by us. But we couldn't stay away from the trial. We're her parents, for better or worse. Mary Claire needs to know we will be there to support her during her time of turmoil, whatever else she thinks of us.

CLEO RAY: From an early age I knew it wasn't for me. I didn't have anything against Jesus or the Bible or the church. I believe in God. But the fanaticism, the relentless preaching, the one-dimensional world view. They neglected their own daughters because Jesus needed them more?
Daughters, plural. You know I had a sister.

ELVA GRIFFITH: The love of Christ will prevail. That's our faith, that's what keeps us going. We prayed and prayed and were so thankful when Mary Claire asked to visit with us.

CLEO RAY: Elizabeth was eight years older than me. Which sometimes made me think I was a mistake. I idolized her. She was more like a mom than a big sister. My most vivid childhood memories are of Elizabeth, not of Asa or Elva.
My sister was there when my parents weren't. I remember feeling really safe with her. When we'd be out on the streets preaching and singing hymns, she was the one looking out for me, making sure I didn't walk into traffic or get stolen by a stranger.
When my parents were out teaching Bible study or volunteering

at the mission house, Elizabeth would make hot chocolate and take out her hidden stash of mini-marshmallows. She'd say, "Let's make this our secret." I loved having a secret with my sister. It made me feel closer to her.

ELVA GRIFFITH: Elizabeth was a good girl. We never had any problems with her. Until... until...

CLEO RAY: When she was supposed to be reading me Scripture, Elizabeth would pull out other books to read to me. *Island of the Blue Dolphins*, I loved that one. And comics with female superheroes. And Harry Potter, which our parents had forbidden.

She read and talked to me about Jesus, too, about his human side. Her favorite verses were from John chapter 8.

> *And Jesus said unto her, Neither do I condemn thee: go, and sin no more.*

Elizabeth said, "That's about forgiveness. And that's the hardest thing in the world, to forgive."

ELVA GRIFFITH: We trusted Elizabeth completely. She'd given us no reason not to.

CLEO RAY: I sensed Elizabeth was unhappy, but she never complained to me or said anything critical of our parents. I had my own weird feelings about what kind of family we were. Surviving on handouts, wearing Goodwill hand-me-downs, never going to the doctor unless it was an emergency.

I noticed Elizabeth being away from home more. Once I looked out the window and saw her in a parked car with a boy. I knew the boys in church stared at her because she was beautiful, supermodel beautiful. I could feel her growing more distant, but I didn't know how to talk to her about it. I was only nine.

One Saturday night after regular services—Elizabeth had stopped going to church with us months earlier—we came home and she was gone. Clothes in closet gone, suitcase gone. I saw the note on her pillow, but my mom took it before I could read it. She turned away and read it to herself, and I could see her hand shaking. She passed it to my dad, and he read it and shook his head. I said, "What does it say? Where did she go?" My mom told me to go do my Bible lessons. Then she tore the note into pieces.

That's the moment I knew someday I would run away, too.

ELVA GRIFFITH: All those years doing the Lord's work, and my oldest runs off with a drug dealer. I did look to God and ask why. How could He let this happen? Where was His mercy? This happens to godless families, not devout ones like ours.

It had to be a test. We were being tested. And then . . . I still find it difficult to talk about.

ALANA BELKNAP, DEFENSE COUNSEL: Three women in the box, and I freely admit we're going for their hearts. In my experience, it is generally true women jurors are more empathetic than men jurors. Of course there's a spectrum. Some women are going to have less empathy than your average man. But I thought we had a chance with these three. It only takes one.

JAKE CROWE, *INYO REGISTER*: O. J. Simpson, Scott Peterson, Casey Anthony, three dramatic, sensational murder trials, and none of them took the stand. The day the defense called Cleo Ray, it felt like we were entering a new dimension. Who wouldn't tune in for that? Everyone lucky enough to have a seat in that courtroom knew this was something special. I would never have a bigger audience for my reporting than this story, I knew that.

> **BAILIFF:** Please raise your right hand. Do you solemnly state that the testimony you give in the case now pending before this court is the truth, the whole truth, and nothing but the truth, so help you God?
>
> **MS. GRIFFITH:** I do.

SAMSON GRIFFITH: Cleo worked harder than anyone I've known at being an influencer. She was not the most natural talent, but she made the most of her ability and learned to engage people in a way that built their trust. I was not a fan of the last-minute shift in strategy, but that didn't mean I lacked faith in Cleo. If anyone could win over that jury, it would be her.

BRIAN BURLEIGH, ASSISTANT D.A.: You never know how someone will perform on the witness stand until they testify. No matter how strong she was at "influencing," given how high the stakes were, it could have gone either way.

ERIN NEWCOMB, CHIEF DEPUTY: She was wearing black slacks that fit like a glove, a simple blue-and-white-checked blouse, with a little blush and lip gloss and her blond hair back in a ponytail. She looked pretty. And she was humble. Different from her social media videos, but still sincere. So much pressure. I wouldn't say I was rooting for her, but I wasn't rooting against her.

TITUS ALDEN: We kept our eyes on her the whole time she was up there, to let her know we were representing our daughter and holding her accountable for every word.

MS. BELKNAP: Good morning, Cleo—may I call you Cleo?
MS. GRIFFITH: Yes, that's the name I prefer, thank you. Good morning.
MS. BELKNAP: I'm going to take you through some of your life experiences so we can get the jury to know you better. How does that sound?
MS. GRIFFITH: Great. I want that, too.

CLEO RAY: I'd gone day after day with the spectators behind me. Now I was facing a hundred people all staring at me. Alana suggested I keep my eyes on her the whole time unless the judge spoke to me, and that's what I did.

MS. BELKNAP: Let's start at the beginning. Where were you born?
MS. GRIFFITH: Grand Rapids, Michigan. My parents were on a mission for their church. My mother was bearing witness when her water broke. At least that's what I was always told.

GILLIAN GRIFFITH: Cleo hadn't shared any of this on social media. She never talked about how she grew up, never mentioned her parents. This was a very different person than her followers were familiar with.

MS. BELKNAP: And how did your parents earn their living?
MS. GRIFFITH: I don't remember them ever having real jobs. They'd go to street corners, set out a donations jar, and start preaching.
MS. BELKNAP: So you didn't have much in the way of clothing or toys?
MS. GRIFFITH: We got our clothes secondhand and had to wear them whether they fit or not. And I can only remember having one doll growing up. I held on to her until she completely fell apart.
MS. BELKNAP: How about food?
MS. GRIFFITH: I remember a church person who was better off would give us restaurant boxes of frozen sirloin. Mom cut it up into smaller pieces and made that last for weeks between the four of us. Many times we had plain pasta for breakfast. Sometimes we'd have to skip meals.

MS. BELKNAP: So it wouldn't be exaggerating to say your family was poor.

MS. GRIFFITH: More than once I heard us described as "dirt poor."

MS. BELKNAP: Very poor and very religious.

MS. GRIFFITH: I heard us called "Jesus freaks."

JAKE CROWE, *INYO REGISTER*: They dealt with the fundamentalist Christian upbringing head-on. Cleo's parents were in the first row behind the defense table—stoic, showing no emotions. A few of the jurors kept glancing between Cleo and her parents, checking for reactions. I'm sure they caught a wince or two.

MS. BELKNAP: Tell us about your relationship with your older sister.

MS. GRIFFITH: She was funny, made me laugh a lot, gave me permission to be silly and act my age. I remember her encouraging me to be creative, to use my imagination. We pretended to go on adventures around the world and acted out being freezing cold at the North Pole and burning hot in the Sahara Desert.

MS. BELKNAP: Tell us what happened to your sister, Elizabeth.

MS. GRIFFITH: She ran away from home. Straight up packed a bag, left a note on her pillow, and ran off with a guy who sold drugs.

MS. BELKNAP: How old was she?

MS. GRIFFITH: Seventeen.

MS. BELKNAP: Then what happened to Elizabeth?

MS. GRIFFITH: I remember getting called out of fifth period and going into the office. They handed me a phone and it was my mom, and she said that Elizabeth had gone to heaven. At first I didn't know what she meant. "Heaven? Where's heaven?" It was the school counselor who told me my sister had overdosed on OxyContin.

MS. BELKNAP: I'm so sorry. That must've been very difficult for you.

MS. GRIFFITH: Even though she's gone, my sister never left me.

SAMSON GRIFFITH: I never met Elizabeth. The one time my brother and sister-in-law came to visit on their way to a mission, she'd already passed away. But I do remember Claire. She was twelve, quiet, hardly said a word. Gillian and I got her out and walked her around Santa Monica Canyon. Her eyes were this big, looking around, taking everything in. She loved all the stairs.

Four years later she came back saying she wanted to live here.

REUBEN JEPHSON, CO-DEFENSE COUNSEL: Alana and I plotted out where she and I would be most effective. In the areas that dealt with Cleo's abusive male relationships, we thought my country-boy manner would make this content easier for the jury to process.

MR. JEPHSON: Did the account Mr. Sparser gave here coincide with your own memories of the incident?

MS. GRIFFITH: Well, I did sneak out of my room and meet him on the street. I didn't know he'd been drinking until after I was inside the car and he started driving.

MR. JEPHSON: Did you ask him to stop so you could get out of the car?

MS. GRIFFITH: No.

MR. JEPHSON: So you were aware he was driving under the influence and there was a greater risk to getting in an accident or getting pulled over?

MS. GRIFFITH: Yes.

MR. JEPHSON: His testimony that you reached over and masturbated him, did that happen?

MS. GRIFFITH: I want to set the record straight. He said he'd help me get a job if I gave him oral sex and asked for it while he was driving. I said no. Then he asked if I'd give him hand sex. Which I did. But he asked for it.

MR. JEPHSON: When he asked that, why didn't you tell him to stop the car and let you out?

MS. GRIFFITH: I wanted a job so I could make my own money.

MR. JEPHSON: So you willingly reached over and masturbated him while he was driving? Did you think that would make his driving even more dangerous, since he'd also been drinking?

BRIAN BURLEIGH, ASSISTANT D.A.: Their strategy was not to pull any punches. They knew if they didn't go there, we would. They wanted to get all the bad stuff out in front of the jury so their client would look as transparent as possible. It was smart.

MS. GRIFFITH: He was a hot guy with money and status. In that world. I wanted him to like me. I wanted him to help me get a job so I could get out of my life.
MR. JEPHSON: After he hit the girl and was driving away, what was going through your mind?
MS. GRIFFITH: For a moment I was in total shock. I was like, *Did that really happen?* And then I started screaming at him to stop and let me out. I thought about opening the door and jumping, but he was going too fast. I thought about grabbing the steering wheel, but that would've caused a crash. There was nothing I could do but keep screaming at him to stop. He took a curve too fast, lost control, and we flipped over. I thought I was dead.
MR. JEPHSON: When the car came to rest, can you tell us what you did?
MS. GRIFFITH: I wasn't dead, but I was hurt pretty bad. My brain started screaming at me to get out of there. There was a small opening I crawled through. I stood up and my legs weren't broken. I heard the sirens and saw the flashing lights coming. Instinct kicked in. No thought or planning, I ran away from the wreck and the police cars. And kept going.
MR. JEPHSON: After running away from the wreck, what did you do?
MS. GRIFFITH: I thought Will would tell the cops I was in the car and they'd come looking for me at home. I thought I'd get arrested and go to jail

and it would be in the news and on my record and follow me for the rest of my life. I didn't want—I didn't want to end up like my sister.

JAKE CROWE, *INYO REGISTER*: First time she came to tears on the stand. At that moment there was a lot of sympathy coming at her. I even noticed Beck's mom wipe a tear on her sleeve.

MR. JEPHSON: How badly hurt were you from the accident?
MS. GRIFFITH: My body felt numb for a while. When that started wearing off, I was in a lot of pain. I was able to buy aspirin and bandages to stop the bleeding.
MR. JEPHSON: Do you still have scars from accident?
MS. GRIFFITH: The worst one is on my right hip. Which is why you'll never see me in a thong.
MR. JEPHSON: After you ran away from the accident, where did you go?
MS. GRIFFITH: I crossed the state hitchhiking and ended up in St. Louis.
MR. JEPHSON: How did you eat and get a roof over your head?
MS. GRIFFITH: I didn't. I was homeless on the streets for almost two weeks. Then I met a guy who offered to take me in and help me find work. Seemed like a nice regular guy. Late thirties, I guess. He treated me well for a while. Got my injuries from the crash taken care of by a doctor. Fed me, bought me new clothes. I wasn't totally naive, I knew he'd want payback. And honestly, I didn't mind returning the favor. He was actually pretty nice.
MR. JEPHSON: So you had sexual intercourse with him?
MS. GRIFFITH: Yes. It wasn't horrible. But then he said I could make good money if I would go to these parties he and his friends put on. He said all I'd have to do was dress in sexy lingerie and dance a little. If I didn't want to go any further, that would be my choice.
MR. JEPHSON: Did you say yes and go to the party?
MS. GRIFFITH: I did. And I was gang-raped there.

JAKE CROWE, *INYO REGISTER*: You've heard the expression "Then came a gasp in the courtroom"?

SAMSON GRIFFITH: I hadn't known that. Shit. The poor kid. I mean, I thought I knew what drove her. But I guess nobody knew the real Cleo. Not even Cleo.

BRIAN BURLEIGH, ASSISTANT D.A.: Everyone was feeling for the defendant, including the prosecution.

ELVA GRIFFITH: I don't know what to say.

ERIN NEWCOMB, CHIEF DEPUTY: Damn, girl. Damn.

> **MR. JEPHSON:** Did you try to run away from this man or call the police?
> **MS. GRIFFITH:** He said he would kill me if I tried to tell anyone. He locked me inside a room in his house with no windows. He kept giving me Percocets, which I pretended to swallow. I'd act like I was drugged up and he believed it. But I knew from what happened to my sister if I took the pills once, that would be my death. And I didn't want to die. I wanted to do something with my life. So I carefully planned my escape, waited for the right moment, and I was gone. Gone to L.A. and to my uncle Samson and this family of blood relatives I'd only met once in my life.

JAKE CROWE, *INYO REGISTER*: When we came back from the recess, Alana Belknap took over the questioning. She would be the one to lead Cleo into the areas about her relationship with Beck, a woman questioning a woman about an affair between two women.

MS. BELKNAP: Tell us how your relationship with Rebecca Alden started.

MS. GRIFFITH: I was the PA and she was doing hair and makeup on an advertising shoot. I thought she was cute and sweet, and we chatted on and off. I said, "You want to grab a coffee sometime?" because that's just what you say, and she was like, "After work?" I said sure. Over lattes I told her about my ambition to become one of the top fitness influencers and I showed her a couple of my Instagram videos. She told me they were great and she had a feeling I would be a huge success. That was music to my ears.

MS. BELKNAP: At what point did the relationship turn romantic?

MS. GRIFFITH: I could feel we were attracted to each other. She was so interested in me and what I had to say and what I thought. That was flattering. And after that first coffee, as I walked her to her car I said, "Please don't take this the wrong way, but can I kiss you?" She seemed shocked—for about two seconds. We kissed and it felt good. And we met again for coffee, and she invited me over to her place. And we ended up making love.

MS. BELKNAP: Was that the first time you'd made love to a woman?

MS. GRIFFITH: No. But it was the first time I got to be the experienced one.

MS. BELKNAP: And when did Beck tell you she had never made love to a woman?

MS. GRIFFITH: Right before our first time.

ELVA GRIFFITH: The church teaches that homosexuality is a sin. But we're all sinners, and God loves us all equally. And we love our daughter. It's not for us to judge her.

MS. BELKNAP: You decided together to keep your relationship a secret. Tell us about that.

MS. GRIFFITH: We both had our reasons. Beck wasn't ready to come out to her parents. I don't think anyone in her circle knew that about her, and she was a shy person by nature.

MS. BELKNAP: And your reasons for wanting to keep it a secret?

MS. GRIFFITH: I was trying to build a social media following and didn't want that label.

MS. BELKNAP: You felt a lesbian relationship would impede your social media growth?

MS. GRIFFITH: I don't consider myself lesbian. If I posted I was in a relationship with another woman, that's how people would see me, and that's all they would see.

MS. BELKNAP: You thought you'd be more acceptable to followers if you were heterosexual?

MS. GRIFFITH: No, I just didn't want to put out anything sexual. That wasn't my message. I was about fitness and lifestyle. Sexuality's not my thing online.

MS. BELKNAP: Now tell us about the first time you met Sandy Finch.

JAKE CROWE, *INYO REGISTER*: You could hear the pace of the questioning build, the testimony was coming to the reason she was on trial. The gallery was silent and you could feel the electricity.

MS. GRIFFITH: I'd been attracted to guys before. I'd slept with guys before. With Sandy, there was so much more. On my way home from the restaurant that night, a little voice was saying this could be a game changer.

MS. BELKNAP: And as you found yourself spending more time with Sandy and your feelings for him deepened, what effect did it have on your relationship with Beck?

MS. GRIFFITH: It wasn't like, *Oh, now I like this guy and I don't like Beck anymore.* I loved Beck. For a while I was able to keep them apart in my mind. Each had their own space and I didn't let them cross over.

MS. BELKNAP: You were seeing both at the same time without the other knowing it?

MS. GRIFFITH: Beck was my girlfriend, I wasn't ready to break up with her. But something kept drawing me back to Sandy. He introduced me to his friends, people I had a lot in common with. Some were represented by my uncle's company. I'm sorry, the answer is yes, I was seeing both at the same time—and neither knew about the other.
MS. BELKNAP: When and how did Beck find out you'd cheated on her with Sandy Finch?

SAMSON GRIFFITH: Sandy did not come to court other than the day he testified. He knew it would be painful for Cleo to have this stuff coming out with him sitting there. He was getting his experience of the trial through the media.

MS. GRIFFITH: She came across photos of me with Sandy on Facebook, and she caught me in a lie. When I walked through the door of her apartment, she attacked me.
MS. BELKNAP: How did she attack you?
MS. GRIFFITH: She started screaming at me. Then she hit me—slapped me in the face.
MS. BELKNAP: Did you hit her back?
MS. GRIFFITH: No, I could never. I've never—it's not me.
MS. BELKNAP: What happened then?
MS. GRIFFITH: I was upset, I felt blindsided. I told her I was sorry and that I was confused and didn't know what I wanted.
MS. BELKNAP: Did you stay or did you go?
MS. GRIFFITH: I told her I needed time to think everything through. I'd do the right thing, but first I needed a few days to get my head straight. And I left.
MS. BELKNAP: And what did you do then?
MS. GRIFFITH: I drove up the coast to Santa Barbara to give myself space.
MS. BELKNAP: Did you see Sandy during this time?

MS. GRIFFITH: No, I was by myself.

MS. BELKNAP: And during this time, did you come up with an idea for how to solve the Beck/Sandy problem?

MS. GRIFFITH: I was looking at the news feed on my phone and saw an article about a canoe accident on a lake in upstate New York, where two people drowned. And for a moment I thought, *That's the solution.* Because I knew Beck couldn't swim.

BRIAN BURLEIGH, ASSISTANT D.A.: I had to stifle a gasp—what? We hadn't known Rebecca couldn't swim. Is the defendant going to confess now? What the heck's going on here?

MS. BELKNAP: Are you saying that's when you decided to drown Beck?

MS. GRIFFITH: No, that's when I knew I'd gone too far. This is crazy, I can't even start to think this way. It made me realize I had to face Beck and tell her we were over and I was going to be with Sandy. I called her and asked if I could come over to talk to her.

MS. BELKNAP: So you went back to her apartment and what happened?

MS. GRIFFITH: My mind was made up a hundred percent to break up with her. When I came in and we sat on the couch, she had this odd look on her face. She said, "Before you say anything, I have something to tell you. I just got back from Missouri where I visited a prison inmate named William Sparser. He confirmed you were in the car when he hit that little girl." And then she said, "So what did you want to tell me?"

MS. BELKNAP: And what did you tell her?

MS. GRIFFITH: I looked in her eyes and said I'd chosen her over Sandy and that the thing I wanted most in the world was to marry her.

MS. BELKNAP: Was that the truth?

MS. GRIFFITH: No. It was not. What I was really thinking was, *I changed my mind, Beck. You are going to drown, and that's how I'm going to solve my problem.*

JAKE CROWE, *INYO REGISTER*: And like on cue, Judge Oberwaltzer called recess for the day. Nobody in the gallery moved. Then the judge asked the bailiff to clear the courtroom.

DUNCAN MCMILLAN: *The night after Cleo's first day of testimony, I was inundated with calls from friends and colleagues around the world—the word was out I was making a documentary. I knew there was international interest in the trial, but now the defendant was actually testifying, it ignited a whole new level of engagement. I heard from the BBC, New Delhi TV, DN Stockholm, KBS in South Korea, on and on. They wanted to know what it was like to be in the courtroom on Cleo Day One. Would I be willing to do a video chat to preview Cleo Day Two? I turned down the interviews and said they'd be welcome to license our series once it was ready.*

Here was a twenty-five-year-old social media personality whose biggest platform in her life would not be YouTube or Instagram or Twitter—it would be the witness stand.

> **MS. BELKNAP:** Good morning, Cleo. Yesterday was a big day.
> **MS. GRIFFITH:** It sure was.
> **MS. BELKNAP:** Ready to do it again?
> **MS. GRIFFITH:** I think so. Yes, I am.

FRED HITE, COUNTY SHERIFF: Must've had twenty people ask if I could get them a seat in the courtroom for her testimony. I said, "Just watch the damn thing on your computer."

> **MS. GRIFFITH:** We looked at Serene Lake online together and made a plan to drive up there . . .

ERIN NEWCOMB, CHIEF DEPUTY: Had to stand at the back of the courtroom, but I wasn't missing that.

MS. GRIFFITH: We pulled in and parked and I let her go rent the canoe . . .

TITUS ALDEN: That day was the worst for Grace and me.

MS. GRIFFITH: Her life vest came off and my arms were around her and . . .

OWEN MASON, DISTRICT ATTORNEY: There the defense paused and wheeled into court a seventy-two-inch Ultra HD screen for their CGI Evidence Simulation. Of course they knew we'd vigorously object. The judge called a recess and ordered us to his chambers.

ALANA BELKNAP, DEFENSE COUNSEL: The software was created by Sim-Tech, a company whose computer-generated evidence has been accepted in dozens of trials, and this particular simulation had been vetted by three independent medical experts.

BRIAN BURLEIGH, ASSISTANT D.A.: Come *on,* it was a company that did visual effects for movies and television. The defense knew they couldn't rely on their client's testimony. They needed to give the jury Hollywood-style visual aids to have any chance of convincing them.

REUBEN JEPHSON, CO-DEFENSE COUNSEL: We showed the simulation to the judge and the prosecution. Since it came down to those moments in the canoe and how precisely the injuries to Beck's face and head happened, and given the visuals followed the exact details of the incident as Cleo had been telling it over and over, it should absolutely be seen by the jury.

OWEN MASON, DISTRICT ATTORNEY: We had discussed conducting our own reenactment but knew the defense would never allow it. Then, because they wanted to show their computer simulation, it provided an opportunity for a horse trade.

BRIAN BURLEIGH, ASSISTANT D.A.: "We'll let you show yours if you let us show ours." And they said okay, and the judge said fine, and we went back into the courtroom.

> MS. BELKNAP: What caused you to back off from Beck at that exact moment?
> MS. GRIFFITH: My body just quit me. I lost all power in my arms and legs. I couldn't do it. I could not harm her. I felt nauseous and stepped back and fell into my seat.

JAKE CROWE, *INYO REGISTER*: At first the screen was set up for the jury in a way that the gallery and the pool camera couldn't see it. The judge heard the grumbling and called the attorneys to the bar.

REUBEN JEPHSON, CO-DEFENSE COUNSEL: The bailiff and the deputies were the ones who positioned the screen, not us. The judge said either set the screen where it's visible to the gallery or he'd have it wheeled back to the jury room, show them how to hit pause and rewind, and shut the door.

BRIAN BURLEIGH, ASSISTANT D.A.: The defense never wants the narrative out of their control, so they dragged the screen around until the whole courtroom could see it. The spectators in back had to stand up, but the judge allowed it.

> MS. BELKNAP: Then what happened, Cleo?
> MS. GRIFFITH: The truth came pouring out of me. I told her I was in love with Sandy, and there was no way I could marry her. We were over, and I'd just deal with whatever she posted on social media about me.
> MS. BELKNAP: How did Beck react to that?
> MS. GRIFFITH: She got really angry and came at me. I grabbed my paddle

and held it up to protect myself. She stumbled on that center bar and fell face-first into the shaft of my paddle.
MS. BELKNAP: Would you demonstrate with your hands how you were holding the paddle?
MS. GRIFFITH: The paddle was on my right, I grabbed it with my right hand, then my left, and braced my arms in front of me.
MS. BELKNAP: And then?
MS. GRIFFITH: Her face hit the shaft hard, and she fell to the side and hit her head on the rim of the canoe. And that impact made the canoe tip over, and we both went into the water.

JAKE CROWE, *INYO REGISTER*: The simulation was all done from Cleo's point of view. They added realistic sound effects of the canoe and water. Beck's face was rendered somewhat out of focus, on purpose. To see a super-realistic Beck would have been even more painful for her parents and might have unfavorably influenced the jury.

MS. BELKNAP: What happened when you fell into the water?
MS. GRIFFITH: I went down way over my head and my body was shocked by how cold the lake was. I swallowed water and my instincts told me to get back up to the air. And I kicked up, broke the surface, swallowed more water, coughed it out, and grabbed the side of the canoe.

BRIAN BURLEIGH, ASSISTANT D.A.: The clarity of the picture was like looking through a window. It wasn't cheap to produce, and there was the defense's advantage. They could outspend us by whatever amount they needed to.

MS. BELKNAP: Looking at the simulation on screen, is that how you remember it?
MS. GRIFFITH: Exactly how I remember it.

SAMSON GRIFFITH: Yes, the infamous tech glitch.

MR. MASON: Objection. The video is repeating over and over, there's no need for that, they should stop it. Your Honor?
THE COURT: Mr. Jephson?

SAMSON GRIFFITH: Reuben was working the remote and had gone back to the moment when Beck's face hit the shaft of the paddle. And the CGI got stuck in a loop. Whether a glitch or accidentally on purpose, I can't say, but those images of Beck stumbling, hitting it face-first, then falling and hitting her head on the edge of the canoe repeated at least a dozen times.

MS. BELKNAP: When you looked around for Beck, what did you see?
MS. GRIFFITH: I didn't see her anywhere. I swam around to the other side of the canoe, thinking maybe she'd grabbed on, but she wasn't there. I ducked under the canoe, searched the inside from one end to the other. I swam around in a wider circle, calling her name, diving down and looking all around. She wasn't anywhere.

ERIN NEWCOMB, CHIEF DEPUTY: What was on that screen exactly mirrored what she was describing. We can't know for certain what she did or didn't do at that point because there were no witnesses and no physical evidence to support her story. But as a visual presentation, it was impressive.

MS. BELKNAP: How long did you keep looking for her?
MS. GRIFFITH: I don't know. Some moments felt speeded up, some like slow motion. I know that I swam around the canoe two or three times, checked underneath again, swam out farther in the lake—but the water was ice cold and my legs were cramping.

BRIAN BURLEIGH, ASSISTANT D.A.: And the defendant wept. As witness-stand weepers go, she was top five, maybe top three. Was she believable? Not to us.

JAKE CROWE, *INYO REGISTER*: Then came the defense's toughest challenge—to explain why Cleo ran away from the scene.

> MS. GRIFFITH: I got to shore and I was crying and shivering. It felt like I was inside a bad dream I couldn't wake up from. I knew if Beck hadn't come up by then, she wasn't going to make it. I thought about running back to the boathouse and telling them. But a voice inside my head was saying, *No one will believe you. They'll think you killed her. They'll arrest you, you'll go to jail, you'll lose everything. And you'll never see Sandy again.*
> MS. BELKNAP: So what did you do?
> MS. GRIFFITH: I shoved the whole experience inside a closet and locked the door.
> MS. BELKNAP: You were able to completely put the experience out of your mind?
> MS. GRIFFITH: No, it was banging on the door. I just kept turning my attention to other things—positive things, happy things. Like being in nature with my friends and being physically close with my boyfriend. I kept trying to convince myself that I was fine, that everything would be fine.

JAKE CROWE, *INYO REGISTER*: The defense's psychologist testified that Cleo had a strong ability to compartmentalize emotional trauma. That's what she'd used to survive her childhood, her sister's overdose, the car crash, her gang rape. In those fitness videos she presents herself as this blissful, together person. You see no hint of any of this other stuff.

> MS. BELKNAP: How do you see those actions you took now, looking back at them?

MS. GRIFFITH: I totally messed up. It was a terrible mistake not to go for help right away. I knew I hadn't caused her death, but I was afraid people wouldn't believe me and I'd lose everything.
MS. BELKNAP: *Everything* meaning your social media following, your endorsement deals, your income, your reputation, your boyfriend?
MS. GRIFFITH: All of it. I'd fall back to the bottom and never be able to build it back up again. I'd be tainted forever. Once you're canceled, you're canceled. But what I did was wrong in every way. And I'd give anything to go back and do it differently.

SANDY FINCH: I didn't watch her on the stand. I hiked up to the top of Temescal Canyon, found a spot where I could be alone, looked out over the ocean, and listened to the livestream. When she said, "I'd give anything to go back and do it differently," I said out loud, "Me too. Anything."

JAKE CROWE, *INYO REGISTER*: After a day and a half of examining the life story of Cleo Ray, in all its dark twists and turns, from the beginning to paddling the canoe out on Serene Lake to the present moment, the defense rested.

And now it was the prosecution's turn to cross-examine.

BRIAN BURLEIGH, ASSISTANT D.A.: The judge called an afternoon recess. He gave us until the next morning to get ready.

ERIN NEWCOMB, CHIEF DEPUTY: We got started around two in the afternoon and barely made it in time for when court started again at nine A.M. Eighteen hours of nonstop prep.

OWEN MASON, DISTRICT ATTORNEY: It would be a complex cross. There were a lot of details to keep organized. But I could trust in the Holy Spirit to guide me and in the image of the Aldens standing over their murdered daughter to motivate me. Justice was on our side, I felt confident in that.

SAMSON GRIFFITH: Most thought the real fight would be between Mason and Alana. But the main event turned out to be the Inyo County district attorney versus Cleo Ray on the witness stand.

> MR. MASON: Good morning, Ms. Griffith. Do you mind if I call you Ms. Griffith?
> MS. GRIFFITH: That's fine. Good morning.
> MR. MASON: As I take you through these questions, I will be trying to make a distinction between what's true and what's not true. You've admitted in your testimony that you lied consistently and abundantly to just about everybody.
> MS. BELKNAP: Objection, argumentative. Is the prosecutor making his closing argument or asking a question?
> MR. MASON: Pardon me, Your Honor, here is the question. When you told Rebecca you were choosing her over Sandy and wanted to marry her, was that the truth or a lie?
> MS. GRIFFITH: A lie.
> MR. MASON: And when you told Rebecca you wanted to take her up to the mountains to make the marriage proposal on a lake, was that the truth or a lie?
> MS. GRIFFITH: A lie.
> MR. MASON: And when you bought the bottle of champagne with Rebecca to celebrate your engagement up at the lake, was that true or were you lying?
> MS. GRIFFITH: Lying.

JAKE CROWE, *INYO REGISTER*: Cleo was the opposite of defensive, admitting to lie after lie.

> **MR. MASON:** And the first story you told about going up to the lake to break up with Rebecca and let her down gently, truth or lie?
>
> **MS. GRIFFITH:** Lie.
>
> **MR. MASON:** And the real reason you told her you wanted to marry her and take her up to the lake to propose, the real reason was that you intended to drown her, truth or lie?
>
> **MS. GRIFFITH:** But I didn't . . .
>
> **MR. MASON:** You intended to drown her, truth or lie!
>
> **MS. BELKNAP:** Objection. The prosecutor is badgering her.
>
> **THE COURT:** Soften your tone, Mr. Mason.
>
> **MR. MASON:** When you made the plan to go to Serene Lake with Rebecca, was your intent to drown her?
>
> **MS. GRIFFITH:** Yes.
>
> **MR. MASON:** And when you packed and loaded up the car and drove off with her to the lake, was your intent to drown her?
>
> **MS. GRIFFITH:** Yes.
>
> **MR. MASON:** And on the drive up, while you were playing music and singing and talking about your future together, was your intent to drown her?
>
> **MS. GRIFFITH:** Yes.

SAMSON GRIFFITH: I started feeling shaky again on Alana's strategy. Cleo had lied to everybody and planned a murder. Mason amplified that for the jury by limiting her to one-and-two-word answers. Punching and landing, *bam-bam, bam-bam*. Then he doubles down with their counter-simulation play.

> **MR. MASON:** Your Honor, may Mr. Burleigh and the deputies bring in the canoe?

JAKE CROWE, *INYO REGISTER*: The defense and prosecution had agreed to it behind closed doors, but not made it public. The first clue was the two-foot-high plywood platform that had been set up in front of the witness stand before the court opened.

ERIN NEWCOMB, CHIEF DEPUTY: Those risers came from Mrs. Peoples's eighth-grade choir class.

SAMSON GRIFFITH: So all heads turn to the door of the courtroom, and first comes this big wooden rack built with two-by-fours, carried by two deputies. Next comes this cherry-red sixteen-foot-long canoe, carried by a deputy at each end, holding it up above their heads. No one had been told this was coming, and there was a noticeable murmur of surprise from the gallery.

BRIAN BURLEIGH, ASSISTANT D.A.: We'd done a dry run at five in the morning, so we knew everything fit together. The canoe was at the right level and stable. The defense went high tech with their visual effects. We were old school and proud of it.

MR. MASON: Ms. Griffith, thank you for your patience. Let's resume, shall we? Now, what you see here is the same canoe rented by Rebecca Alden on the day of her death. It's a Mad River Canoe, two-person Explorer model. It has a length of sixteen feet, a width of thirty-five inches, and a depth of fourteen inches. Ms. Griffith, do you recognize this as the canoe you and Rebecca paddled out into Serene Lake?
MS. GRIFFITH: I wouldn't know if it was the exact one, but if you say so, okay.
MR. MASON: In addition, there were two wooden paddles made from Douglas fir. Two nylon life vests with double front buckles. Also please note the bottle of Moët & Chandon, unopened. These items look familiar to you, Ms. Griffith?

MS. GRIFFITH: They look close enough.

MR. MASON: Good. Now, would you please step over here and show the jury exactly where you were sitting as you and Rebecca pushed off from the dock?

JAKE CROWE, *INYO REGISTER*: Mason took Cleo's hand and helped her step into the canoe. He actually looked chivalrous at that moment. As she settled into the rear seat, he stepped over to an enlarged map of Serene Lake that had been placed on an easel between the witness stand and the jury box. He picked up a wooden pointing stick that looked like it hadn't been used since the 1970s.

MR. MASON: Take a look at this map of Serene Lake, Ms. Griffith. Here's where you drove in, here is the boathouse, and here is the dock you launched from. Are you oriented now in terms of how you remember it?
MS. GRIFFITH: Yes.
MR. MASON: Hang on, there's something missing in the canoe. Chief Deputy?

ERIN NEWCOMB, CHIEF DEPUTY: Got to say, I was proud of my craftsmanship. Half-inch foam core with a photo image front and back, life-size to within the inch. The pictures we used came from her parents. For the front we picked one where she was smiling. Rebecca had a pretty smile.

REUBEN JEPHSON, CO-DEFENSE COUNSEL: The prosecution had said nothing about placing a foam-board cutout of Beck in the front seat of the canoe. That was their October surprise. Alana and I leaned our heads together and discussed objecting, but on what grounds? So we kept looking supportively at Cleo, because that was their whole game, getting her to react.

MR. MASON: And this is where Rebecca was sitting, in the bow or front seat of the canoe?

MS. GRIFFITH: Yes.

BRIAN BURLEIGH, ASSISTANT D.A.: We positioned the cutout so the defendant could see only the back of Rebecca, what she would have seen from her seat. And the foam core was thick enough to hang a life vest on.

MR. MASON: Ms. Griffith, you were wearing your life vest when you paddled out into the lake, correct? Would you mind putting the life vest on, so we have everything as it was?

REUBEN JEPHSON, CO-DEFENSE COUNSEL: Cleo looked at us, like "Should I?" We nodded. This was the deal we made, and we had to live with it.

MR. MASON: Now Ms. Griffith, does everything look correctly positioned to you? Where the champagne bottle is placed? Where the paddles are located?

MS. GRIFFITH: Pretty much.

MR. MASON: When you started out from the dock, did you have a destination in mind?

MS. GRIFFITH: Yes. Looking at the lake online, I'd seen a small cove up there to the left.

MR. MASON: Here?

MS. GRIFFITH: Yes.

MR. MASON: And you chose that location why?

MS. GRIFFITH: Because it looked like a secluded spot.

MR. MASON: What was the reason you wanted a secluded spot?

MS. GRIFFITH: Less likely to draw attention.

MR. MASON: Less likely to draw attention when you threw Rebecca into the lake?

MS. BELKNAP: Objection!

MR. MASON: I withdraw it. How long approximately did it take you to reach this cove?

MS. GRIFFITH: Ten, fifteen minutes.

MR. MASON: And when you'd reached this secluded cove, what did you do?

MS. GRIFFITH: I stopped paddling and said this looked like a good spot to do it.

MR. MASON: To do what?

MS. GRIFFITH: To have me propose.

MR. MASON: That's what Rebecca assumed you were going to do.

MS. GRIFFITH: Yes.

MR. MASON: And now can you show the jury what transpired in the canoe leading up to the point it tipped over?

SAMSON GRIFFITH: That's what it sounds like when a hundred people all hold their breath.

MS. GRIFFITH: I took off my life vest.

MR. MASON: Beg your pardon. You know how to swim, correct?

MS. GRIFFITH: Correct.

MR. MASON: Continue, please.

MS. GRIFFITH: I got up from my seat, came forward, kneeled behind her, and started kissing her neck.

MR. MASON: I understand it's awkward with the cutout. Do the best you can.

MS. GRIFFITH: I reached under her life vest to touch her breasts and I kept kissing her. Then she unbuckled her life vest and took it off herself.

MR. MASON: That was your goal, correct? To get her life vest off?

MS. GRIFFITH: Yes.

MR. MASON: How were you planning to get her into the water?

MS. GRIFFITH: I didn't have a plan.

MR. MASON: You knew you were going to drown her.

MS. GRIFFITH: I didn't have an exact plan. I thought I would just tip the canoe over.

MR. MASON: You had all that time and hadn't thought through the most critical part?

MS. GRIFFITH: No, I hadn't planned the actual . . . doing it.

MR. MASON: Let me read back your testimony: "What I was really thinking was, *I changed my mind, Beck. You are going to drown, and that's how I'm going to solve my problem.*" Now you're asking us to believe you never visualized how you would drown her?

MS. GRIFFITH: I was going to tip the canoe over. That's the extent of the how. But as I had my arms around her, everything came to a stop.

MR. MASON: What stopped you?

MS. GRIFFITH: As I said, my body stopped me. It shut down. I totally froze and dropped my arms. I just couldn't do it. I couldn't hurt Beck.

MR. MASON: And what did Rebecca do at that point?

MS. GRIFFITH: She turned around to face me and asked what was wrong.

ERIN NEWCOMB, CHIEF DEPUTY: The district attorney nodded to me, and I turned the cutout around so it was facing her.

ALANA BELKNAP, DEFENSE COUNSEL: They wanted the jury to see Cleo's reaction when Beck's face was twelve inches away. How could she not react under those circumstances? I mean, really.

MR. MASON: What happened next?

MS. GRIFFITH: I backed away from her and dropped into my seat.

MR. MASON: Will you show us?

MS. BELKNAP: Objection, the defendant could hurt herself.

ERIN NEWCOMB, CHIEF DEPUTY: It was too late for the objection. Cleo had already taken a step and tripped backward over that center bar. Landed right on her bottom, short of the seat.

THE ANATOMY OF DESIRE

MR. MASON: Are you okay? I'm sorry.

MS. GRIFFITH: I'm okay, I'm fine.

MR. MASON: Ms. Griffith, as you moved back, you tripped over the center bar, the yoke as it's called. Yet in your previous testimony, you never mentioned that.

MS. GRIFFITH: I don't remember tripping over it.

MR. MASON: Don't remember? Falling like that would have upset the canoe, wouldn't it?

MS. GRIFFITH: I don't remember, I only remember dropping into my seat.

MR. MASON: But if you tripped over the yoke and fell on the bottom of the canoe, you would have had to push yourself back up to your seat, correct?

MS. GRIFFITH: I don't remember that. Maybe I stepped over the bar.

MR. MASON: With your back to it? You couldn't see it. It was behind you. Yet you had the presence of mind to carefully step over the yoke as you moved backward?

MS. GRIFFITH: I don't know. I just know I didn't fall backward, I dropped into my seat.

MR. MASON: You said you don't remember tripping. Now are you saying you *do* remember not tripping over the yoke, as you just did here? Could it be that you didn't trip and fall backward because you did not go back to your seat? Because you stayed up front to make sure Rebecca went into the water?

MS. BELKNAP: Objection, Your Honor!

THE COURT: Mr. Mason, I heard three questions in there.

MR. MASON: All withdrawn. After you found your seat, Ms. Griffith, what happened then?

MS. GRIFFITH: I started telling Beck the truth, that I wasn't in love with her anymore, that I couldn't marry her.

MR. MASON: After all this time deceiving her, planning to drown her, you do a sudden one-eighty and start telling the truth?

MS. GRIFFITH: Yes.

MR. MASON: Did you tell Rebecca you had intended to drown her?

MS. GRIFFITH: No, I said I couldn't be with her, that I wanted to be with Sandy.

MR. MASON: Did Rebecca ask, "Then why did you bring me up here?" Would've been a natural question, wouldn't it?

MS. GRIFFITH: I was speaking really fast and didn't give her a chance to say anything.

MR. MASON: What happened next?

MS. GRIFFITH: She got really angry and came at me.

MR. MASON: Would you be more specific about how she came at you?

MS. GRIFFITH: She got up from her seat and lunged toward me with her fingers out like she wanted to claw my face. And she stumbled over that bar.

MR. MASON: The bar that was right in front of her? She stumbled moving forward over the same bar that you magically avoided while moving backward?

MS. BELKNAP: Objection.

MR. MASON: Withdrawn. So your testimony is that Rebecca got up from her seat, lunged at you, tripped on the yoke, and fell toward you. Was her life vest on or off at this moment?

MS. GRIFFITH: Off.

MR. MASON: Her lunging must have upset the stability of the canoe. You've told us Rebecca couldn't swim, and she didn't have her life vest on, so what you're describing would have been extremely reckless of her, yes?

MS. GRIFFITH: She wasn't thinking, she was just reacting.

MR. MASON: Reacting in a way that endangered her life?

MS. GRIFFITH: She was filled with rage.

MR. MASON: Did she verbally express her rage?

MS. GRIFFITH: You mean like say, "I'm so angry at you"? No.

MR. MASON: You interpreted her actions as anger, but she made no verbal communication expressing anger. What if she was coming forward to embrace you?

MS. GRIFFITH: No.

MR. MASON: You were passionately kissing and fondling her moments before, yes?

MS. GRIFFITH: When I said I didn't love her and wasn't going to marry her, her feelings changed. I could see her become very upset.

MR. MASON: Would you show us what you did in reaction to Rebecca lunging at you?

BRIAN BURLEIGH, ASSISTANT D.A.: We'd been doing our own simulations into the wee hours of the morning. Everyone took multiple turns trying to do what the defendant claimed to have done.

MR. MASON: You're telling us that as Rebecca lunged at you without warning, you had time to locate your paddle, grab it with both hands, bring it up and brace your arms defensively before she reached you?

MS. GRIFFITH: The paddle was by my seat—I instinctively grabbed it.

MR. MASON: Your testimony is that you didn't reach for the paddle until after Rebecca began lunging at you. And you're telling us you had time to put your hands on the paddle, grip it, lift it, and brace your arms before Rebecca hurtled across a span of not more than six feet?

MS. GRIFFITH: Yes, that's what happened.

SAMSON GRIFFITH: I caught one of the jury members shaking her head right then. I thought—I won't tell you what I thought.

MR. MASON: Your testimony is that Rebecca hit the shaft of the paddle face-first, then fell and hit her head on the edge of the canoe. Did she fall to the right or the left?

MS. GRIFFITH: To my right.

MR. MASON: You hesitated.

MS. GRIFFITH: I needed a moment to visualize it.

MR. MASON: And the force of her falling on the edge of the canoe caused it to tip sideways to your right?

MS. GRIFFITH: Yes, it caused me to lose my balance and fall to my right.

JAKE CROWE, *INYO REGISTER*: We'd done our own informal simulation in the pressroom. According to a stopwatch, the whole confrontation must have transpired in under a minute.

MR. MASON: You and Rebecca fell into the water at almost the same time?

MS. GRIFFITH: She went in first and I followed right after.

MR. MASON: You hit the water on top of where she fell in?

MS. GRIFFITH: To the side of where she fell.

MR. MASON: But within a foot or two?

MS. GRIFFITH: Or three.

MR. MASON: And you knew she couldn't swim?

MS. GRIFFITH: Yes.

MR. MASON: And you knew she wasn't wearing her life vest?

MS. GRIFFITH: Yes.

MR. MASON: And you testified that you went down into the water, then kicked to the surface and took a breath of air?

MS. GRIFFITH: Yes.

MR. MASON: At what point did you think you should look for Rebecca?

MS. GRIFFITH: Immediately.

MR. MASON: Immediately. So you fall in the water, sink down several feet, kick to the surface, and within a second or two, you have it in mind to find Rebecca. How many seconds would you say elapsed between when you hit the water and when you started looking for her?

MS. GRIFFITH: Maybe ten, maybe less.

MR. MASON: Any idea how long it takes for a healthy adult to drown?

MS. GRIFFITH: No idea.

THE ANATOMY OF DESIRE

MR. MASON: According to multiple medical sources, it can take as little as sixty seconds. Which means you had at least fifty seconds to save her life. Where was your first instinct to look for her?

MS. GRIFFITH: I thought she might be holding on to the other side of the canoe.

MR. MASON: That would assume Rebecca was able to kick to the surface, and since she couldn't swim, wouldn't it be more likely she'd still be under the water?

MS. GRIFFITH: I looked underwater, too. I looked under the canoe and all around it.

MR. MASON: Ms. Griffith, here are some high-resolution photos of the area of Serene Lake where your canoe turned over and Rebecca drowned. These were taken on the day it happened, within a few hours. Does this water look pretty clear to you?

MS. GRIFFITH: I didn't see her in the water.

MR. MASON: My question is, looking at these photos taken on the day your canoe turned over and Rebecca drowned, does this water look clear to you?

MS. GRIFFITH: Those were taken from *above* the water. I was *in* the water.

MR. MASON: Okay, let's try it your way. From where you were in the water, how far down could you see?

MS. GRIFFITH: I don't know, I didn't measure it.

MR. MASON: Could you see down to your feet?

MS. GRIFFITH: Yes.

MR. MASON: Could you see down below your feet?

MS. GRIFFITH: I don't know how far down I could see.

MR. MASON: Could you see down to the bottom?

MS. GRIFFITH: No.

MR. MASON: Did you try swimming down to the bottom to find Rebecca?

MS. GRIFFITH: I dove down, but I didn't reach the bottom.

SAMSON GRIFFITH: Where they went into the lake, it was twenty-five feet deep. There's no way Cleo could have gone down that far without bursting an eardrum.

MR. MASON: In your testimony you stated that at some point you gave up searching for Rebecca and swam to shore. In minutes, how much time elapsed between the canoe turning over, your searching for and not finding Rebecca, and your swimming to shore?

MS. GRIFFITH: I'm not sure. The water was so cold I couldn't stand it any longer, so maybe ten, twelve minutes.

MR. MASON: And when you reached the shore, did it occur to you that you should call for help?

MS. BELKNAP: Your Honor, if the prosecutor has completed his questioning involving the canoe, my client should be able to resume her place on the witness stand.

MR. MASON: I will have more about the canoe. Isn't it better she not go back and forth?

THE COURT: Overruled. The witness can continue to testify from where she is.

MR. MASON: Ms. Griffith, did it occur to you that Rebecca might still be saved if you got help in time?

MS. GRIFFITH: No, I thought she was dead.

MR. MASON: But if you didn't see her, and you couldn't find her, and you looked everywhere and she was gone, you could not be a hundred percent sure she was dead, could you?

MS. GRIFFITH: Not a hundred percent.

MR. MASON: If only seconds before you'd been so intent on helping her, why didn't you call for help then?

MS. GRIFFITH: Because I got scared.

MR. MASON: Scared of Rebecca being revived and accusing you of trying to kill her?

MS. BELKNAP: Objection!

THE ANATOMY OF DESIRE

MR. MASON: I'll rephrase. Ms. Griffith, when you swam to shore and didn't call for help because you were scared, what were you scared of?
MS. GRIFFITH: Of being blamed for what happened.
MR. MASON: You didn't go for help on behalf of Rebecca Alden. Instead you did what?
MS. GRIFFITH: I left.
MR. MASON: Where did you go?
MS. GRIFFITH: To my boyfriend.
MR. MASON: Now that you bring it up: Was it a coincidence Sandy Finch and your friends were up in the mountains the same weekend you were planning to drown Rebecca in Serene Lake?
MS. GRIFFITH: Coincidence?
MR. MASON: You made the plan with Rebecca to drive up to the lake knowing that Sandy and your other friends were going to Mammoth for a camping weekend. So leaving from Serene Lake to go join them was part of your plan all along, yes?
MS. GRIFFITH: I knew Sandy would be up there, and I did go to meet him.
MR. MASON: You told him you'd meet him in Mammoth before you left for Serene Lake with Rebecca, yes?
MS. GRIFFITH: Yes.

JAKE CROWE, *INYO REGISTER*: Mason kept her in the canoe for the optics, then grilled her about going off with her boyfriend while Rebecca was dead at the bottom of a lake. No way around her looking extremely callous and duplicitous or in a state of morbid denial. This was always going to be the defense's Achilles' heel.

MR. MASON: Ms. Griffith, you may take your seat back on the stand.
MS. GRIFFITH: Thank you.
MR. MASON: Ms. Griffith, here is the problem I need your help with. You went up to the lake with the intent to kill Rebecca Alden. Everything was going according to your plan. You got her into a canoe, made sure she

was seated right in front of you. You had to get her life vest off, so you came forward and pretended to be affectionate so that she—or you—would unbuckle it. The moment her vest came off, that was your green light. And according to our medical experts, Rebecca suffered a blow to the bridge of her nose and right brow . . .

SAMSON GRIFFITH: I see Mason stepping into the canoe, and I'm thinking, *The son of a bitch is going to do it.*

MR. MASON: . . . the injuries indicated an offensive rather than defensive blow, which matches with everything you've told us except the part about you losing your nerve. So my question is, as soon as Rebecca's vest came off, did you not reach back, grab your paddle, stand up, and swing it at her head with all your strength?

REUBEN JEPHSON, CO-DEFENSE COUNSEL: Alana and I were stunned. He totally took advantage of the moment. That was shameless grandstanding in front of the jury.

JAKE CROWE, *INYO REGISTER*: Oh, it was a cheap shot. But as cheap shots go, it was pretty spectacular.

BRIAN BURLEIGH, ASSISTANT D.A.: Owen had not told any of us what he was going to do. Was I upset he did it? Not at all.

ERIN NEWCOMB, CHIEF DEPUTY: Our D.A. took a full baseball swing with that wooden paddle and demolished my beautiful artwork—*bam!*

> **THE COURT:** Mr. Mason! That kind of conduct has no place in this courtroom.
> **MR. MASON:** I'm sorry, Your Honor, I truly am. But the question still stands, Ms. Griffith. Isn't that what really happened?
> **MS. GRIFFITH:** No, it was not, no, that's not what happened. No.

BRIAN BURLEIGH, ASSISTANT D.A.: Owen's cross-examination will be taught to aspiring prosecutors until the cows come home. It was a masterpiece.

MR. MASON: Just a couple more questions, Ms. Griffith. I do appreciate you bearing with me. Now, would it be fair to say that over the last ten years, since arriving in Los Angeles and starting a new life, you were firmly on the path to achieving the things you most desired—prior to the events on Serene Lake?

MS. GRIFFITH: I'd say yes.

MR. MASON: Hundreds of thousands of followers on social media, endorsement deals, a rising income, a growing celebrity, and a man who seems like every woman's idea of a prince. Did you have those things prior to the events on Serene Lake?

MS. GRIFFITH: I did.

MR. MASON: So no matter what version of events we believe took place in that canoe, your choice to run from the scene and not tell anyone, ducking the fishermen in the woods, passing the boathouse without reporting what happened, driving away and not using your phone to notify someone—those choices set in motion all the events that followed, do you agree with that?

MS. GRIFFITH: Yes.

MR. MASON: One more question, Ms. Griffith. With all you had achieved and all you had to lose, what else would have prevented you from reporting what happened on the lake—unless it was a guilty conscience?

MS. GRIFFITH: I made a mistake. My behavior was inexcusable. But it wasn't because I'd killed Beck. It was because I was afraid I would be blamed for killing Beck.

MR. MASON: That's all I have.

SAMSON GRIFFITH: When Mason said, "That's all," the courtroom stayed dead quiet. Cleo sat there in the witness stand, white as a sheet.

Alana should have spoken right up to begin her redirect. That silence only lasted about five seconds, but by the time Alana got started, the damage was done.

JAKE CROWE, *INYO REGISTER*: The judge told the attorneys to be ready the next morning with final arguments. As I walked out of the courthouse it was getting dark and I could feel everyone's exhaustion. We'd been on this roller coaster day after day for weeks and we were all numb.

OWEN MASON, DISTRICT ATTORNEY: People in the media want to make it about winning and losing. I don't see it that way. Either justice is done or it's not. It's been that way for thousands of years. "Follow justice and justice alone, so that you may live and possess the land the Lord your God is giving you." It's an ancient obligation, and we've convoluted it into a spectator sport where all that matters is the score when the clock runs out.

BRIAN BURLEIGH, ASSISTANT D.A.: Our district attorney knows in his heart he's serving a higher purpose. And we love him for it.

REUBEN JEPHSON, CO-DEFENSE COUNSEL: Personally? I'll never regret the choice to have Cleo tell the truth.

ALANA BELKNAP, DEFENSE COUNSEL: I do like closing arguments. It's where I get to tell the whole story beginning to end and convey a perspective that is equal parts law and humanity. Yes, we're here to see our laws are followed and upheld, but we can't subtract out the human factor, or we might as well be AI robots functioning in a single dimension of rationality absent wisdom.

THE COURT: Ladies and gentlemen, I'm going to read the jury instructions first because it will provide the legal framework within which to consider the evidence and reach your verdict. After the attorneys complete their arguments, I'll finish by giving you direction about how to deliberate, what you need to do in reaching a verdict. All right? Here we go. The defendant is guilty of first-degree murder if the People have proved she acted willfully, deliberately, and with premeditation . . .

SAMSON GRIFFITH: Final round. Neither combatant was leaving anything in the locker room. These closing arguments would be a fixed point in the arc of their legal careers, that day their legacies were on the line. Maybe that's a little grand, but it's my occupational preset to see most things through a lens of drama and narrative.

MR. MASON: You heard the testimony of a medical expert who said the injuries to the bridge of Rebecca's nose and above her right eye were consistent with being hit by a wooden paddle swung horizontally, like a baseball bat. You heard further expert testimony that the wound on the back side of Rebecca's skull showed an up-to-down striking motion and was consistent with the dimensions of the blade on the paddle held in the defendant's hands. You may ask, if the defendant knew her victim couldn't swim, why didn't she just tip the boat over and let nature take its course? For the simple reason that it would have given Rebecca a chance to yell out, to make noise that would draw attention from people in the vicinity of Serene Lake. The defendant needed to stun her victim so she would go quietly into the water, so she would go straight down into the lake without resisting or crying for help. The defendant had made a conscious decision to kill Rebecca Alden. Why else would she have taken two hard swings at her head? It was insurance. It gave the defendant confidence that there would be minimal struggle, and that with her first gasp for breath, Rebecca would gulp water into her lungs. In her panic for air, Rebecca would swallow more water and her panic would escalate as water filled her lungs. Her brain, deprived of oxygen, would systematically malfunction. Imagine the terror of a young woman who experiences her lover turning on her, smashing her twice in the head, and flinging her into the water. Within seconds Rebecca would lose all motor control. For several frantic moments she would have known with utter and terrifying certainty that she was going to die. Only a minute earlier, Rebecca was living out her dream of a marriage proposal, of a beautiful, loving celebration, and now her body was suffering hypoxic convulsions as her beating heart came to a stop.

In closing, we want you to remember Rebecca Alden by her final words:

> *Hi mom. We're up in the Sierras and I want to share a secret—we're getting engaged! Please don't tell anyone, especially not dad. I want to tell him myself. I'm ready to do it, finally. You can say you heard from me at the lake and everything's fine. Please don't worry about me. This was meant to be and I've never been happier. We'll be back late Sunday. Big hug and kiss. Love you—Beck.*

JAKE CROWE, *INYO REGISTER*: Saving Beck's unsent text for the end was genius. There are things about Owen Mason I have issues with, but give the man his due. His closing argument for that trial was everything it needed to be.

MS. BELKNAP: What if my intention is to go to the grocery store, but I end up going to a restaurant instead? What if my intention is to go to the gym, but I end up riding my bike around the neighborhood instead? What if my intention is to go on vacation, but I use that money to help out my parents instead? In each example, I arrive at the result of my action—

going to a restaurant, riding my bike, and helping my parents. The going to the grocery store, to the gym, and on vacation exist only in my mind as ideas, immaterial desires, unrealized, unperformed.

    Now, if my intention is to drown Rebecca Alden, but I end up confessing the truth to her instead, I cannot be found legally guilty of my intention. Intention does not equal action. So what has the prosecution proved? That Cleo had the intention of drowning Rebecca Alden? No, because Cleo admitted this herself on direct examination. The prosecution did not get Cleo to admit a single thing that she hasn't already admitted under oath. They didn't get her to change, reframe, or rearrange anything in her account. She gave the exact same testimony under questioning by the defense and the prosecution. When it comes to the character of Cleo Ray, judge her however you will. She acknowledges making mistakes. She recognizes her behavior led to catastrophic consequences. There is no moral justification for her making love to her boyfriend while telling no one about what happened to Rebecca Alden on Serene Lake. You may find her guilty of lacking remorse, or incredible carelessness, or an incomprehensible denial of reality—but to find her guilty of first-degree murder, you must believe that the prosecution proved she transformed her intention into action. You must have no doubt that she willfully and viciously struck Ms. Alden in the face and head, then willfully and ruthlessly tipped over their canoe, then willfully and cruelly watched a woman she had loved drown.

    Cleo has been completely truthful and transparent about her intentions leading up to those moments before the canoe tipped over. Intention does not equal action. Being guilty of the desire does not equal being guilty of the deed. The prosecution presented to you its theory of the crime, but they did not prove the only thing on trial here—that Cleo transformed her intention into action in those moments on Serene Lake. The prosecution did not present a single witness who saw what happened in the canoe, nor did they present conclusive physical evidence that Cleo committed an act of violence against Rebecca. No witnesses, inconclusive physical evidence, a defendant who took the stand and under oath readily admitted she planned to commit a crime but resolutely denied she carried it out. If those things added together cause even a glimmer of reasonable doubt in your minds, then your duty as impartial seekers of fact is to find this defendant not guilty.

SAMSON GRIFFITH: I'd known Alana was a strong closer, and she did not disappoint. She was great. Expensive, but great.

DUNCAN MCMILLAN, INTERVIEWER: What was your reaction as you sat there listening to Alana's closing argument?

CLEO RAY: The words repeating inside my head were *an incomprehensible denial of reality*. I looked down at my hands on the table, saw my feet on the floor, saw the prosecutors, the judge, the jury. I felt an urgent desire to step outside of my body and observe Cleo Ray from a distance. I consciously resisted doing that. *This* was my reality. *I* was on trial for murder. And here was this exceptionally articulate woman doing everything she could to save my life.

I had to stay in this experience and not run away. I had to find a way to forgive myself—to forgive Mary Claire Griffith.

EPISODE SEVEN

GIRL LOST

You've got this! I'm so darn proud of you! Catch your breath, hydrate, and come to a comfortable seat. Deep inhale, full exhale. Now make your hands into fists, lift your chest, punch one arm forward, then the other. One two, one two, faster, like you're hitting away at the things holding you back! You're strong, you're worthy! Pause, deep inhale. Hold. Release and be still. Allow your heart to open and receive all the love you have to give yourself. You've worked hard, you deserve it.

IGTV, CleoRayFitness

CLEO RAY: It was morning and I was in the exercise yard doing modified sprints that fit the smaller space. By making myself breathless, I could shift my feelings of anxiety to feelings of physical exhaustion. The jury was starting its third day of deliberation. I couldn't think about that, so it was distraction by endorphins.

Then one of the deputies came out and said the jury had reached a verdict.

Leti was running with me when we heard. She was scheduled for release in twenty-four hours. We were joking that I'd get out before her and meet her at Glenn's food truck the next day. I'd have a plate of shrimp tacos waiting.

DUNCAN MCMILLAN, INTERVIEWER: Did you have any feeling about what the verdict would be?

CLEO RAY: I knew the true verdict in my heart. Would the jury come to the same answer? I was about fifty-fifty on that. I think Uncle Samson and Alana and Reuben were more optimistic. There were jurors they thought would vote not guilty. The foreperson of the jury was a woman with a college degree. They thought that was positive. I wasn't as optimistic, but I wasn't pessimistic, either.

I was more like, "Let's get this over with."

DUNCAN MCMILLAN, INTERVIEWER: After they told you a verdict had been reached, what did you do?

CLEO RAY: They let me rinse off in the shower. I was grateful for that. I did what I could to make my hair look nice and put on lip gloss and blush. Alana had gotten me a dark blue dress from a store in Beverly Hills, conservative yet sophisticated. Hearing a verdict that would determine the rest of my life seemed like an occasion for wearing a dress, don't you think?

DUNCAN MCMILLAN, INTERVIEWER: Describe the trip from the jail to the courtroom on that day.

CLEO RAY: Physically it wasn't different from the other thirty days I'd gone to court. I had counted the number of steps from my cell to the van, and they were exactly the same that day. When I got out of the van at the courthouse, I could see a dusting of snow on the mountaintops, first of the season.

DUNCAN MCMILLAN, INTERVIEWER: What was the vibe like when you entered the building?

CLEO RAY: Most days I tried not to look into people's faces as I went up the stairs, but that day I did and I tried to smile. People seemed receptive. Most smiled back. Whether those were smiles of hope that I'd walk out of there a free woman or of sympathy because I'd be spending the rest of my life in prison, I could not tell you. Maybe they were just returning a smile with a smile.

BAILIFF: All rise. The Superior Court of Inyo County, State of California, is now in session. The Honorable Judge Roy Oberwaltzer presiding. Please be seated.
THE COURT: Good morning, ladies and gentlemen. I understand you have reached a verdict?
JURY FOREPERSON: Yes, Your Honor, we have.

JAKE CROWE, *INYO REGISTER*: The jury had deliberated for two full days, their verdict came on the morning of the third day. We figured they'd come to it the day before and gave themselves a chance to sleep on it.

SAMSON GRIFFITH: Before turning off my phone, I checked an online gambling site that was taking bets on the verdict. Guilty was +110, not guilty, –120. Not guilty was a slim favorite. There was a lot of money being put down, more than on an NFL game. Did I bet? No. Or rather, *yes*. I'd bet pretty much everything I had on not guilty. I was all in on this hand.

REUBEN JEPHSON, CO-DEFENSE COUNSEL: I mean, we've sat a few feet away from these people day after day, looked them in the eyes a hundred times, had many moments where we thought we could read their faces. But trying to guess which way they'd go as a group, that's futile.

THE COURT: I will caution the spectators, if any disruption occurs during the reading of the verdict or the polling of the individual jurors, the bailiff will remove the offender or offenders from the courthouse, no exceptions. Understood? All right, will the defendant and her counsel stand and face the jury? Court clerk, will you read the verdict?

CLEO RAY: Breathe.

COURT CLERK: Superior Court of the State of California, county of Inyo, in the matter of *The People v. Mary Claire Griffith*. We the jury in the above titled action find the defendant guilty of murder in the first degree, in violation of Penal Code 187, a felony, upon Rebecca Grace Alden, a human being, with malice aforethought.

JAKE CROWE, *INYO REGISTER*: There were moans and groans all over. It was just shocking to hear those words. I saw Mr. and Mrs. Alden embrace. And I saw Samson Griffith hang his head. I couldn't see Cleo Ray's face because her back was turned, but I did see her shoulders tense up.

SAMSON GRIFFITH: That's it? It comes down to twelve strangers and a single word, starts with *g*, ends with *y*? I don't like this game.
  Oh, Cleo. I'm sorry for me, but I am so, so sorry for you.

THE COURT: Ladies and gentlemen of the jury, I will now poll each of you individually. Juror 1, did you find the defendant Mary Claire Griffith guilty or not guilty?
JUROR NO. 1: Guilty.
THE COURT: Juror 2, did you find the defendant Mary Claire Griffith guilty or not guilty?
JUROR NO. 2: Guilty.

CLEO RAY: I heard it once. Then I had to listen to it twelve more times. I do remember hoping each time that one of the twelve would say "Not guilty." None of them did.

ALANA BELKNAP, DEFENSE COUNSEL: Sometimes juries get it right, sometimes they get it wrong. Or were you expecting something more philosophical? Do I say they got it wrong because it went against my client? No. There was a big, inescapable shadow of reasonable doubt there, and the prosecution had not erased it. I'm not saying we didn't make mistakes. Cleo had done most everything she was accused of, except for willfully hitting Beck with the paddle and tipping over the canoe. No one saw it happen, the physical evidence wasn't conclusive, and she was a hundred percent convincing on the stand. That's all I have to say.

OWEN MASON, DISTRICT ATTORNEY: I think you can predict my answer—justice was done. Did that make it a joyous occasion? Of course not. One young person was dead, and another was going to spend the majority of her life in a penal institution. Two young women with all the promise in the world, and two tragic outcomes. Not a cause for celebration.

ELVA GRIFFITH: I grabbed Asa's hand and said, "The Lord has a plan." *The Lord has a plan.*

> **THE COURT:** Ladies and gentlemen of the jury, at this time I would like to publicly thank you for your service in this case. The burdens you have carried over these weeks were big. You kept your focus and exercised your duties with integrity and diligence. As you are well aware, there has been intense media interest in this case. I will be imploring the media to act responsibly and refrain from harassing any of you or identifying you without your consent. I can only ask you to hope for the best but expect the worst. The court is truly sorry for whatever distress you experience in this regard.

ERIN NEWCOMB, CHIEF DEPUTY: Owen Mason, Brian Burleigh, Sheriff Hite, and I went for a drink after court that day, to a bar the media wouldn't be caught dead in, the kind with dollar bills tacked to the walls. Believe me, we were not whooping it up. But we'd done our jobs, and despite the big money and celebrity factor, the system worked. We felt we'd earned respect for Inyo County. That was important to us.

DUNCAN MCMILLAN, INTERVIEWER: Where were you when you heard the verdict?

SANDY FINCH: In my kitchen, making coffee. I had a feeling it would come that morning. When they showed Cleo on TV, it was overwhelming. I didn't just feel for her, I felt her, like I was physically there next to her. I know she wasn't guilty of first-degree murder. She wasn't guilty. I mean, she was guilty of other things, but not that.

DUNCAN MCMILLAN, INTERVIEWER: Did you think about going up there and trying to see her?

SANDY FINCH: Sure, yes. But I had reporters staked out in front of my house 24/7. If I headed north on the 405, they'd follow me up there. By the time I arrived, a mob would be waiting. And the only way I could see her would be behind glass with wall phones.

So I wrote out an email, sent it to Samson, who was up there, and I asked him to print it and hand-deliver it to the jail. That way she'd have it on the same day she got the verdict.

CLEO RAY: I knew he wouldn't be there, but I still looked for him. Right after the verdict they took me out of court, down the stairs, back into the van, and drove the three blocks to the jail. Then straight back to my cell.

Leti was being so encouraging. I was in shock, but I could hear her words, and that she was making the effort to make me feel better helped a lot.

Just before dinner, the deputy delivered an envelope addressed to me from Uncle Samson. I pulled out the note, unfolded it, and saw that it was from Sandy. My heart stopped. I read it once. Then I read it again. I have it here with me.

DUNCAN MCMILLAN, INTERVIEWER: You okay with sharing it?

CLEO RAY: I hope I can keep it together. Here goes.

> *My dear Cleo—I just heard the verdict. My heart is breaking. Writing these words is hard, but I want this to reach you by end of day. I know beyond any doubt you are not guilty. I will never be able to comprehend how devastating that moment must have been for you. I love you. You don't need to know a person for a long time to say that and mean it. And I mean it.*
>
> *Though I made the choice not to come to court, I have followed you throughout this ordeal, and I'm so proud of the courage you have shown. When I was there to testify, I had to use every ounce of willpower not to reach out for you, not to rush over and take you in my arms. When I didn't come to visit you at the jail afterwards, it was my failure of courage because I knew there would be the partition between us, and I feared I wouldn't be as strong as you needed me to be. Forgive me for where I have failed you.*
>
> *I can't predict the future, our future, but I have every hope we will get another chance at being together someday. You have come through so much and survived. That's a gift that can help you continue to survive and even find a way to thrive in the face of this injustice. Your spirit is my inspiration, Cleo, and though I'm not physically there with you, I'm keeping you close in my heart. You have my love today, tomorrow, forever—Sandy*

DUNCAN MCMILLAN, INTERVIEWER: Do you remember what you were feeling when you first read that?

CLEO RAY: It made me more aware of the pain *he* was feeling. I stayed in my cell and missed dinner. Leti brought me back a sourdough roll and an apple. And I was reminded I was losing her the next day. She said, "If you want, I'll go shoplift a six-pack and get put right back here to keep you company." What a sweetheart.

You know what's weird? That night, after I was found guilty and got the letter from Sandy, that was the best night's sleep I had the whole time I was in the county jail.

DUNCAN MCMILLAN, INTERVIEWER: Because the outcome was finally settled?

CLEO RAY: That's probably it. I knew the next day would be my last of having to go in front of a gazillion people and be concerned about every gesture and facial expression, about being appropriate and not doing something dumb—unmindful—and have it cause a Twitter meltdown. I was so exhausted. I just wanted to sleep.

JAKE CROWE, *INYO REGISTER*: The state allows the defendant, now the convicted felon, to make a statement to the court at her sentencing and/or have witnesses speak on her behalf. The prosecution also has the opportunity to bring witnesses to speak on why the judge should not give any leniency.

On the final day of this drama the court was as packed as ever, and there were even more people outside than usual. They had one last chance to be part of the biggest event in Inyo County for generations, to be able to say, "I was there at the Influencer Murder Trial."

> **THE COURT:** At this time and prior to sentencing, we will hear a statement from the victim's father. Sir, you may direct your statement to the court or to the defendant, as you see fit.
> **MR. TITUS ALDEN:** Thank you, Your Honor. My name is Titus Alden, and the victim, Rebecca—we called her Beck—was our daughter. Our only daughter, our only child.

REUBEN JEPHSON, CO-DEFENSE COUNSEL: Mr. Alden turned to Cleo and stared at her. To Cleo's credit, she did not look away. She met his stare and gave back compassion. The only time she took her eyes off him was to wipe away tears.

MR. TITUS ALDEN: Not only did we lose our daughter, but we've had to sit here for weeks and listen to her deepest secrets and most private thoughts exposed to the world. And she was not present to explain or defend herself. All her words were given a meaning to fit what the defense attorneys wanted you to believe, and they made her look like an awful person. They accused her of blackmail and physical abuse and vengefulness and malice. Many times, I had to ask myself, *Who's on trial here?* Because our daughter was none of those things. She was good and gentle and caring, a wonderful person. Were any of these positives brought out by the defense? Did they say anything about her good qualities?

Her mother and I have had to sit here and listen to her character get trashed over and over so their client's actions could be justified. That has been a sickening and enraging experience, and it's added a lot to our pain. It felt like Beck was getting murdered all over again, but this time it was her character getting thrown in the lake. Our sweet and beautiful girl got slandered inside this court, and her memory is tainted forever. Why? Because of legal tactics, to win a court case. And that's a shameful thing. A shameful thing.

TITUS ALDEN: I don't know what I said, tell you the truth. I didn't watch the video or read about it after. I let my heart empty out the feelings that'd been building up.

SAMSON GRIFFITH: Mr. Alden wasn't wrong. It's how the system works. I never thought Beck was a bad person. I don't think most people thought that. But she knew what she was doing when she went to visit Sparser in prison and used that to keep her hold on Cleo.

REUBEN JEPHSON, CO-DEFENSE COUNSEL: Elva Griffith wanted to speak at the sentencing. You can imagine that made us nervous, given their family history and the practically nonexistent mother-daughter relationship. But Elva had written a letter to Cleo beforehand, and Cleo told us she was okay with her making a statement. She wanted to give her mother a chance to say her piece.

MS. ELVA GRIFFITH: Hello, my name is Elva Griffith, and Mary Claire is my daughter. As you may know, my husband and I have not been close or had much contact with our daughter for about ten years. A lot of our history has come out at this trial and in the media, so there's no need to go back into that now. We have attended every day of the trial because she is our daughter and we would go to the ends of the earth to be there for her in her time of need. She's told us from her heart she is not guilty, and we believe her. We believe her because she is our daughter and because we raised her as a child of God. And we know that when she was under our roof, she never committed a single act of cruelty or evil. She loved all living things and never hurt anything or anybody. When she was six, the mission house where we were staying had a rat infestation. My husband placed traps around the house and in the basement. One day we heard Mary Claire screaming from downstairs. We found her trying to set free a rat that had gotten caught in a trap but was still alive. She was crying, "Let it go, Daddy, let it go!" My husband pushed her out of the way, stomped on the rat with his boot, and killed it. And Mary Claire became hysterical. She was screaming, "The Lord told Noah to save all the animals, not kill them!"

I'm not standing here as a perfect parent. But a mother knows her child. And when my child says her heart would not let her strike a blow against this woman Rebecca, I know it's true. Because I have seen Mary Claire's goodness and gentleness and been a witness to her love for all living things. I trust the jury made the best decision they could, given what they saw and heard, but I tell you in the sight of God my daughter is not a killer.

THE ANATOMY OF DESIRE

Our hearts go out in sympathy and love to Rebecca's mother and father. I pray they can find peace. And I ask you, Your Honor, please have mercy on our daughter. She is a risk to nobody and can still do so much good with her life.

JAKE CROWE, *INYO REGISTER*: The last person given an opportunity to speak pre-sentencing is the defendant. We weren't sure whether Cleo Ray would speak or not. Moments before the judge moved on, she stood up and faced him.

MS. GRIFFITH: Your Honor, I would like to address my statement to Mr. and Mrs. Alden.
THE COURT: The Aldens have indicated they don't want you to address them directly, so you may address the court, Ms. Griffith.
MS. GRIFFITH: Okay, I understand. I want to talk about Beck—Rebecca Alden. I agree with her dad, a lot of negative things have been said about her here. For that I am deeply, deeply sorry. Her dad was so right, Beck was a wonderful person. She was everything he said she was. And I want to add she was funny, too. She had a great dry sense of humor that she didn't share until you got to know her. Her little comments about situations, her observations about people would make me laugh so hard. We laughed a lot together. And we talked about the future. She told me she had her heart set on adopting babies and becoming a mom. She said she knew she'd be a great mom because she'd had a great mom. And I want to say this because it's true and something I envied about her—she adored her parents. She loved you guys so much. You know that because she didn't hold it back. The Beck I got to know was a hundred percent loving, caring, and loyal. I'd say to her, "You're a beautiful person," and she would say back: "Thanks to Grace and Titus." I want her parents to know that.

SAMSON GRIFFITH: At the time I thought, *Cleo, say something about yourself, speak from your heart about who you are*. But afterward, I realized that was the best statement she could have made. In speaking about Beck to her parents with such real affection, Cleo said everything about herself you needed to know.

THE COURT: Will the defendant please stand? Ms. Griffith, as I am sure you've been informed, your conviction for murder in the first degree can result in one of three sentences. One is death, however, in California capital punishment is currently under suspension by order of the governor; two is life in state prison without the possibility of parole; and three is twenty-five years to life in state prison. The court is taking into consideration several factors, perhaps most prominently your age and lack of a prior criminal history.

JAKE CROWE, *INYO REGISTER*: Can't say there was much suspense about the sentencing. It was more how the judge would characterize his decision. Keep in mind, he hadn't publicly expressed his opinion about the case or the defendant for the entire trial.

THE COURT: In sentencing you to twenty-five years to life, I am aware that serving the minimum would take you to the age of fifty and leave you with two or three decades to live a free and productive life. Some people make good use of their time in prison, and I can see you being one of them. I believe you have those better angels of your nature within your grasp and I would hope you reach for them and heed their voices. I do believe there is every possibility you will come out of this a better person and a better citizen. I wish you good luck with that, Ms. Griffith, I truly do. Court is adjourned.

DUNCAN MCMILLAN, INTERVIEWER: Thank you for agreeing to be interviewed. Per your request, we will not be giving out your name. You will be referred to as Juror 7. You were the foreperson elected by the jury in the Mary Claire Griffith murder trial?

JUROR NO. 7: Yes. In my job I am responsible for managing a team of people, so it was a natural role for me.

DUNCAN MCMILLAN, INTERVIEWER: It took two days of deliberation to reach your verdict. Were there differing opinions about the defendant's guilt at the beginning of your discussions?

JUROR NO. 7: I'd say everyone felt a big responsibility not to rush to judgment. Both the prosecution and the defense presented a lot of evidence, and we all agreed we needed to evaluate it in an organized and rational manner.

DUNCAN MCMILLAN, INTERVIEWER: When you took that first vote, how many were against conviction?

JUROR NO. 7: Votes were taken, but I can't tell you the results.

DUNCAN MCMILLAN, INTERVIEWER: What testimony turned out to be the most persuasive?

JUROR NO. 7: Well, the fact the defendant admitted she planned to kill the victim was a big deal to us. The intent was there all the way to the final moments.

DUNCAN MCMILLAN, INTERVIEWER: So you didn't believe the defendant when she said she backed off at the last moment and couldn't follow through with her plan?

JUROR NO. 7: If that were true, why didn't she call for help? If she was in shock and it took a moderate length of time to come to her senses, okay. But she ran away and went to meet her boyfriend. Our consensus was, the behavior she showed after the canoe turned over was the behavior of a guilty person.

DUNCAN MCMILLAN, INTERVIEWER: Were there any jurors who believed she was not guilty and needed convincing?

JUROR NO. 7: I would say we started out wanting to hear arguments for and against, so some of us spoke in the defendant's favor and walked through the events from her point of view. But we kept coming back to how she acted after the event, how that undercut her credibility.

DUNCAN MCMILLAN, INTERVIEWER: Were any jurors influenced by the defendant's troubled past?

JUROR NO. 7: I think we all felt sympathetic toward her. Personally I was quite moved by her testimony. But it wasn't applicable to her actions and the law. Bad life experiences do not justify taking the life of another human being.

DUNCAN MCMILLAN: *The twenty-four-hour news cycle following the verdict produced a range of headlines, editorials, and opinion pieces across the spectrum of mainstream media. It was one of those rare moments when the culture's attention collectively focuses on a single story and a single protagonist.*

Los Angeles Times
INFLUENCER MURDER TRIAL SHINES
SPOTLIGHT ON SMALL-TOWN JUSTICE

The Wall Street Journal
CLEO RAY VERDICT SPLITS SOCIAL
MEDIA OVER GUILT, INNOCENCE

New York Post Page Six
PROTESTERS CLASH WITH SHERIFF'S
DEPUTIES OVER CLEO'S FATE

THE ANATOMY OF DESIRE

USA Today

INFLUENCER CULTURE EXPOSED:
WHERE THE HARDBODIES ARE BURIED

NPR

MURDER ON SERENE LAKE,
FIT-FLUENCER FOUND GUILTY

ABC News

SOCIAL CLIMBING IN THE DIGITAL AGE:
A NEW AMERICAN DREAM

DUNCAN MCMILLAN, INTERVIEWER: Describe the experience of leaving the county jail and your transition to state prison.

CLEO RAY: I didn't realize how much I'd gotten used to that jail and the staff. No one was breaking the rules, but they'd give me an extra ten minutes in the exercise yard and they were nice to me—or they weren't mean, put it that way. The air's clean, the views are spectacular, and the jail's not very big. While I was there, they had, like, sixty total inmates and only ten to fifteen women. Alana tried to prepare me for what was ahead, and I knew it would be a major adjustment, but my choices were to be upbeat or suicidal.

The day I was leaving, a few of the staff came to my cell to say goodbye. They brought chocolate chip cookies. I was touched.

ERIN NEWCOMB, CHIEF DEPUTY: We all make mistakes, some worse than others, but I don't think it's fair to label a person for the worst mistake they ever made. Cleo Ray made a positive contribution to a lot of people's lives through her social media coaching. At her core she was a decent person—in my opinion. On the day she was being transferred, I went to the jail to say goodbye. I told her I had faith she could turn things around. She thanked me and said she was sorry for causing everyone so much trouble.

CLEO RAY: When the van taking me to the prison pulled out of the jail parking lot, there was a group of thirty or forty people on the sidewalk holding signs: WE LOVE YOU, CLEO; WE'RE WITH YOU, CLEO; WE BELIEVE YOU, CLEO—sorry, give me a moment.

DUNCAN MCMILLAN, INTERVIEWER: Take your time.

JAKE CROWE, *INYO REGISTER*: I came to the jail to cover Cleo's departure and asked a few of her supporters for comments. I recorded these on my phone:

"I was going through a tough time in my life when I found her on Instagram, and following her helped me through it—she inspired me to get in shape *and* to be a better person."

"I miss her so much. I keep replaying her videos. It's so sad there won't be any new ones."

"As the sun offers rays of light, Cleo offered rays of well-being. This is a tragedy."

CLEO RAY: I didn't know they were out there. It caught me by surprise. I could see out, but they couldn't see in because of the tinted windows. I wish I could've thanked them or at least acknowledged them. One sign said, WE'LL NEVER FORGET YOU, CLEO. I'll never forget that sign.

The Reception Center for Female Offenders—I was officially designated an *offender*—is in Central California, a five-hour drive from Independence. Two state officers drove me in a Department of Corrections van. I was the only prisoner, so I had the whole rear compartment to myself. It was a spectacular fall day, crystal clear, just gorgeous. We went past Mount Whitney and down through Mojave and up to Tehachapi and along the western side of the Sierras. My senses were extra sharp, and I was noticing everything, like the people in other cars and out on the streets of the small towns we drove through. The parade of ordinary everyday life, but it seemed so extraordinary. I mean, do these people even realize how blessed they are to have their freedom? To be able to choose whether to turn right or left, to go to the market or to the park, to walk down the block without walls surrounding them?

Can't say it was the *best* road trip I'd ever taken, but it was the most profound.

DUNCAN MCMILLAN, INTERVIEWER: I can see that.

CLEO RAY: That road trip was followed by a brutal reality check: back into isolation. They put me in a six-by-eight-foot cell with no window and a steel door with a narrow slot that looked out at another cell door. This was not solitary confinement; this is where they had to keep me until they could decide which prison in California would be the best fit—based on my classification score. For the first week, no visitors were allowed and I could make only one phone call. I was assigned a counselor and we filled out form after form. I got a complete medical exam and a psychological evaluation. It felt like I had to go through a hundred times more processing than when I was booked into the Inyo County Jail.

Any upbeatness I felt was gone by the second night.

DUNCAN MCMILLAN, INTERVIEWER: How did you end up in the state's maximum security prison for female inmates?

CLEO RAY: According to my permanent record, I had run away from two crime scenes, the car crash and the lake, and also when they came to arrest me with the hiking party. Didn't matter that I had no criminal record, that I'd been a taxpaying, contributing member of society, no lower security dormitory for Cleo. She gets a concrete cell and electrified fences, guard towers with sharpshooters and armed officers inside and out. She gets Level Four, with all the violent offenders and hardcases.

DUNCAN MCMILLAN, INTERVIEWER: What was it like emotionally during those first few weeks?

CLEO RAY: I tried hard to focus on the positives: a free bar of soap, eight ounces of shampoo, and five sanitary pads per month. Yeah, those first weeks were the darkest of the dark.

SAMSON GRIFFITH: My clients didn't all leave at once. There was a trickle after Cleo's arrest. Some more during the pretrial hearings. More each week of the trial. Several more after the verdict. And in the month following the trial, our list went from over a hundred to less than ten. I reduced staff, but suddenly there wasn't enough money coming in to afford the office rent. I started working out of my house with a minimal staff, but we weren't bringing in any new business. Pretty soon I couldn't afford the house, so we had to put it up for sale. The real estate market was soft, and I had to take less than what I'd paid for it.

Griffith All Media became one of those companies that gets toxically branded for being associated with a scandal. I had to shut it down. But hey, this business is filled with redemption and comeback stories. And I've got grit. So I'll be relevant again. Hell yes I will.

DUNCAN MCMILLAN, INTERVIEWER: Any regrets for backing Cleo's defense and supporting her through the trial?

SAMSON GRIFFITH: No regrets. Maybe I should have pushed more vigorously for not changing our defense strategy, but that's water under the bridge. Fact is, Cleo was not guilty of first-degree murder. I put my money on the truth. Unfortunately, in this world today, truth is at best a fifty-fifty proposition.

GILLIAN GRIFFITH: Had my dad not taken her in, given her a job, promoted her career, supported her at her murder trial, and paid for her legal defense, my family would still own one of the most successful social media agencies in the country. We'd still have our family home. We'd still have our reputation.

So yeah, I feel bitterness toward Cleo—Mary Claire, my cousin—for the impact she had on our family. I'm not saying Cleo didn't have it hard, but her troubles were of her own making.

SANDY FINCH: I drove up to see Cleo during her second month of *incarceration*.

CLEO RAY: We hadn't spoken in a couple of weeks. He'd handwritten me three letters, and they were filled with affection—but also kind of unsettled. I knew he'd been going through a lot.

SANDY FINCH: I read about the Central California Women's Facility before driving up there, so I thought I'd be prepared. But it was still a shock. Cleo's in there? This place made the Inyo County Jail look like an elementary school. Another exercise in extreme cognitive dissonance.

CLEO RAY: So my personal property that was taken and kept for me when I was booked in the county jail followed me to prison. It wasn't much, believe me, but there was something I wanted for his visit and I made a special request ahead of time. I did everything I could to make it happen.

This would be our first "contact visit" since I was arrested, meaning we were allowed to exchange a *brief hug*. That's how it's described in the prisoner manual and on a sign posted in the visitation room. What's the definition of brief, guys? Two seconds? Three? Can it be a full body hug? Can we kiss? We're told if there's a violation, the visit will be terminated and privileges will be suspended.

There was a lot riding on that first hug.

SANDY FINCH: I knew the rule about keeping the hug brief. I was afraid that once I had her in my arms, I wouldn't be able to let go.

CLEO RAY: When I came into the room, he was already there at one of the tables. He looked so good—such a beautiful man.

I walked straight to him, and when we hugged, I felt this incredible release of energy. Everything that had been building up inside me went whoosh out into the universe.

SANDY FINCH: It lasted just a few seconds, but the feeling I had was that we'd never been apart.

CLEO RAY: We broke off before the guard could hassle us, so we were okay. We sat down opposite each other, hands on the table where they were visible. I was dying to reach out and hold his hand, but it's not allowed. Then he saw it.

SANDY FINCH: She was wearing the promise ring. The one I'd given her a lifetime ago.

CLEO RAY: I said, "They won't let me wear it here, but I got them to make an exception for your visit."

And he said, "Thank you. That means a lot to me."

"To me, too," I said.

For a good long minute, we stared in each other's eyes. Both of us teared up. He said, "Breathe." That made me smile.

SANDY FINCH: She had a prison haircut and no makeup, she was wearing that shapeless jumpsuit, and she looked fantastic. I'm not just saying that. There was something inside her that was shining through. It stunned me.

CLEO RAY: What do I say? How was the drive up? What's the weather been like in L.A.? Have you been sleeping with anyone else? Of course you have. And of course I'd never ask you that.

SANDY FINCH: We didn't have a lot of time, so I started telling her about the trip I took to Yellowstone in Wyoming, to a spot miles from the nearest road. I'd printed maps, loaded my gear, and drove up by myself. The weather had turned cold, but I was determined to get as far off the grid as possible.

CLEO RAY: I asked, "What did you do when you got there?"
  He said, "I meditated."
  And I was like, "Right on."

SANDY FINCH: I needed a reset, but I didn't realize how life-changing it would be. After a few days of losing myself in nature, where I could scream at the top of my lungs and no one would hear me, where my phone was cut off from any connection, I experienced something big. I said to Cleo, "I know it sounds cliché, but through all those hours of being still and silent, I had a revelation."

CLEO RAY: "Tell me."

SANDY FINCH: It was my time to be in service to others. My friend David said to me, "You're already in service to others through your influencing." But was I really? All the followers and fans and endorsement deals—that was me feeding my ego. I'd strayed away from my real self, and it was time for a truing up.

CLEO RAY: He'd completely quit social media. Took down his pages, deleted himself from all the platforms, dropped his remaining deals, gave people their money back. He kept a calendar app, an email account, and a reading app on his phone. That was it.

SANDY FINCH: I signed up with an organization that builds and installs toilets in developing nations. It's mind-blowing, actually.

CLEO RAY: I was like, "You'll be installing toilets?" And he went into this whole thing about how 4.5 billion people in the world don't have safe sanitation, and how there are so many places where human waste is allowed to flow into rivers and streams and causes diseases like typhoid fever that a lot of people die from.

SANDY FINCH: They're called non-sewered sanitation systems. Basically, it's a toilet that doesn't need plumbing to process the waste. Because it produces clean water as a by-product, this is an invention that's leading a global revolution in safe sanitation practices. And they need people to truck them into these remote places, assemble them, and show the locals how they work.

CLEO RAY: As he was explaining it, I was thinking, *Okay, I get it. This is extremely important to the wellness of people. It's promoting global hygiene and health. Really pretty awesome.*
  Wow, Sandy.

SANDY FINCH: I told her I'd volunteered for eighteen months, and it was like the Peace Corps or the military. I could be deployed anywhere, and the first place they were sending me was northern India.

CLEO RAY: My jaw dropped. Eighteen months? And then I thought, *He could have said eighteen years and I'd still be right here when he got back.*

SANDY FINCH: I said, "I don't know what comes after this. I just know this is what I need to be doing for now."

CLEO RAY: I told him I respected that and was happy he'd found this path. "Maybe you can write me once in a while? I'd love to hear about your experiences. Because if I wasn't in here, I would probably be volunteering right next to you."

SANDY FINCH: I said, "I know you would. And I will write you."

CLEO RAY: We smiled. Then we chatted about his drive up and the weather in L.A. That was okay. I didn't mind having a normal conversation with Sandy.

SANDY FINCH: When our time was up, I said, "Are we allowed a parting hug?" She turned to the woman guard standing a few feet away and said, "I'm going to hug him goodbye, okay?" The guard didn't say anything, so we got up and put our arms around each other and held tight. That's a moment I'll keep with me a long time.

CLEO RAY: I waved to him and turned away, and the guard escorted me out of the room. I reached in my pocket and found a clump of tissues I'd brought with me. I hadn't had to use any.

I took the ring off and handed it to the guard. Yes, my heart hurt. But it didn't feel like it was being ripped out, the way it did before. I loved him. And I couldn't be with him. That's all.

ELVA GRIFFITH: The trial from start to finish had been unfair. Our daughter was not guilty, it was that simple, and therefore the fault had been in the judge or prosecution or jury—or all three. An appeal had to be filed. And a new trial would have to be granted.

I let Mary Claire know she could depend on me. What I lacked in legal knowledge I could make up for by reading and studying and asking questions. When I visited her in prison, I told our girl, "I've got this. I let you down in the past, I know that, but not anymore. I've got this."

ALANA BELKNAP, DEFENSE COUNSEL: I was not quitting. There are simply people better equipped to handle the appeals process in California. I sent the Griffiths to Olivia Nevins, the best criminal appeals lawyer in the state. And you know what, a fresh set of eyes and new blood helps energize a case. Reuben and I gave it everything we had. Cleo needed a specialist who could analyze what had taken place with objectivity and who knew the Fourth District Court of Appeal inside out. I placed them in great hands. Whatever else they needed, I was ready to help.

This was a tough one. It's stayed with me.

ELVA GRIFFITH: I understood that Samson had nothing left to give. Bless him for all he did. The appeal was going to be expensive, so he set up a crowdfunding page for us. That kind of thing is my brother-in-law's specialty. He did a great job putting it together with Mary Claire's videos and—what's it called?—optimized search, and media ads. I didn't know how to get around online, but he had his people teach me, and I picked it up pretty quick.

Asa and I agreed to do a few paid television interviews, and all the money went into the appeal. Then came setting up a tour of California churches where I could plead Mary Claire's case and ask for contributions to her legal fund. We started down in San Diego, where the appeals court is. They have these incredible megachurches down there. We met a number of good and decent people who wanted to help us.

CLEO RAY: My mother, the unworldly street preacher, turned out to be a badass—a badass on a crusade to get her daughter set free. "Oh, Lord, have mercy on our Mary Claire, and grant her another chance at getting a fair trial and a just verdict." She learned how to run a fundraising page, she went on the news and on faith-based cable shows, she made appearances at Sunday sermons every week. She was my number one champion.

And she was my first visitor in prison.

ELVA GRIFFITH: I did ask my daughter for her forgiveness. If she was willing, I was certainly willing to make a clean start. I wouldn't try to push anything on her, I'd respect her . . . independence. We both had a lot of healing to do.

CLEO RAY: And it finally dawned on me how horribly I'd treated her—both my parents. I'd gone for weeks refusing to let them visit me in jail. Day after day I would not even acknowledge their presence in the courtroom. They sacrificed everything to come support me, they slept in people's garages and on their floors, they gave up their mission work. And I froze them out.

When I first entered state prison, one of the staff therapists asked to see me. She'd followed the trial, and you know her first question? "Why'd you behave that way toward your parents?"

"Uh, well, I hated the way they raised me."

"What did you hate about it?"

"God came first, and their kids came second. Or God came first, their church second, their kids third. Or everything came before their kids, and their kids came dead last."

"Do you feel you weren't loved?"

"They loved me. But they loved Jesus more."

"Do you still think that's true?"

They'd showed up for me like they never had before. That was a fact. My mom gained a new superpower in raising money for her daughter's cause.

My dad ended up getting sick and stopped coming to the prison for visits. Then it was just Mom and me for sixty minutes, once a week. So much anger, and I had to let it all go.

You know what? Wasn't as hard as I thought it would be.

ELVA GRIFFITH: During one of my visits, Mary Claire told me she'd started going to a prison Bible study. That made me happy. Very happy. But all I said was "Good for you," and then I dropped it. When she had more to tell me, she would.

CLEO RAY: They sing gospel songs at these Bible studies. And I got to amaze my prison sisters with my ability to recite the majority of the lyrics in their songbook. I even taught them a few new hymns—from memory.

> *I heard the voice of Jesus say*
> *"I am this dark world's Light;*
> *Look unto Me, thy morn shall rise*
> *And all thy day be bright."*

ELVA GRIFFITH: Ms. Nevins filed the appeal within sixty days of the verdict. Then she had to file a brief, which was another sixty days. Then we had to wait for the appeals judges to read it and schedule the oral arguments. We were told all that could take from twelve to twenty-four months. Asa and I rented a small house outside of Fresno, down the road from Mary Claire. We found a nice church to join, with a congregation that was very welcoming. Then Asa became ill and he couldn't get out of the house much. I had my daughter in prison and my husband in a sickbed. The Lord would see us through. "The Lord is my strength and my shield; my heart trusts in Him."

DUNCAN MCMILLAN, INTERVIEWER: This interview is being conducted inside the visiting room of the state prison where Cleo Ray is currently incarcerated. We thank the officials both here and with the California Department of Corrections and Rehabilitation who granted this request, though for security reasons we have been limited to recording audio only. Because this is an open room, you will be hearing different acoustics. And with that bit of stage setting, here I am sitting across from Cleo Ray, who just passed her fourteenth month of confinement in this facility.

The natural first question is, how are you doing?

CLEO RAY: So many layers to that question. Before I answer, may I ask you a question?

DUNCAN MCMILLAN, INTERVIEWER: You may.

CLEO RAY: Have you decided on an ending for the docuseries?

DUNCAN MCMILLAN, INTERVIEWER: Short answer: no. Longer answer: we're considering a few choices. It's an ongoing conversation with my editor and producer.

CLEO RAY: Do you have a favorite?

DUNCAN MCMILLAN, INTERVIEWER: More than one. We're not locking picture for three weeks, so there's time. I'm not worried, we'll have a good one—a *strong* one. Maybe something will come from this interview.

CLEO RAY: Have you decided on a title?

DUNCAN MCMILLAN, INTERVIEWER: Our working title is still *The Two Lives of Cleo Ray*.

CLEO RAY: I might have a suggestion, and it leads back to your first question. I've been here a little over a year, and I'm already feeling a major transformation. This life couldn't be more different from the life I had before, obviously. But it's given me the distance to look at things and make some big shifts in perspective.

DUNCAN MCMILLAN, INTERVIEWER: Are you referring to your spiritual transformation, finding God?

CLEO RAY: That's part of it. I love the Bible studies we do here, and it's a great group of women. I've been reading the Bible more than ever and thinking about Jesus in ways I hadn't before. But I've also been spending a lot of time in the library reading philosophy and history and poetry. And there's a program where we can get used schoolbooks delivered right to our cells for free. This morning, I read a line that struck me: "You, earth and life, till the last ray gleams, I sing."

DUNCAN MCMILLAN, INTERVIEWER: Walt Whitman?

CLEO RAY: You're good.

DUNCAN MCMILLAN, INTERVIEWER: I see your influencer name in there, "Till the last *ray* gleams."

You spent so much time and energy to be an influencer. If you could have your platform back for one more post, what would it be?

CLEO RAY: Hmm. Okay, it would be a selfie, and I'm smiling, an authentic smile, from inside, and the caption would read: "Don't feel sorry for me. I'm alive and living this moment. That's what I want to say to you and the people who followed me and heard my message. Be alive and live this moment."

So along with *The Two Lives of Cleo Ray*, you might consider *The Three Lives*.

DUNCAN MCMILLAN, INTERVIEWER: You're getting the hang of this interview thing, aren't you?

CLEO RAY: I don't know about that, but I have been keeping a journal. I never did that before, writing down my private thoughts every day. Before this happened, I was recording myself every day, with selfies and videos and posts, but those were designed to go out to the public, to build my brand. The beauty of a journal is it's so personal. I'm not trying to get someone to like me or follow me. I can be more real—with myself.

DUNCAN MCMILLAN, INTERVIEWER: Maybe you could share some of your entries? We're still open to finding the perfect ending.

CLEO RAY: I might have something for you.

DUNCAN MCMILLAN, INTERVIEWER: Terrific. You do seem more—gleaming.

CLEO RAY: I've been reading about Buddhism and thinking about the difference between fate and karma. I've been studying these things, and as I'm coming to understand it, fate means a predetermined outcome, and karma allows for an evolving outcome that develops as a result of individual will. When I think back to what happened on Serene Lake, even though I didn't hit Beck willfully and the canoe tipped over by accident, and I looked for her but couldn't find her, her death was an outcome I was responsible for. I desired her to die. Even if my direct actions weren't the cause, I have to own the consequences. Her drowning in that lake wasn't her fate, and it wasn't mine. The choices were mine to make, and my choices let everyone down, most of all me.

DUNCAN MCMILLAN, INTERVIEWER: You're saying if you had to do it over again . . . ?

CLEO RAY: There aren't any do-overs. There is only this moment and the next, and the next is not even guaranteed. What is past is past. What will come will come. And I'm sure none of this will make it into the docuseries because I sound like I'm trying to channel an Indian guru.

DUNCAN MCMILLAN, INTERVIEWER: You never know.

CLEO RAY: Before I forget, would you do something for me? Would you mail me a pack of different-colored highlighters? Like the pink, orange, and blue in addition to yellow? I want to be able to highlight some of these things I'm reading.

DUNCAN MCMILLAN: This is Duncan McMillan, director of the docuseries, and right now I am alone in my apartment recording this on Wednesday morning, January thirteenth. I just got a call from Elva Griffith, Cleo Ray's mother, and she informed me that her daughter died last night in the Central California Women's Facility, where she was serving her sentence for first-degree murder.

Elva didn't have many details. The warden told her it appeared the death was due to natural causes. Which is hard to imagine because Cleo was so fit and health conscious. I literally just hung up the phone and am in a state of shock. I mean, I picked up this pack of highlighters for Cleo because she asked me for them during our last interview, which was only a few days ago. I was going to mail them to her today. Pink, orange, blue, and yellow.

My God, I'm thinking about the people I need to call. About how this impacts the ending of our series. I have to stop that. I have to think about the person, about Cleo, about my... my friend. Okay, I'm sitting down. And breathing. My first instinct was to record this moment because, well, I'm a documentarian. But I'm also a human being. So I'm going to turn it off now.

DUNCAN MCMILLAN: Me again, from my L.A. apartment, recording myself. It's been three weeks since I got the call about Cleo Ray passing away in prison at the age of twenty-six. An autopsy report has now been released and we have an official account of the cause. I'll do my best to lay out what we've learned about Cleo's shockingly abrupt death.

According to her cellmate, Cleo came back from dinner that Tuesday night complaining of a pressure in her upper chest. The cellmate reported that Cleo started coughing and gasping for breath. After lying down on her bunk for a minute, Cleo stood up and then collapsed on the floor. By the time the guards responded to her cellmate's cries for help, Cleo had stopped breathing. Prison staff performed CPR, but she was unresponsive. Cleo was rushed to the nearest hospital emergency room, where she was pronounced dead on arrival. Her body was transported to the county medical examiner for an autopsy, which is routine when someone so young and in such apparent good health suddenly dies.

The medical examiner found a blood clot that had caused a catastrophic artery blockage in Cleo's lungs, making her unable to breathe. The clot was traced to a vein inside Cleo's right knee. The official cause of death was listed as a pulmonary embolism resulting from deep vein thrombosis.

Having followed Cleo's court case in the media, the examiner recalled she had been involved in a serious car accident years earlier. The examiner speculated that Cleo had sustained an injury to her knee as a result of the accident, and that it initially would have caused pain and swelling. But there was no external wound, and as had been brought out at the trial, Cleo went for weeks without medical treatment. A clot then developed behind her knee that Cleo would not have been able to see or feel. When she filled out medical forms for jail and prison, she never listed the knee problem because she assumed the injury had healed. The clot remained there for years, invisible, until that Tuesday evening when it broke loose and traveled up her bloodstream to her lungs. The blood flow to her lungs was cut off, severely restricting her air supply. At that point she would've needed immediate medical intervention to survive.

A second, nationally recognized medical expert was brought in to review the first M.E.'s findings. She concurred that the cause of death was acute pulmonary embolism from a clot that had formed from a prior injury to Cleo's right knee. The CDC estimates that between 60,000 and 100,000 Americans die annually from deep vein thrombosis, and I was surprised to learn it's the leading cause of sudden death in people in their twenties with no chronic medical conditions or diseases.

In our last interview, Cleo talked about fate and karma. Many will see her life as defined by two bad choices made ten years apart. The second landed her in prison. The first, it appears, led to her death. Did she just draw the wrong card? Flip a coin and have it land on the losing side? Or did those bad choices determine her fate?

I know this. More than anything, she strived to do better. And there are many people who, because of Cleo Ray, do better.

DUNCAN MCMILLAN: I am recording this ten weeks after the death of Cleo Ray. On the last day of her life, Cleo made an entry in her journal. With the permission of her mother, who received the journal from the prison along with Cleo's personal effects, I'll read it now.

"At mail call this afternoon, the C.O. handed me a small package I thought might have been the highlighters I asked Duncan for. I took it back to my cell, and opening it, I found an old print photo with a note from my mom. Not wanting the photo to be damaged in handling, she'd placed it between two pieces of cardboard and taped the sides. The photo was of me and my sister, Elizabeth, and we were eating ice cream cones. No date on it, but I guessed I was around eight or nine, which means Elizabeth was sixteen or seventeen, close to when she ran away from home. I don't remember this photo, but I do remember that rare treat when our parents allowed us to get a soft-serve cone from Dairy Queen. I could see in my face a look of pure enjoyment.

"My mom had written: 'A missionary friend found this in a drawer of one of our old houses and sent it to us. I am passing it on to you. I hope you find some comfort in the memory. For me, it made me realize we should have let you and your sister have more ice cream cones. It's trivial, I know, but that's what I thought when I looked at the two of you. Much love, Mom.'

"I wanted to say to her: No, Mom, it's not trivial, not at all. And thank you."

The entry ended there.

Cleo said something during our final visit that felt significant then and all the more so now.

CLEO RAY: Don't feel sorry for me. I'm alive and living this moment. That's what I want to say to you and the people who followed me and heard my message. Be alive and live this moment.

L. R. DORN

THE THREE LIVES OF CLEO RAY

A SEVEN-PART DOCUSERIES
Directed by Duncan McMillan

SERIES CREDITS

Produced by
Jane Early   Allison Strader   Scott Tsou   Antonio Gunn

Cinematography by
Noah Scharf   Lucas Delia

Editing by
Ilana Akerman   Vita Kapoor

Music by
LeRoy Elkins

Art Department
Mackenzie Layfield   Freida Ibanez   Brock Walker III

Sound Department
Sebastian Chaney   Wilma Kael   Adam P. Adams   Greg Bartkowski

THE ANATOMY OF DESIRE

Camera and Electrical Department
Marlee Cantor   Diego Chen   Hanson Tucker   Jerome Boyce

Production Management
Hank Kingman   Sharon Soliah

Special thanks to Inyo County Superior Court, Independence; Inyo County Sheriff's Office; Mono County Sheriff's Office; Public Information Officer of Inyo County; California Department of Corrections and Rehabilitation; Inyo County Free Library; Inyo County Parks and Recreation; U.S. Forest Service, Inyo National Forest; Eastern California Museum; Bishop Airport; Bishop Tourist Information Office; Westin Monache Resort at Mammoth Lakes; Winnedumah Hotel; Mt. Williamson Motel and Basecamp; Best Western Frontier Motel of Lone Pine; Tom's Place General Store, Café & Bar; and Glenn's Taqueria for those world-class tacos!

A PRODUCTION OF D-MAC MEDIA

A NOTE FROM THE AUTHORS

Theodore Dreiser's fascination with the real-life drowning of Grace Brown at the hands of her lover, Chester Gillette, led to the creation of the author's most iconic work, *An American Tragedy*. That novel inspired movies (including 1951's *A Place in the Sun*), radio dramas, TV shows, stage plays, a musical, and adaptations in other languages. Its timeless crime narrative of ambition and desire leading to murder inspired us to reimagine the story, characters, and themes through a contemporary lens. From the 1906 murder case to the 1925 fictional telling to our current retelling, here is the true crime/literary lineage of the key characters:

Chester Gillette—Clyde Griffiths—Cleo Ray (Mary Claire Griffith)
Grace Brown—Roberta Alden—Rebecca Alden
Harriet Benedict—Sondra Finchley—Sandy Finch
Noah Gillette—Samuel Griffiths—Samson Griffith
District Attorney George Ward—Orville Mason—Owen Mason
Defense Counsel Albert Mills—Alvin Belknap—Alana Belknap

Many thanks to Paul Bresnick, David Highfill, Tessa James, Jessica Rozler, Elina Cohen, Caitlin Garing, Suzanne Mitchell, Kate Falkoff, Tavia Kowalchuk, Sharyn Rosenblum, Wayne Alexander, Joel Gotler, Jacob Walker, Lance Bogart, Carma Roper, Nancy Masters, and Samson Dorff.